The Things That Knock

Volume One

by

Christopher Winterberg

Published by fu-X Publishing Company.

This is a work of fiction. Names, characters, places, and incidents are either products of the author's imagination or used fictitiously. Any resemblance to actual persons, living or dead, events, or locales is entirely coincidental.

First edition. Volume One.

ISBN: 978-0-9894483-1-4

Dedication

For those who believed in and appreciated my writing along the way. You know who you are.

And, for those who read.

Contents

I'm Me, You're You

Rina Martinez meets herself in the parking lot of a closed laundromat at 1:13 in the morning, which feels insulting.

Not poetic.

Not cinematic.

Not on a rooftop under lightning while the city trembles beneath the weight of destiny.

A laundromat.

With one flickering sign.

And a homeless man asleep beside a vending machine that sells off-brand barbecue chips.

Rina stands beside the time machine, which looks less like a miracle of science and more like a commercial freezer that lost a fight with a radio tower. It hisses behind her. Steam leaks from the seams. A blue light pulses from under the door, sickly and nervous, like the machine itself regrets participating.

"Fantastic," Rina mutters. "I invented a midlife crisis with a power cord."

Technically, she doesn't invent it.

Dr. Leonard Vorn invents it.

Rina steals access, threatens a grad student, guesses a password, and makes several choices her therapist would describe as "classic Rina."

Her phone buzzes in her jacket pocket.

Lila.

Of course.

Rina answers because she's stupid, lonely, and apparently in the business of making history worse.

"Please tell me," Lila says, "that the loud bang I heard before you hung up was not you violating spacetime."

Rina looks around the parking lot. Same cracked asphalt. Same dead laundromat. Same taco truck across the street, still open because God loves drunk people.

"I'd describe it more as lightly inconveniencing spacetime."

"Oh my God."

"Don't be dramatic."

"You used the machine."

"No."

"Rina."

"Fine. Yes."

There's a silence on the other end. Not a normal silence. A disappointed, muscular silence. The kind Lila has perfected over twenty years of watching Rina make decisions like a raccoon with a credit card.

"You went back," Lila says.

"I went adjacent."

"That's not a thing."

"It is now."

"Where are you?"

Rina squints at the laundromat sign.

"San Pedro Avenue. Same neighborhood. Nineteen years ago."

Lila makes a sound between a laugh and a scream. "You went to 2007? Why?"

Rina doesn't answer right away.

Because Mateo leaves tomorrow.

Because she lets him.

Because she remembers wanting to win the fight more than she wants to save the love.

Because every good thing in her life has a door-shaped bruise where he walks out.

Instead she says, "Research."

"You don't do research. You do crimes with stationery."

"Look, I'm not changing anything major."

"You are standing in the past."

"I'm standing in a parking lot."

"Same problem."

The laundromat door swings open.

Rina turns.

A young woman steps out carrying a laundry basket against one hip and a cigarette behind one ear. Long dark hair. Red leather jacket. Cheap black boots. Hoop earrings big enough to start a fight with. Her eyeliner is a little crooked. Her mouth is already arranged into a scowl, like the world has disappointed her before breakfast and plans to keep going.

Rina's breath goes hard and shallow.

The young woman stops under the flickering sign.

They stare at each other.

The phone slips slightly in Rina's hand.

Lila's voice crackles from the speaker. "Rina? What happened?"

Rina can't move.

The young woman tilts her head.

Then she says, "Okay, either I'm drunker than I thought, or that is the ugliest future I've ever seen."

Rina closes her eyes.

"Jesus," she whispers. "I was unbearable."

Younger Rina looks her up and down. "Was?"

The machine behind them gives a deep metallic groan.

Both Rinas turn toward it.

The blue light inside goes red.

Lila's voice becomes thin and far away. "Rina, what was that sound?"

Older Rina swallows.

The laundromat windows reflect the parking lot, the street, the taco truck, the two women facing each other.

And between them, in the glass, stands a third Rina.

Smiling.

"Tell me you see that," older Rina says.

Younger Rina keeps staring at the laundromat window. Her laundry basket slides lower on her hip.

"I see a lot of things," she says. "A broken freezer. A woman dressed like a divorced cat burglar. My own face looking tired enough to qualify for federal aid."

"In the glass."

Younger Rina leans forward, squinting.

The third Rina in the reflection leans forward too.

Not perfectly.

A half-second late.

Like bad reception.

Younger Rina steps back so fast she nearly drops the basket.

"Nope."

"Good. You see it."

"I said nope."

"That's not how seeing works."

"It is when I don't want to be involved."

The third Rina smiles wider.

Older Rina raises the phone back to her ear. "Lila?"

Static.

"Lila?"

The line pops. Hisses. Then Lila's voice comes through, stretched thin like it's being pulled down a hallway.

"Rina… don't… talk to…"

"What?"

"Don't… talk… to yourself…"

Older Rina looks at younger Rina.

Younger Rina lifts a finger. "For the record, I hate that sentence."

The call dies.

The time machine gives another groan, louder this time, a sound like an elevator cable snapping somewhere underground. The blue light pulses red again, then black, then red.

Younger Rina points at it.

"What's that?"

"A time machine."

Younger Rina stares.

Older Rina sighs. "Yes, I know how that sounds."

"No, actually, I don't think you do. Because from my side, some middle-aged woman who looks like my sleep paralysis demon just appears next to a haunted Frigidaire and announces time travel like she's giving me bus directions."

"I'm forty-two."

"That's middle-aged."

"That's hateful."

"It's just math."

Older Rina steps toward the machine. The metal casing is hot. Not warm. Hot enough that she feels it through her sleeve when she pulls the handle.

The door doesn't open.

"Great," she says. "Great, great, great."

Younger Rina edges toward the sidewalk.

"Okay. Well. This has been disgusting. I'm going home."

"No, you're not."

"Excuse me?"

"You have to stay where I can see you."

Younger Rina laughs once, sharp and mean. "Lady, I don't stay where anyone can see me unless there's money, food, or emotional damage involved."

"I'm serious."

"So am I."

"You walk away, and something worse happens."

"You mean worse than meeting myself and finding out I become someone who shops entirely from the witness protection section?"

Older Rina turns on her. "Do you ever stop?"

Younger Rina blinks.

For one quick second, the sarcasm drops. Not far. Just enough to show the girl underneath, startled and a little hurt.

Then it slams back into place.

"Apparently not," she says. "You're still doing it."

That lands harder than Rina likes.

The laundromat sign flickers above them. WASH-N-FOLD becomes WASH-N-OLD, then ASH-N-OLD, then just OLD buzzing in pink neon.

Older Rina glares at it.

"Subtle," she says.

Younger Rina looks at the sign, then at her. "Did the sign just insult you?"

"Time is having a tantrum."

"Time can get in line."

Across the street, the taco truck's generator sputters. The cook leans out the service window, annoyed.

"Hey! You ladies okay?"

Both Rinas turn.

The cook freezes.

His eyes bounce from one Rina to the other. Young. Older. Same bones. Same eyes. Same expression that promises a bad Yelp review and possibly violence.

He pulls himself slowly back inside the truck.

The service window slides shut.

Younger Rina snorts. "Coward."

"He's the smartest person here."

A sharp pop cracks through the air.

Every streetlight on the block goes out at once.

Darkness drops over the parking lot like a bag.

Younger Rina says, "Nope," again, but this time there's less attitude in it.

Older Rina grabs her arm.

Younger Rina jerks back. "Do not touch me."

"Then move."

"Where?"

"Inside."

"The laundromat?"

"It has walls."

"It also has three washers that smell like murder and stale water."

"Then hold your breath."

Another sound comes from the machine.

Not mechanical this time.

A voice.

Low. Wet. Familiar.

"Rina."

Both women go still.

Younger Rina whispers, "Tell me that was you."

Older Rina whispers back, "I'd love to."

The voice comes again, from inside the time machine.

"Rina."

Younger Rina's face loses color. "Why does it sound like us?"

"Because apparently the universe has no imagination."

Older Rina pushes younger Rina toward the laundromat door. "Inside. Now."

They run.

The laundromat smells like detergent, mildew, coins, and the stale loneliness of people washing socks after midnight. Fluorescent lights buzz overhead. Two machines churn near the back, though no one is inside. Clothes tumble behind round glass doors, waiting to be freed. A vending machine glows in the corner.

Younger Rina drops her basket on a folding table.

"Okay," she says, pacing. "Okay. Let's establish some rules. Are you a ghost?"

"No."

"Demon?"

"No."

"Government experiment?"

"No."

"Amway?"

"What?"

"I don't know. Your life."

Older Rina goes to the front window and peers out. The parking lot is black except for the red pulse leaking from the time machine.

Younger Rina follows but keeps a careful distance from the glass. "What year are you from?"

"2026."

Younger Rina makes a face. "That sounds fake."

"It feels fake."

"Who's president?"

"You don't want to know."

"Is Jennifer Lopez okay?"

"Depends what you mean by okay."

"Do I get rich?"

Older Rina looks at her.

Younger Rina groans. "Oh my God. I get poor."

"You get employed."

"That's worse."

"You get stable."

"That's worse with health insurance."

Older Rina turns from the window. "Listen to me. I didn't come here to catch up."

"Clearly. You came dressed for a burglary."

"I came because tomorrow you make a mistake."

Younger Rina goes still.

There it is.

The hook in the meat.

She tries to laugh it off. "I make a mistake every day. Be specific."

"Mateo."

Younger Rina's expression changes before she can stop it.

A small flicker of panic. Then anger. Then the smug little smile she uses when she wants to hurt someone before they can hurt her.

"Oh, wow," younger Rina says. "You're one of those."

"One of what?"

"A sad future woman with a man-shaped hole in her life."

Older Rina's jaw tightens. "Careful."

"No, you be careful. You don't get to step out of your murder fridge and start giving me relationship advice."

"You don't know what happens."

"You don't know what's happening now."

"I was you."

"You were a version of me."

The words hit the room and seem to stay there.

The washers stop turning.

All at once.

The hum of the fluorescent lights cuts out.

Silence.

Then the vending machine display flashes.

NO

Younger Rina stares at it. "Did the snack robot just disagree with me?"

Older Rina's mouth goes dry.

The display blinks again.

NO NO NO NO NO NO NO

The glass door of the nearest dryer fogs from the inside.

Something drags a finger across it.

Backward letters appear in the condensation.

I'M ME

Younger Rina steps behind older Rina, then immediately seems offended by her own survival instinct and steps sideways instead.

"What does that mean?"

Older Rina whispers, "I think it means we have a problem."

The dryer door clicks.

The handle turns.

There is no hand on it.

Younger Rina grabs the laundry basket and lifts it like a weapon and a shield at once.

Older Rina looks at her. "Really?"

"What? It's full of jeans."

"That's your plan?"

"What's yours?"

Older Rina scans the room, finds a metal coin tray on the folding table, and picks it up.

Younger Rina gives it a flat look. "Wow. Future combat is elegant."

"Shut up."

The dryer door opens an inch.

Cold air spills out.

Not normal cold.

Not air-conditioning cold.

Grave cold.

The kind of cold that makes teeth ache and old bones remember themselves.

A woman's fingers curl around the edge from inside.

They are Rina's fingers.

Older Rina swings the coin tray.

The dryer door slams shut with a bang.

Younger Rina screams, then tries to convert it into a cough halfway through, badly.

"I didn't scream."

"I didn't hear anything."

"Good."

The dryer starts shaking. The whole machine bucks against the wall. Coins rattle in the change slots. The vending machine display keeps flashing.

I'M ME

I'M ME

I'M ME

Then the front door opens.

Both Rinas spin.

Carmen Martinez enters carrying a purse big enough to hide a ham and wearing the expression of a woman who has already decided everyone is guilty.

She is forty-six here. Younger than older Rina remembers. Stronger too. Hair dyed black, lipstick bright, gold hoops swinging. Her floral blouse is tucked into high-waisted jeans. She smells like rose lotion and cigarette smoke from other people's bad habits.

She stops when she sees them.

Her eyes go to younger Rina.

Then older Rina.

Then younger Rina again.

Nobody speaks.

The dryer pounds against the wall behind them.

Carmen raises one eyebrow.

"Rina," she says.

Both women answer, "Yeah?"

Carmen's eyes narrow.

"Oh," she says. "Absolutely not."

Younger Rina points at older Rina. "She started it."

Older Rina points back. "You existed first."

"That's not my fault."

"It is a little your fault."

Carmen lifts a hand. "Enough."

The dryer slams once.

Twice.

Three times.

Carmen doesn't even look at it. "And whatever demon is in the Whirlpool, it can also wait."

The dryer stops.

Older Rina looks at it, then at her mother. "How did you do that?"

Carmen sets her purse on the folding table. "I raised you. Twice, apparently. Appliances are nothing."

Younger Rina turns to older Rina. "You told Mom before me?"

"I didn't tell anyone."

Carmen looks at older Rina for a long, uncomfortable second.

Her face changes.

Just slightly.

The irritation remains, but something else slips beneath it.

Recognition.

Fear.

Something old enough to have roots.

"You," Carmen says quietly.

Older Rina frowns. "Me?"

Carmen's hand tightens around the purse strap.

"I dreamed you," she says.

The lights flicker back on.

Younger Rina laughs nervously. "Okay, so everyone's insane. Cool."

Carmen ignores her. She steps closer to older Rina, studying her face the way mothers do, like they can read every bad decision from the wrinkles and pores.

"You were older in the dream," Carmen says. "Standing in my kitchen. Bleeding from the nose. Telling me not to let you leave."

Younger Rina's smile disappears.

Older Rina feels the room tilt.

"I never did that," she says.

"Not yet," Carmen replies.

The vending machine display goes black.

Then green letters crawl across it again.

SHE REMEMBERS

Younger Rina backs away. "I don't like snack prophecy."

Older Rina looks at Carmen. "What else did I say?"

Carmen's lips press together.

Outside, the time machine starts humming. The sound crawls through the laundromat floor, up through the soles of their shoes.

The front windows frost over from the edges inward.

Carmen looks at both Rinas.

"You said if two of you ever stood in the same room," she says, "time would make room by removing one."

The dryer door opens.

This time, no one touches it.

Inside, curled impossibly in the drum, is the third Rina.

Her neck bends wrong. Her smile is bright but crooked. One eye flutters like it is trying to wake from a bad dream.

"I'm me," she says.

Then she looks straight at younger Rina.

"You're you."

Older Rina grabs younger Rina by the sleeve and yanks her back.

The thing in the dryer spills out onto the laundromat floor.

That is the only word for it.

Spills.

Like her bones have not agreed on a structure yet. Like she has been poured into the shape of Rina Martinez but the mold came cracked. Her head lolls, snaps upright, then jerks sideways. Her smile stays where it is, too wide and too patient.

Younger Rina makes a small sound.

Older Rina tightens her grip. "Don't."

"I wasn't going to."

"You were."

"I was thinking about it."

"You were about to say something stupid."

Younger Rina stares at the thing crawling out of the dryer. "To be fair, there's a lot of pressure."

The third Rina plants both palms on the tile, backward, and rises.

She wears older Rina's black jacket, younger Rina's red leather, Carmen's gold hoops, Lila's eyeliner, Mateo's old blue work shirt.

Pieces of people.

Pieces of choices.

All stitched onto Rina's face.

Carmen crosses herself.

The third Rina watches the motion.

"That doesn't work," it says.

Carmen's mouth tightens. "Maybe not, but it makes me feel organized."

Older Rina backs toward the front door, pulling younger Rina with her. "Mom, move."

Carmen reaches into her purse.

Younger Rina whispers, "Why is Mom grabbing her purse?"

Older Rina whispers back, "Because if there's one thing scarier than that thing, it's whatever your mother keeps in there."

Carmen pulls out pepper spray.

The third Rina steps forward.

The fluorescent light above her burns red.

"I'm me," she says again.

"No," older Rina says. Her voice shakes, and she hates that. "You're not."

The third Rina looks almost amused. "You came back because you wanted to replace her."

Younger Rina turns sharply. "Excuse me?"

Older Rina doesn't answer fast enough.

Younger Rina's face hardens. "Oh, wow."

"That's not what this is."

"That's exactly what this is."

"I came to warn you."

"No, you came to edit me."

The third Rina smiles.

The laundromat windows rattle.

Older Rina points at the monster. "Can we fight about my emotional defects after we deal with the dryer goblin?"

"You don't get to call it a goblin when it has our cheekbones."

"Fine. Temporal cheekbone goblin."

"It's not better."

"It's a little better."

The third Rina laughs.

Not loudly.

Not naturally.

She laughs like someone plays the sound from another room.

"You both think you're the original," she says. "That's sweet."

Carmen steps between them and the thing.

Older Rina's stomach drops. "Mom, no."

Carmen's eyes don't leave the third Rina. "You don't talk to my daughter like that."

"I am your daughter."

Carmen lifts the pepper spray. "You are something wearing her bad attitude."

The third Rina moves.

Fast.

A blur of red leather and black jacket.

Carmen sprays.

The mist hits the creature's face.

It stops.

Blinks.

Then smiles through streaming orange chemical tears.

"You used that on Mr. Delacruz's dog in 1998," it says. "You cried after."

Carmen's arm falters.

The third Rina tilts her head. "You told no one."

Carmen whispers, "How do you know that?"

"It knows what we remember," older Rina says. "Maybe what we almost remember."

The thing turns toward her.

"And what you bury."

The front door slams shut behind them.

The deadbolt twists by itself.

Younger Rina runs to it and yanks the handle. It doesn't move. She kicks it. Once. Twice.

"Open, you cheap glass bastard."

Older Rina snatches up the metal coin tray again. "We have to get back to the machine."

"It's outside," younger Rina snaps.

"Thank you. I thought it was in the soup aisle."

"There is no soup aisle."

"Exactly, genius."

"Girls," Carmen says.

Both Rinas look at her.

Carmen points.

Every washing machine door along the wall is fogging over.

One by one.

Words appear.

I'M ME

YOU'RE YOU

I'M ME

YOU'RE YOU

I'M ME

YOU'RE YOU

Then the glass circles begin to show faces.

Not full faces.

Fragments.

Rina at thirty, crying in a bathroom stall.

Rina at sixteen, stealing lipstick from a drugstore and looking terrified when she gets away with it.

Rina at fifty-five, maybe, hair white at the temples, mouth bloody, laughing at something burning behind her.

Rina as a child in Carmen's kitchen.

Rina old.

Rina dead.

Rina never born.

Younger Rina goes very still.

Older Rina feels the fight leave the room for one dangerous second.

The third Rina uses it.

She lunges for younger Rina.

Older Rina shoves the coin tray into the thing's face. Metal cracks against teeth. The third Rina's head snaps sideways, too far, then slowly rotates back into place.

Crack by slow crack.

"Rude," the thing says.

"Runs in the family," older Rina says.

Carmen grabs a bottle of detergent from a folding table and hurls it.

It hits the third Rina in the shoulder and bursts, blue liquid splashing across the tile.

Younger Rina looks at Carmen. "That was your plan?"

Carmen grabs another bottle. "I'm improvising."

Older Rina grabs younger Rina's hand.

This time, younger Rina lets her.

That matters.

A little.

"Back room," older Rina says.

They run past the folding tables and into the employees-only area, Carmen close behind. The back room is tiny, packed with boxes of detergent, cleaning supplies, mop buckets, and a stained office chair that looks like it knows secrets and hopes no one owns a black light. A rear exit waits on the far wall.

Younger Rina grabs the knob.

Locked.

"Of course," she says. "Because God hates cardio."

Older Rina scans the shelves. Bleach. Ammonia. Industrial detergent. A toolbox on the bottom shelf.

"Move."

She drops to her knees, grabs the toolbox, and dumps it open. Screwdrivers, wrench, pliers, a utility knife.

Younger Rina snatches the knife first.

Older Rina looks at her.

"What?" younger Rina says. "You got a tray. I want a thing."

Carmen takes the wrench. "Nobody cuts anybody unless I say."

The door to the laundromat floor creaks.

The third Rina appears in the doorway, one hand on the frame.

Her face is changing.

Not melting.

Correcting.

Her features flicker between older and younger. Lines appear, vanish. Skin tightens, loosens. Her hair shortens, lengthens. She is trying on versions.

Trying to settle.

"You can stop this," she says.

Older Rina grips the screwdriver. "By killing one of us. That's the pitch, right?"

The third Rina smiles. "By choosing."

Younger Rina's fingers whiten around the utility knife.

"Choosing what?"

"Which one gets to be Rina."

The room seems to contract.

Carmen says, "No."

The third Rina doesn't look at her. "One life. One path. One body. One set of memories. That's how it works."

Older Rina feels something cold open under her ribs.

Because some part of her knows.

Maybe the part that comes back here with too much regret clinging to her.

Maybe the part that watches younger Rina step out of the laundromat and thinks, for one horrible heartbeat, I could stop her from becoming me.

Younger Rina sees it.

Of course she does.

Her voice lowers. "You were thinking about it."

Older Rina says nothing.

Younger Rina laughs, but it breaks in the middle. "Jesus. You really did come to murder me with life advice."

"No," older Rina says.

"You came to save Mateo from me."

"I came to save us."

"Don't make it pretty."

"I'm not."

"You are. That's what old people do when they screw up. They rename it."

Older Rina flinches.

Carmen turns toward her. "Rina."

"I wasn't going to hurt her," older Rina says.

The third Rina leans in and whispers, "Not with your hands."

The words hit worse than any accusation.

Because they are true enough to sting.

Older Rina looks at younger Rina.

Really looks at her.

Not as the idiot girl who ruins things.

Not as a mistake in a red jacket.

As herself before the bruises harden into personality. Herself before she learns to make every room laugh so no one notices she is bleeding under the table.

Younger Rina is terrified.

And still standing.

Still holding a utility knife like she might stab physics if it comes close enough.

Older Rina lowers the screwdriver.

"I'm sorry," she says.

Younger Rina frowns. "That's it?"

"I'm sorry."

"No speech?"

"I'm trying something new."

"Gross."

"I know."

The third Rina's smile fades.

Older Rina keeps her eyes on younger Rina. "I came back because I thought you made the wrong choice. With Mateo. With Mom. With me. I thought if I could correct the moment, I could stop becoming someone I don't like."

Younger Rina swallows.

"And?"

Older Rina glances at the creature in the doorway. "And apparently time hears replace myself and gets ambitious."

The third Rina hisses.

The shelves tremble. Detergent bottles topple. The fluorescent light bursts overhead, showering the room with sparks.

Carmen shoves both Rinas down. Glass rains over her shoulders.

Younger Rina grabs her mother. "Mom!"

"I'm fine," Carmen snaps, which means she is not.

Blood runs from a cut near her temple.

Older Rina stares at it.

A memory moves.

Not hers.

Not yet.

Carmen in a kitchen, older, bleeding from the nose.

Carmen saying, "You told me not to let you leave."

Older Rina suddenly understands.

Not all of it.

But enough.

"The machine doesn't need both of us," older Rina says.

Younger Rina's face tightens. "What's that mean?"

"It brought me here. It can take me back."

"The haunted freezer is outside and currently doing demon karaoke."

"I know."

"No, you don't get to do brave and stupid after apologizing. That's manipulative."

Older Rina almost laughs.

God, she likes this girl.

She forgot that.

She forgot liking herself.

The third Rina steps into the back room.

Its shoulders scrape the doorframe.

Too tall now.

Too many angles under the skin.

"You don't go back," it says.

Older Rina looks at the bleach.

Then at the utility knife in younger Rina's hand.

Then at Carmen's wrench.

The third Rina rushes.

Carmen swings the wrench into its knees. Younger Rina slashes with the utility knife, catching the creature's arm. Older Rina hurls the open bleach bottle into its face.

The third Rina shrieks.

This time, the sound is not Rina.

It is every version of her screaming at once.

Older Rina shoulder-checks the rear door.

Pain shoots through her arm.

The door holds.

Younger Rina yells, "Move."

She kicks beside the lock with the full stupid fury of twenty-three. Once. Twice. On the third kick, the frame splinters.

The rear door flies open.

Cold night air blasts in.

They spill into the alley behind the laundromat, stumbling over crates and trash bags. The red pulse from the time machine spills around the corner, painting the brick walls like blood.

The third Rina crawls through the broken doorway behind them.

Her face is ruined now.

Not from the bleach.

From indecision.

Too many Rinas fighting for one skin.

Older Rina pulls Carmen along. Younger Rina runs ahead, then stops and turns back.

Older Rina barks, "Keep moving."

Younger Rina doesn't.

"Mateo," she says.

"What?"

"You came because of Mateo. Tell me what happens."

"No."

"Tell me."

The third Rina drags herself closer.

Older Rina wants to scream. "This is not the time."

"It's exactly the time. If you're leaving, then tell me the damn warning."

Older Rina stares at her.

The old answer is easy.

Don't let him go.

Call him.

Apologize.

Don't turn cruel because you're scared.

But standing in the alley with a monster made from regret clawing toward them, Rina finally understands the shape of the trap.

Any specific warning becomes a cage.

Any instruction becomes a theft.

Younger Rina doesn't need orders from a future she hasn't chosen.

She needs something harder.

Something kinder.

Older Rina says, "Tomorrow, you'll be scared. You'll want to win the fight more than save the love. Don't."

Younger Rina's eyes shine.

"That's it?"

"That's it."

"Do we end up with him?"

Older Rina's throat tightens.

"I'm not telling you that."

"That means no."

"It means I'm me," older Rina says. "You're you."

Younger Rina looks at her.

The words land between them.

Not as a curse this time.

As a boundary.

As a mercy.

The third Rina screams behind them.

"No."

Older Rina grabs a trash bin and shoves it hard. It rolls into the creature, knocking her sideways.

They sprint around the corner into the parking lot.

The time machine bucks on the asphalt, red light blasting through every seam. The metal skin peels back in strips. Inside there is no seat, no console, no tidy science. Just a dark opening full of wind and whispering.

Older Rina runs to it.

The door will not open.

She yanks the handle once.

Twice.

The machine screams back at her.

Her phone buzzes in her pocket.

She pulls it out with shaking fingers.

The screen flickers.

Lila's name appears.

Then vanishes.

Then another name replaces it.

DR. VORN

Rina answers.

"What?" she snaps.

Vorn's voice crackles through, high and panicked. "Rina? Rina, listen to me. The machine is not built for identity recursion."

"You think?"

"If you've made contact with yourself, the system may attempt to correct for duplicate presence."

"It grew a third me in a dryer."

There is a brief silence.

Then Vorn says, "That is worse than I predicted."

"I hate you more with every sentence."

"Only one displaced subject can return. One. After that, the aperture collapses."

Older Rina looks at younger Rina.

Younger Rina hears enough. She points at older Rina. "Her. Send her."

The third Rina rounds the corner.

The sleeping homeless man finally wakes, sees the scene, stands, picks up his chips, and walks away.

"Valid," younger Rina says.

Older Rina grips the phone. "What happens to her if I leave?"

"To who?" Vorn asks.

"To me. The first me. The young me."

"She continues. In theory."

"In theory?"

"Science is a series of humiliating surprises."

Carmen lifts the wrench. "Put him on speaker so I can threaten him properly."

The third Rina runs. It's wobbly and awkward, like a newborn colt.

The time machine opens wider.

Wind tears through the parking lot, ripping flyers from telephone poles, spinning trash into the air, dragging younger Rina's laundry across the asphalt like surrender flags.

Older Rina grabs younger Rina and hugs her.

It's awkward.

Hard.

Brief.

Younger Rina freezes, then grips back with one arm.

"Don't become boring," younger Rina says into her shoulder.

Older Rina chokes on a laugh. "Don't become a warning label."

"No promises."

Carmen grabs older Rina's face in both hands.

For one second, older Rina is not forty-two. She is every age she has ever been under her mother's touch.

Carmen kisses her forehead.

"Go," she says. "And when you see me, don't act weird."

"I always act weird."

"Less weird."

The third Rina slams into them.

Everyone goes down.

Older Rina's phone skids across the asphalt.

The machine pulses red.

Then white.

The third Rina crawls over older Rina, fingers digging into her jacket.

Her face is closer now.

Almost right.

Almost Rina.

For one instant, the horror drops away.

What remains is grief.

Pure and bottomless.

All the lives not lived. All the choices cut off. All the versions that never get a body. Never get a mother's kiss. Never get to be stupid in a red jacket or tired in black boots or loved badly and still survive.

"I'm me," the third Rina whispers.

Older Rina's hand hovers over the machine's emergency lever.

Maybe she is.

Maybe that is the worst part.

"I know," older Rina says.

Then she pulls the lever.

The machine screams.

Red light turns white.

Younger Rina's voice cuts through the wind. "Hey, old me!"

Older Rina looks back.

Younger Rina stands with Carmen, hair whipping across her face, eyes wet, utility knife still in hand because of course.

"You're not that ugly," she yells.

Older Rina laughs as the light takes her.

"Liar!"

The world folds.

For a moment there is no laundromat, no parking lot, no body.

Only memory turned inside out.

Rina sees Mateo standing by his truck in 2007, waiting for an apology that may or may not come.

She sees Carmen in a kitchen, pausing with a spoon in her hand as if remembering a dream.

She sees Lila in 2026, phone pressed to her ear, saying Rina's name like a curse and a prayer.

She sees the third Rina reaching for her.

Not angry now.

Hungry.

Lonely.

Then Rina hits the floor of Dr. Leonard Vorn's laboratory hard enough to knock the breath from her lungs.

Alarms scream.

Sprinklers rain from the ceiling.

The time machine stands smoking in the center of the room, its metal shell split open like rotten fruit. The blue light is gone. The red light is gone. Everything is gray.

Lila Park stands ten feet away holding a fire extinguisher.

Her sleek bob is damp. Her eyeliner betrays her. She looks furious enough to become legislation.

Rina coughs. "Good news."

Lila lowers the extinguisher. "I swear to God."

"I learned a lot about myself."

Lila marches over, drops to her knees, and grabs Rina by the collar. "Did you meet yourself?"

"Yes."

"Did you talk to yourself?"

"A little."

"Define a little."

"Several emotionally irresponsible conversations."

"Did anything come back with you?"

Rina opens her mouth.

The lab goes silent.

One sprinkler drips steadily.

Plink.

Plink.

Plink.

Rina turns her head.

On the far wall, behind the cracked observation glass, her reflection looks back at her.

Just one reflection.

Tired.

Soaked.

Forty-two.

Alive.

It raises its hand when she raises hers.

No delay.

No smile.

Rina exhales.

"No," she says. "I don't think so."

Lila closes her eyes. "You don't think so."

"That's the strongest statement science allows."

Lila lets go of her collar and hugs her instead.

Hard.

Rina allows it for three seconds before becoming uncomfortable.

Then four.

Then five.

"Okay," Rina mutters. "We're moisturizing each other with sprinkler water."

"Shut up."

"Beautiful moment. Terrible texture."

"I said shut up."

Rina does.

For once.

Across the lab, a phone begins ringing.

Vorn's office phone.

Lila pulls back. "Absolutely not."

Rina stares at it.

The phone rings again.

Every alarm stops. Every machine is dead. The building has no reason to let a landline ring.

Rina pushes herself up.

Lila grabs her arm. "No."

"I have to."

"No, you don't. That's how white people die in horror movies."

"I'm not white."

"You're acting white-adjacent."

Rina limps across the lab anyway.

The phone sits on Vorn's desk, black and old-fashioned, because Leonard apparently likes his science with a side of haunted hotel. The caller ID screen shows no number.

Just words.

I'M ME

Rina's blood turns cold.

Lila whispers from behind her, "Rina."

The phone rings again.

Rina picks it up.

For a long second there is only static.

Then a younger voice comes through.

Hers.

Breathless.

Shaky.

Alive.

"Okay," younger Rina says. "So, first of all, rude exit."

Older Rina grips the receiver.

Her knees nearly go.

"You shouldn't be able to call me."

"Yeah, I got that from Mom screaming, 'Do not touch the demon phone,' but here we are."

Behind younger Rina, Carmen's voice shouts, "Hang up before you get possessed by yourself."

Younger Rina muffles the receiver. "I'm not getting possessed, I'm gathering information."

Older Rina laughs.

It comes out half sob.

Lila mouths, What the hell?

Rina waves uselessly.

Younger Rina's voice drops. "It's gone. I think. The machine folded in on itself. Your scientist ran away crying, which was nice."

"Good."

"You're okay?"

Older Rina looks at the ruined lab. At Lila. At her shaking hands.

"No," she says. "But I'm here."

There is a pause.

Younger Rina says, "I called Mateo."

Older Rina closes her eyes.

"And?"

"And I told him I was scared."

Older Rina presses a hand over her mouth.

Younger Rina keeps talking, faster now, embarrassed by honesty. "Which was disgusting. I hated it. He got quiet. Then he said he knew. Then I called him an emotionally smug bastard, but softly, so I think it counts as growth."

Older Rina laughs again.

"That counts."

"Do we get married?"

"I'm not telling you."

"Do we get rich?"

"No."

"You answered that too fast."

"Sorry."
"Do we at least get better hair?"
"Eventually, yes."
"Thank God."
The static thickens.
Younger Rina's voice begins to fade.
"Hey," she says.
"Yeah?"
"I don't think you're pathetic."
Older Rina can't speak.
Younger Rina fills the silence the way she always does.
"I mean, you're definitely a lot. Like, medically a lot. But not pathetic."
Older Rina wipes her face. "You're not unbearable."
"That's obviously false, but thank you."
The static grows louder.
Somewhere behind younger Rina, Carmen says, softer now, "Tell her I love her."
Younger Rina groans. "Mom says she loves you."
Older Rina smiles through tears. "Tell her I know."
Younger Rina is quiet for one beat too long.
Then she says, "I'm me."
Older Rina looks at her reflection in the dark office window.
This time, it is only her.
"You're you," she says.
The line cuts.
The phone goes dead.
Rina stands there holding the receiver until Lila gently takes it from her hand and sets it down.
Neither of them speaks for a while.
Then Lila says, "So. Therapy tomorrow?"
Rina nods. "Yeah."
"Actual therapy? Not time-crime therapy?"
"Actual therapy."
"Good."
Rina looks at the ruined machine.
Then at the cracked glass.
Then at herself.

For the first time in years, she does not feel like a bad ending wearing boots.

She feels unfinished.

Dangerous, probably.

Messy, definitely.

But unfinished.

And that, well, it's something.

Lila helps her toward the exit.

Behind them, in the silent lab, the broken time machine gives one last soft click.

Both women freeze.

Rina turns.

Nothing moves.

No light pulses.

No voice calls.

No reflection smiles.

On the floor beside the machine, something small glints under the emergency lights.

Rina walks back despite Lila whispering several excellent reasons not to.

She crouches.

It is a hoop earring.

Cheap gold.

The kind younger Rina wears outside the laundromat.

Rina picks it up.

It is warm.

Lila stares at it. "Please tell me that's yours."

Rina closes her fingers around the earring.

She thinks of younger Rina in the parking lot, alive and angry and still possible.

She thinks of the third Rina, hungry for a life.

She thinks of time, not as a line or a machine, but as a mouth.

Then she slips the earring into her jacket pocket.

"No," Rina says. "But I'm keeping it."

Lila makes a pained sound. "Of course you are."

They leave the lab just before dawn.

Outside, the city is wet and gray and unremarkable. Traffic moves. Birds scream at each other from power lines. Somewhere, someone burns coffee. Somewhere else, someone ruins their life and gets another chance later.

Or doesn't.

Rina steps onto the sidewalk.

For a moment, in the dark glass of the laboratory door, her reflection lingers half a second after she moves.

Rina stops.

Lila turns. "What?"

Rina looks again.

The reflection looks back.

Tired.

Soaked.

Forty-two.

Hers.

Then it raises one hand exactly when she does.

Rina lets out a slow breath.

"Nothing," she says.

But in her jacket pocket, the earring is still warm.

6 in the Morning

Outside, it's bright. Already scorching. Already close to one hundred degrees, and the day has barely started.

In the front yard, a red-headed woodpecker taps away at a queen palm, transforming from bird to hammer drill. Every strike of its chisel beak repeats like a machine gun. The back-and-forth flash of crimson on its head and neck glistens fiery red in the drenching sun.

A lone shaft of sunlight pokes through a sliver of open curtain. Its ray catches dust particles dancing in the air, twitching like puppets on invisible strings. Each one rises, drifts one way, then the other. That single beam, like it's splitting the universe, makes its way along the beige carpet toward the kitchen, where it stops at the white doorframe, never reaching its final destination until later in the day.

Lynette sits in the middle of the plush couch in pink Juicy terry shorts, the front drawstring too long on one side and untied. It reaches the outline of her crotch as she sips fresh coffee. The java is so hot that thick, opaque clouds of steam waft from the surface, one after another, each disappearing into the living room air. Mixing with the oxygen she breathes.

She scratches at one braless breast beneath a black Metallica T-shirt. Her nipple pokes against the fabric.

One leg extends. Thick in the right spots. Her toes, nails brushed shiny azure, just reach the cherrywood coffee table. They cling there like a cat on a branch. The lone ray of sunshine splashes across her smooth thigh before resuming its trajectory.

And she stares at the wall.

A once-lifeless crack runs halfway from the baseboard to the middle. There, it branches three ways like a tree. She knows it needs fixing. Wants to fix it. Has the desire to fix it.

But fuck it.

There are other things that need doing.

And right now, one is at the top of her mind.

Adam saunters in from the kitchen and places an oversized black mug on a too-small cork coaster. The cup hides the protective covering almost completely. He plops down on the gray leather recliner and lets out a long sigh as his ass lands. Ocean-blue eyes blink, gathering in the morning.

His sleep pants, sheer and already short, ride up and uncover half a calf. At over six and a half feet tall, not much really fits. He scratches his shirtless, hairy chest, right across a chiseled pec. A gold cross hangs from a necklace around his neck, almost lost in the thicket of curly black hair.

Lynette takes her gaze from the wall and its vein of a crack. She takes a long sip of coffee, careful not to slurp because Lynette hates slurping.

"So," she starts, "wanna tell me why there's a dead body in the bathtub?"

Adam stops blinking.

Just stops.

His fingers stay curled around the mug handle. Steam rises between his knuckles, wetting the black hair there. Outside, the woodpecker hammers.

Tap tap tap tap.

The sound lands in the room like little nails being driven into bone.

Lynette waits.

Adam looks at her. Then toward the hallway. Then back at her.

"What?"

"You heard me."

"I didn't."

"You did."

"No, I mean…" He licks his lips. They're dry. His tongue is pink and slow and too careful. "What are you talking about?"

Lynette smiles without warmth. "Don't do that."

"Do what?"

"That thing where you pretend English is a language you just started learning."

Adam sits forward. The leather recliner wheezes under him. His knees open because the chair is too small, his body is too large, and the room suddenly feels smaller than it did thirty seconds ago. Sweat already shines on his shoulders. A single bead gathers near his collarbone, crawls down through the hair, and disappears behind the gold cross.

Lynette notices it.

Hates that she notices it.

Feels both nipples hardening.

Even now.

Especially now.

"You went into the bathroom?" he asks.

"I live here."

"I mean this morning."

"No, Adam. I smelled coffee, woke up, and levitated straight to the couch."

"Lynette."

She sets the mug down.

Not hard.

Controlled.

That's worse.

"There is a woman in our bathtub. Naked."

He says nothing.

"Black hair. White nails. Little tattoo between her shoulder blades. Looks like a moth or a butterfly or one of those stupid things girls get when they want people to ask about trauma."

Adam swallows.

There it is.

A tiny movement. A guilty muscle. A betrayal under the skin.

Lynette sees it, and the morning tilts.

"You know her," she says.

"No."

"You do."

"I don't."

"You just swallowed like a man trying to eat a felony."

He stands too fast. The recliner slaps back against the wall. Coffee jumps over the lip of his mug and spills onto the cork coaster, then onto the side table, then down in one slow black thread.

Lynette doesn't move.

Adam looks down the hallway.

The hallway is dim. Too dim for this early. The bathroom door sits three-quarters closed at the end of it. Pale yellow light seeps through the gap near the floor. The exhaust fan hums from inside.

Steady.

Low.

Like something breathing through a mask.

"You shouldn't have gone in there," he says.

Her stomach tightens.

Not, There isn't a body.

Not, You're crazy.

Not even, I can explain.

You shouldn't have gone in there.

The woodpecker stops.

The house listens.

Lynette slowly draws her foot off the coffee table. Both feet hit the carpet. Her thighs press together. The untied drawstring falls between them. She feels suddenly aware of her bare legs. Of the softness of her body. Of the way those short shorts ride up. Of Adam's size. Of the front door ten steps away. Of her phone on the kitchen counter because charging it overnight on the couch makes the cord annoying.

"Who is she?" Lynette asks.

Adam runs a hand over his face. His palm rasps against morning stubble. "Her name is Celia."

Lynette laughs once.

No humor in it.

"Of course it is."

"She came here last night."

"That much I figured."

"It's not what you think."

"That's always promising."

"Lynette, shut up for one second."

Her eyes narrow.

His face changes as soon as he says it. Regret flickers. Fear too.

Not fear of her.

Fear of something behind him. Down the hallway. Behind that mostly closed door.

He lowers his voice. "Please."

That gets her.

Not because it's sweet.

Because Adam never says please unless something is already broken.

The bathroom fan keeps humming.

From inside the bathroom comes a soft sound.

Water moving.

Lynette's gaze snaps to the hallway.

Adam doesn't turn around.

That's how she knows he heard it too.

"Adam," she whispers.

He closes his eyes.

Again, the water shifts. A delicate lap against porcelain. Like someone in the tub adjusting a knee.

Lynette's pulse jumps hard enough to make her throat hurt.

"She's dead," she says.

Adam opens his eyes. They look less blue now. Almost gray.

"She was."

The front doorbell rings.

Both of them flinch.

The sound is too cheerful. Two bright notes.

Ding dong.

Ding dong.

Morning manners. Neighborhood bullshit. The kind of sound that belongs to packages, missionaries, kids selling candy. Not dead women in bathtubs.

"Don't answer," Adam says.

The doorbell rings again.

Then a fist bangs.

"Lynette?" calls a woman from outside. "Honey? It's Marisol."

Lynette looks at Adam.

Adam shakes his head.

Marisol Vega lives next door in the yellow house with the ceramic geese lined along the walkway. She is forty-three, maybe fifty, depending on the lighting and her mood. She wears giant sunglasses, bright house dresses, and enough coconut lotion to grease a frying pan. She knows every dog's name, every recycling-day mistake, every vehicle that doesn't belong.

She also calls everyone honey like she's putting a leash around their neck.

"Lynette?" Marisol calls again. "I know you're up. I see your shadow."

Lynette looks toward the front window.

There, between the curtain and the hot white blade of morning, is the vague shape of Marisol's head. One hand cupped to the glass. Sunglasses dark as beetle shells.

Adam mouths, No.

Lynette mouths back, Fuck you.

He crosses the room faster than she expects. Not running. Not quite. But his body fills the space between her and the door with awful ease. Heat rolls off him. Coffee and sweat and male skin. Last night's sleep still trapped in his chest hair. She has the stupid, insane thought that under any other circumstance she'd bite him.

Or fuck him right there.

Instead, she steps around him.

He catches her wrist.

Not tight enough to bruise.

Enough to warn.

Her eyes drop to his hand.

"Let go."

"Listen to me."

"Let go, Adam."

"Marisol can't come in."

"Then maybe you should've kept dead Celia out of the tub."

His jaw flexes.

For a second, his grip tightens.

Then the bathroom door creaks.

One inch.

Both of them turn.

The yellow light widens across the hallway floor.

The water inside the bathroom drips once.

Then again.

Then something pale presses against the gap at the bottom of the door.

Fingertips.

Four of them.

White nails.

Too long.

Too clean.

Lynette stops breathing.

Adam releases her wrist.

At the front door, Marisol bangs harder.

"Lynette, open up. I saw something weird this morning, and I really think we need to talk."

The fingertips curl against the tile.

Scratch once.

Scratch twice.

From inside the bathroom, wet and small and impossible, a woman's voice whispers, "Six in the morning."

Lynette makes a sound she'll deny later.

Not a scream.

Not a word.

Something worse. Something small and animal that gets caught behind her teeth.

Adam backs up one step, his bare heel sinking into the carpet. His face has gone loose. Not dumb. Not blank. Loose, like whatever holds a man together has started to slip its hooks.

The fingers under the bathroom door flatten.

White nails scrape tile.

Then the hand slides back into the bathroom and disappears.

Marisol bangs on the front door again.

"Lynette, honey, I'm not trying to be a pain in the ass, but I saw a woman in your yard this morning."

Adam's head turns slowly toward Lynette.

Lynette doesn't look at him. She keeps staring down the hall at that band of yellow bathroom light.

Marisol keeps talking, her voice muffled through wood and heat and glass.

"She was soaking wet. Just standing by your palm tree. Barefoot, I think. It was early. I was taking my blood pressure pill because God forbid I sleep past five with these goddamn hot flashes, and there she is. Wet hair. White nails. Looking right at your house."

The bathroom fan hums.

The coffee on the side table drips onto the floor.

Lynette can hear every drop.

Tick.

Tick.

Tick.

The woodpecker starts again outside, frantic now, drilling the palm like it wants inside the tree. Like something has whispered to it too.

Adam grabs Lynette's shoulders and turns her to him.

His hands are hot.

Too hot.

"She isn't dead anymore," he says.

Lynette blinks at him.

"That's your explanation?"

"She was."

"Adam."

"I swear to God."

"Don't bring God into the bathroom with the naked corpse."

"She wasn't naked when she came here."

That hits her harder than it should.

A little jealous spark. Stupid. Rotten. Embarrassing. There's a dead woman in the tub, and still some ugly part of Lynette claws upright, wanting to know what Celia wore, why she came, whether Adam looked at her the way he looks at Lynette when he thinks she isn't watching.

"What was she wearing?" Lynette asks.

Adam stares.

"Seriously?"

"Seriously."

"Jesus Christ."

"What was she wearing?"

"A green dress."

"Pretty?"

"Lynette."

"Was she pretty?"

His mouth opens.

Shuts.

There it is again.

The delay.

The crime behind the pause.

Lynette feels heat rise in her face. Not from the sun. Not from the house. From rage. From humiliation. From fear wearing perfume.

"She came here asking for you," Adam says.

That flips the rage sideways.

"For me?"

He nods.

"Why?"

"I don't know."

"Bullshit."

"I don't know."

Marisol calls through the door again. "And I know Adam's truck is there, so don't act like nobody's home."

Adam lowers his voice. "She said she knew you from before."

"Before what?"

"I asked her the same thing."

"And?"

"She said before six in the morning."

The words land flat.

Then they spread.

Lynette turns toward the bathroom.

The yellow light at the bottom of the door pulses. Not flickers. Pulses. Like the room itself has a heartbeat.

Six in the morning.

She looks at the clock on the cable box below the television.

6:08.

That can't be right.

It was 6:08 when she sat down with coffee. She remembers because she hates being awake before seven unless someone pays her or dies.

And now someone has died.

Maybe.

The clock still reads 6:08.

The little colon between the numbers blinks.

6:08.

6:08.

6:08.

A sour taste fills her mouth.

"Adam," she says.

"I know."

"No. Look."

He follows her gaze.

The clock refuses to move.

Marisol stops knocking.

For one beautiful second, there is only the hum of the fan, the woodpecker, the drip of coffee.

Then Marisol says, quieter now, "Who's that behind you?"

Lynette's skin goes cold.

She turns to the front window.

Marisol is still there, her face pressed close to the glass, sunglasses tilted down now so her eyes can peer over them. Her mouth hangs slightly open.

Lynette doesn't want to turn around.

Her body does it anyway.

At the end of the hallway, the bathroom door is open.

Celia Morrow stands in the doorway.

Or something wearing Celia Morrow does.

She is pale with a blue underwash, the kind meat gets when it's forgotten in the back of a freezer. Wet black hair clings to her cheeks and throat. Her green dress hangs from her in strips, soaked dark and sagging, one strap torn, the fabric plastered to her body in a way that makes Lynette both ashamed and sickened for noticing. Her feet are bare. Water streams off her calves and gathers in the hallway carpet in growing black stains.

The tattoo between her shoulder blades is not visible now.

What is visible is her throat.

A deep purple bruise wraps around it.

Finger marks.

Large ones.

Adam's size.

Lynette looks at Adam.

He shakes his head once.

"No."

Celia smiles.

It isn't big. It isn't theatrical. It's worse because it's almost shy. A dead girl smiling at a bad joke only she heard.

Her lips part.

Water spills out.

Not vomit. Not spit. Bathwater. Clear at first, then pink, then threaded with something darker.

Marisol screams outside.

The sound snaps something loose.

Adam lunges to the front door, not toward Celia.

Lynette grabs his arm.

"Don't open it."

"We have to get her away from the window."

"Are you insane?"

"Marisol saw."

"She saw the dead woman walk out of our bathroom. I think the neighborhood gossip ship has already sailed."

Celia takes one step forward.

Her wet foot lands on the hallway carpet with a soft suck.

The house seems to dim around her. The sunlight beam on the floor bends strange, thinning, like it wants nothing to do with her.

Celia looks at Lynette.

"Lyn."

Lynette's stomach drops.

Nobody calls her that except her mother, and her mother has been dead nine years.

"What did you say?"

Celia's head tilts.

"Lyn," she says again, and the voice isn't Celia's now.

It's older.

Drier.

Familiar enough to hurt.

Adam whispers, "Don't listen to her."

Lynette can't look away.

Celia's face twitches. A ripple moves under the skin from jaw to temple. Her left eye clouds, clears, clouds again.

"Baby," Celia says in Lynette's mother's voice. "Why didn't you answer the phone?"

The room drops away.

Lynette is twenty-two again, standing in a grocery store aisle with a basket full of nothing important. Pasta. Cheap wine. Razors. Her phone buzzing in her purse. Mom flashing on the screen. She lets it ring because she's tired. Because every conversation is a weight. Because love, in her family, always arrives carrying a bill.

Her mother dies forty minutes later from a brain aneurysm in a kitchen with yellow wallpaper.

Lynette never calls back.

Adam's hand closes around hers.

This time she lets him.

"Not her," he whispers. "That isn't her."

Celia's smile widens.

Marisol pounds the window now, not the door.

"Open the door. Open the door, goddammit."

Celia's eyes slide toward the window.

Her smile fades.

She doesn't like Marisol.

Good, Lynette thinks wildly. Finally, common ground.

Then Celia moves.

Not fast.

Worse.

She bends wrong at the waist, too loose, as if bones are suggestions. Her hands hit the carpet. Her knees follow. She crawls down the hallway toward the living room with wet black hair dragging behind her.

Adam yanks Lynette backward.

"Kitchen," he says.

"What?"

"Kitchen. Now."

Celia crawls faster.

Marisol shrieks outside, slapping the glass with both palms.

Lynette and Adam bolt into the kitchen.

The kitchen is white tile, white cabinets, butcher-block counters, sun glaring through the breakfast nook window. Too bright for horror. Too bright for anything supernatural. Dirty dishes sit in the sink. A banana goes brown in a wire basket. A roll of black lawn-debris bags sits on the counter beside yesterday's mail because Adam has been meaning to trim the bougainvillea for three days.

Lynette sees the bags and has a thought so ugly she wants to spit it out.

Adam grabs a chef's knife from the block.

Lynette grabs the cordless phone off the wall charger, then remembers they stopped paying for the landline six months ago because nobody under seventy should have one.

"Fuck."

"Your cell," Adam says.

"Counter."

"In the living room?"

"No. Kitchen counter. It was here."

It isn't.

The charger cord is there.

The phone is not.

From the living room comes Marisol's scream.

Then glass breaks.

Not the big front window.

Smaller.

The side window by the entry table.

Marisol has done the stupid brave thing. Or the stupid nosy thing. With Marisol, there's never much daylight between the two.

"Help me," she screams. "Help me, help me, help me."

Adam grips the knife harder.

Lynette sees the blade tremble.

For a second, he looks like a child holding something too adult for him.

"Tell me what happened last night," Lynette says.

"Not now."

"Yes, now."

"Lynette."

"Because if I die wearing Juicy shorts and no bra, I'd like to at least know the plot."

Celia's wet hands slap the kitchen tile just beyond the doorway.

Adam pulls Lynette behind him.

Celia doesn't enter.

She crouches at the threshold like an animal trained not to cross a line. Her fingers curl on the tile. Her white nails click.

She looks at the knife.

Then at Adam.

Then at Lynette.

"Six in the morning," she whispers.

The cable box in the living room clicks.

The clock changes.

6:09.

Every light in the house goes out.

The air conditioner dies.

The bathroom fan stops.

Silence.

Then, from somewhere outside, Marisol makes a wet choking sound.

Lynette edges sideways until she can see through the doorway, past Celia, into the living room.

Marisol is halfway through the broken side window, her bright orange house dress caught on jagged glass. Her sunglasses are gone. Blood runs down one arm from where the window cut her. She kicks against the outside wall, trying to pull herself in or push herself out. It's impossible to tell which.

Celia turns her head toward Marisol.

Too far.

Almost all the way around.

Marisol freezes.

"Oh, Mother Mary," she says.

Celia rises.

Her knees crack.

Her spine unfolds.

She steps out of the kitchen doorway and moves toward the living room.

Adam whispers, "Back door."

Lynette doesn't move.

Marisol sees her.

"Lynette. Please."

That please is horrible.

It strips all the nosy right off her. Strips away the gossip, the coconut lotion, the sunglasses, the judgment. Leaves only a woman bleeding through a broken window, terrified and stupidly human.

Lynette looks at Adam.

He shakes his head.

"Don't," he says.

But Lynette is already moving.

She snatches the roll of black plastic bags from the counter. She doesn't know why. Maybe because they're heavy. Maybe because the thought is still there, ugly and useful. Those bags are thick. Contractor thick. Thick enough for thorns, palm fronds, dead branches.

Maybe more.

She grabs the cast-iron skillet from the stove with her other hand.

Adam hisses, "Lynette."

She rushes through the doorway.

Celia stands over Marisol.

Marisol sobs, one leg inside the house, one leg still outside. Her belly presses against the broken glass. Blood dots the beige carpet beneath her like spilled beads.

Celia reaches down and touches Marisol's cheek.

Tender.

Almost loving.

Marisol stops crying.

Her eyes go glassy.

Celia leans close to her ear and whispers something Lynette can't hear.

Marisol smiles.

Lynette swings the skillet with both hands.

It connects with Celia's head.

The sound is not a clang.

It's a heavy, wet knock, like hitting a melon wrapped in a towel.

Celia drops sideways.

Lynette doesn't wait to see if it works.

"Move, Marisol!"

Marisol blinks.

"Move, you nosy bitch!"

That gets through.

Marisol claws at the window frame. Adam appears beside Lynette, big hands grabbing Marisol under the arms. He pulls.

Glass slices deeper into the orange dress. Marisol screams. Adam pulls harder. The dress tears. She falls into the living room on top of him, bleeding, sweating, crying, alive.

For three seconds, nobody moves.

Then Celia laughs from the floor.

A quiet laugh.

A bathroom-drain echo laugh.

Lynette looks down.

Celia lies on her side, skull dented above one ear. Black fluid leaks through her hair. Her eye rolls up toward Lynette.

"Again," Celia whispers.

The dent in her skull slowly pushes itself back out.

Adam scrambles upright and drags Marisol away from the window.

"Back door. Go."

"Go where?" Marisol cries.

"Anywhere."

"The heat'll kill me."

Lynette laughs because she can't help it. "Read the room, Marisol."

Celia's fingers twitch.

Adam grabs Lynette.

This time she goes.

The three of them run for the kitchen. Marisol limps, one hand clamped to her torn arm. Blood drips between her fingers. Lynette's feet slap tile. Adam still has the knife. The black bags bounce under Lynette's arm.

They reach the back door.

Adam unlocks it.

Pulls.

It doesn't open.

He yanks harder.

Nothing.

Lynette looks through the glass.

The backyard is sun-drenched and white-hot. The patio furniture shimmers. The pool glows blue and fake, clean enough to look obscene.

On the other side of the door stands a boy.

Barefoot.

Maybe twelve.

Milo from across the street.

He wears oversized basketball shorts and a faded anime shirt. His hair sticks up on one side. His face is pale with heat or fear or both.

He presses one hand flat to the glass.

In the other, he holds Lynette's cell phone.

Lynette lunges to the door.

"Milo!"

He looks past her.

Past Adam.

Past Marisol.

Toward the hallway.

Then he mouths something through the glass.

Lynette can't hear him.

"What?" she shouts.

Milo lifts the phone.

The screen lights.

6:09.

Then his nose begins to bleed.

A thin red line slips over his lip.

Behind Lynette, from the living room, Celia starts singing in Lynette's mother's voice.

"Happy birthday to you."

Lynette's blood turns black.

It isn't her birthday.

It's her mother's.

And her mother died at six in the morning.

Milo's nosebleed hits his chin.

He doesn't wipe it.

He stands outside the locked back door with Lynette's phone in his hand, staring into her house like he already knows how it ends.

Adam pounds the heel of his palm against the glass.

"Milo! Open it!"

The boy doesn't move.

"He can't," Lynette says.

Adam looks at her. "What?"

"He can't hear us."

Marisol sobs behind them, folded against the kitchen island, one hand still clamped around her bleeding arm. Her orange dress is torn across the belly. Sweat runs down her neck into the soft hollow between her breasts. She looks smaller without sunglasses. Less royal pain in the ass. More frightened woman who woke up early and accidentally saw hell in the neighbor's yard.

Milo lifts Lynette's phone higher.

The screen changes.

Not the clock now.

A text message.

Lynette squints through the glass.

The message is from Mom.

Her stomach drops so hard she almost bends.

Adam sees her face.

"What?"

Lynette doesn't answer.

The phone screen glows bright in Milo's small hand.

Answer me.

Lynette's mouth goes dry.

"Your mother?" Adam asks.

She hates him for knowing. Hates herself for having told him the story one drunk night in bed with his arm heavy over her waist, his lips near her ear, his body warm enough to make grief feel temporarily survivable.

Celia keeps singing from the living room.

"Happy birthday, dear Mommy…"

Wrong words.

Wrong voice.

Right pain.

The kitchen lights flicker back on.

Once.

Twice.

When they steady, Celia stands in the kitchen doorway.

No crawling now. No shy dead-girl smile. She stands straight in the torn green dress, wet hair clinging to her face. The dent from the skillet is gone, but one side of her head remains stained black. Her white nails hang at her sides like little pieces of bone.

Adam steps in front of Lynette.

That does something awful to her heart.

Even now.

After the body. After the lies. After Celia.

Even now, his shoulders fill her view and some stupid part of her wants to press her face between them and breathe him in like a place to hide.

Celia's cloudy eyes drop to the knife in his hand.

"Adam," she says.

Her voice is no longer Lynette's mother's voice.

It's Celia's.

Soft. Young. Hurt.

Adam goes still.

Lynette feels it in him, that tiny betrayal again.

Celia smiles.

"You said you'd help me."

"I tried," Adam says.

Lynette turns on him.

"You tried?"

"Not like that."

"Oh, good. There are flavors."

Celia takes a step into the kitchen.

Marisol makes a little whimper.

Celia's eyes slide to her.

Marisol presses herself harder against the island.

"No. No, please."

Celia sniffs.

Just once.

Like an animal catching a scent.

"Nosy," she whispers.

Marisol shakes her head so hard her earrings slap her jaw.

"No. I didn't see anything. I promise. I don't know anything."

"You saw me," Celia says.

"I see lots of things. I don't remember half of them."

That would almost be funny if Marisol weren't crying.

Celia moves so quickly Lynette barely tracks it.

One second Celia is in the doorway.

The next, she is against Marisol.

Her hand plunges into the torn orange dress at Marisol's belly. Not with a blade. With fingers. Those white nails disappear into flesh like they've been waiting all morning for softer material.

Marisol's scream turns huge.

It fills the kitchen. Fills Lynette's skull. Turns the white cabinets and butcher block and banana basket into something underwater and far away.

Adam swings the knife.

Celia turns her head and catches his wrist.

Bone cracks.

Adam grunts and drops the knife.

Lynette grabs the roll of black bags and hits Celia across the face with it.

It's ridiculous.

Pathetic.

A household object against a dead thing.

But the roll is heavy, thick plastic wrapped tight around itself, and it lands hard enough to snap Celia's head sideways.

Celia releases Adam.

Marisol slides down the island, both hands pressed to her stomach. Blood spills between her fingers, too much, too fast, so dark it almost looks purple on the white tile.

Lynette grabs the knife.

No thought.

No speech.

She drives it into Celia's neck.

The blade sinks in halfway.

Celia looks at her.

Not angry.

Interested.

Lynette yanks the knife sideways.

This time the sound is wet.

Celia's throat opens.

Black water pours out first. Then blood. Then something like gray strings. Her mouth opens, but no scream comes. Just a thick gurgle, as if the bathtub is draining inside her.

Adam kicks Celia in the chest.

She flies backward into the hallway and hits the wall hard enough to crack plaster.

The house groans.

The crack Lynette had been staring at earlier splits higher up the living room wall.

Branches spreading.

Veins waking.

Marisol coughs.

Lynette drops beside her.

"No, no, stay with me."

Marisol's eyes flutter. "I told you… I saw something."

"You did. You were right. Congratulations. Biggest pain in the ass on the block, and you were right."

Marisol tries to smile. Blood pinks her teeth.

"I wasn't… judging."

"Bullshit."

That gets the smallest laugh out of her.

Then she coughs again.

More blood.

Adam crouches nearby, one hand holding his broken wrist against his stomach. His face is gray. Sweat drips off his chin. His giant body suddenly seems too vulnerable. Too much bone and skin and breakable meat.

"We have to go," he says.

Lynette looks down at Marisol.

Marisol looks back.

There's no lie available.

They all know.

Celia, in the hallway, starts to sit up.

Adam's voice drops. "Lynette."

Marisol grabs Lynette's wrist.

Her grip is weak, but desperate.

"Don't leave me for her."

"I won't."

Adam says, "Lynette."

"I said I won't."

Celia's neck hangs open, split wide from the knife. She pushes herself to her feet with one hand. Black liquid streams down her green dress. Her head wobbles slightly, like the cut has loosened whatever cable holds it upright.

Lynette grabs the roll of lawn-debris bags.

The ugly thought returns.

Not ugly now.

Practical.

She tears at the perforated edge with shaking fingers. The plastic fights her. Of course it does. Everything in the world opens wrong when someone is bleeding out on your kitchen floor.

Adam understands before she says it.

"No."

Lynette looks at him.

"No what?"

"You're not thinking."

"I am exactly thinking."

"That isn't Marisol anymore if she dies in here."

Marisol hears him.

Her eyes widen.

The horror of that lands harder than the wound.

Not dying.

Coming back.

Becoming something that crawls through someone else's house in a dead girl's dress and sings with a borrowed voice.

Marisol starts crying again. Quiet this time. Almost embarrassed.

"I don't want that," she whispers.

Lynette swallows.

Celia takes one slow step down the hallway.

Then another.

The clock on the stove clicks.

6:10.

A pressure changes in the house.

All at once, the kitchen smells like hot pennies, bleach, bathwater, and roses left too long in a vase.

Milo pounds on the back door.

Once.

Hard.

Lynette turns.

The boy's mouth moves behind the glass.

This time she understands.

Don't let them reach six twelve.

The phone in his hand lights again.

Another text from Mom.

Two minutes.

Celia laughs from the hallway, though her throat is open and ruined.

Adam grabs the knife off the tile.

"We cut her down."

Lynette looks at him. "What?"

"Celia. We take her apart. Bags are thick enough. We separate the pieces. Maybe that slows her."

"You sound way too calm for a man pitching arts and crafts with a corpse."

"I killed her once."

The kitchen goes still.

Even Celia pauses.

Lynette's face turns numb.

"What did you say?"

Adam's eyes close.

There it is.

The truth.

Not all of it.

Not enough.

But the first rotted plank giving way.

"She showed up at five-thirty," he says. "Soaking wet. Bleeding. Half out of her mind. She said she needed you. Said if she didn't get inside before six, something would follow her."

"Why didn't you wake me?"

"Because I thought she was drunk. Or high. Or trying to start something. She kept saying your name, but she wouldn't say how she knew you. Then she grabbed my arm and begged me not to make her wait outside."

"And you just let her in?"

"I thought I was helping."

Lynette laughs once, sharp and bitter.

"Yeah. Men love calling it that."

"I was going to wake you. I swear. But then she saw the bathroom and said she needed water. She pushed past me. Locked herself in. I heard the tub running. Then I heard her talking to someone."

"Someone?"

"I don't know. Someone who wasn't there."

Celia's smile widens through her ruined throat.

Adam keeps going.

"I opened the door. She was in the water with her own hands around her throat."

Lynette stares.

"She wasn't killing herself," he says. "Her hands were making her. Like somebody else had them. I pulled her out, and she grabbed me, and she said six in the morning, over and over. Then she stopped breathing."

"Then why are there finger marks from you?"

"Because I tried to pry her hands loose."

A lie can wear truth like perfume.

Lynette can't tell which part stinks.

Marisol groans.

Her blood reaches the toe of Lynette's foot, warm and slick.

The heat inside the house grows thicker. The air conditioner stays dead. Sweat runs under Lynette's shirt. The cotton fabric sticks to her skin. Adam's eyes flick down for half a second, automatic, ashamed.

Celia sees that too.

Her smile widens.

She lifts one white-nailed hand and touches the split in her own neck.

Then she pulls.

The cut opens farther.

Her head leans to one side.

Not off.

Almost.

"Again," she gurgles.

Lynette tears a black bag free from the roll.

The plastic snaps open with a violent flutter.

Adam steps forward with the knife.

Milo outside pounds again.

The phone screen flashes.

6:11.

Marisol's breathing changes. A rattle now. Wet and deep and wrong.

Lynette kneels beside her.

"Marisol."

Marisol's eyes find hers.

"Don't let me… knock on doors."

That breaks something in Lynette.

She nods.

"I won't."

Marisol's hand slips from her wrist.

Her body gives one little shudder, almost polite, and then the woman from the yellow house with the ceramic geese and beetle sunglasses and coconut lotion is gone.

For half a second.

Only half.

Then Marisol's dead hand clenches around Lynette's ankle.

Hard.

Too hard.

Her eyes snap open.

But they aren't Marisol's eyes anymore.

They are cloudy, filmed with bathwater.

Adam brings the knife down.

Lynette turns her face away.

There is a chop.

A wet crack.

A second sound, worse than the first.

Marisol's hand releases Lynette.

Lynette screams then.

Not because of the blood.

Because Marisol's mouth keeps moving.

No voice comes out.

Just the shape of words.

Six in the morning.

Celia runs.

She comes down the hallway all wrong, head half-loose, throat open, arms wide.

Adam meets her with the knife.

Lynette grabs the skillet from where it landed on the tile.

The kitchen becomes noise.

Knife into flesh.

Skillet into bone.

Adam yelling.

Celia choking laughter through a ruined neck.

Milo pounding outside like a trapped bird.

The clock on the stove changes.

6:12.

Everything stops.

Not pauses.

Stops.

Adam freezes mid-swing.

Celia freezes with her mouth open.

The blood falling from the knife hangs in the air in red beads.

Suspended, as if time has stopped.

The sunlight through the window hardens into white wire.

Lynette alone can move.

She stands in the center of the kitchen with Marisol dead at her feet, Celia split and smiling in front of her, Adam trapped in a moment with terror locked inside his eyes.

The back door unlocks.

Click.

Milo opens it from the outside.

Hot air rolls in.

He steps into the kitchen holding Lynette's phone.

His nose still bleeds.

His eyes are cloudy now too.

He offers her the phone.

"Your mother wants to talk," he says.

Lynette looks at the phone in Milo's hand.

The screen glows white.

No wallpaper. No apps. No time.

Just one button.

Answer.

Everything else stays frozen.

Adam stands with the knife raised, sweat trapped in beads across his chest. His broken wrist hangs wrong against his stomach, but pain has stopped on his face, locked there like a photograph. Celia leans toward him, black water suspended from her open throat. Marisol lies at Lynette's feet, her body folded wrong, her orange dress ruined, one hand still reaching.

The house is a held breath.

Only Lynette moves.

Only Milo moves.

Only the phone waits.

"No," Lynette says.

Milo smiles.

It is not a child's smile.

"You always say that."

His voice sounds like him and not him. Thin. Dry. A little bored.

Lynette steps back. Her heel slides in Marisol's blood, and she almost goes down. She catches herself on the kitchen island. Her fingers land in something warm and slick, and she jerks them away, choking.

Milo keeps the phone out.

"Answer her."

"No."

"She's been calling."

"My mother's dead."

"So is everyone eventually."

That sounds nothing like Milo. That sounds like something wearing him badly. Something that has heard children speak and knows where the mouth is, but not what innocence is supposed to do with it.

Lynette looks at Adam.

His eyes are locked on her.

He can't move, but he can see. She realizes that all at once. He's frozen, but aware. Trapped inside himself. Watching her decide whatever this is.

The sexual heat between them is still there somehow, hideous and alive under the terror. The memory of his hand around her wrist. His breath on her neck. His body in the doorway. The way he stepped in front of her. His eyes dropping to her shirt for one shameful second, even with death in the room.

She hates him.

She wants him alive.

Both things feel true enough to cut with.

"What happens if I answer?" she asks.

Milo's smile grows.

"You get to hear her."

"And if I don't?"

He glances down at Marisol.

Then at Celia.

Then at Adam.

"They finish waking up."

Outside, the woodpecker hammers faster.

Tap-tap.

Tap-tap.

Tappity fucking tap.

Like a countdown.

Lynette wipes her bloody hand on her pink shorts. It smears red across the terry cloth. The sight of it makes her absurdly furious. She bought those stupid shorts on sale eight years ago and refuses to throw them away because the fabric still feels good against her skin.

Now there's blood on them.

Marisol's blood.

Maybe Celia's.

Maybe something older.

"Who are you?" Lynette asks.

Milo lifts one shoulder.

A grown-up shrug on a boy's body.

"Six in the morning."

"That's not a name."

"It is where names go to die."

The house creaks.

The crack in the living room wall spreads another inch. Lynette hears it, even from the kitchen. A dry, splitting sound. Like old teeth breaking.

"Why me?"

Milo's face changes.

For the first time, the smile slips.

He looks toward the living room. Toward the hallway. Toward something beyond walls.

"Because you let it ring."

Lynette's throat tightens.

"No."

"Because she called and called."

"No."

"Because you saw her name and let your phone buzz in the dark of your purse while you touched tomatoes and checked wine prices and pretended needing a minute was the same as love."

"Shut up."

Milo tilts his head.

"You always say that too."

Lynette lunges for the phone.

Milo jerks it back, quick as a spider.

For one second, she sees his eyes clearly. Under the cloudy film, the real boy is there. Terrified. Screaming without sound. Trapped the way Adam is trapped.

Then the thing looks through him again.

"Don't grab," it says. "Rude."

The frozen blood beads hanging from Adam's knife tremble.

Celia's fingers twitch.

Time is starting to soften.

Lynette sees it.

Milo sees her see it.

"Answer."

The phone vibrates in his hand.

Once.

Twice.

The sound punches straight through her bones.

Mom.

Mom.

Mom.

She remembers the grocery-store aisle. The cheap wine. The screen lighting up. She remembers being tired in a way that felt righteous. She remembers thinking, I'll call back when I can be nice.

When I can be nice.

Her mother dies while Lynette is choosing between merlot and pinot noir.

The phone vibrates again.

Lynette reaches for it.

This time, Milo lets her take it.

The plastic is warm.

No.

Not warm.

Body temperature.

Like it has been carried under someone's tongue.

She looks once more at Adam.

His eyes beg.

Not don't answer.

Not answer.

Just live.

Lynette presses the button.

The phone goes black.

Then her mother breathes in her ear.

Not a voice at first.

A breath.

Wet, shallow, familiar. The breath from childhood sickbeds, cigarettes on the porch, laughing too hard during bad movies, crying quietly in the kitchen when she thought Lynette was asleep.

"Baby?"

Lynette's knees weaken.

Her hand tightens around the phone.

"Mom?"

The kitchen changes.

Not visually.

Everything remains frozen. Adam. Celia. Marisol. Milo. The white cabinets. The black garbage bags on the floor. The cast-iron skillet. The knife. Blood in beads and smears and puddles.

But the air changes.

It becomes her mother's kitchen.

Yellow wallpaper.

Coffee burnt on the burner.

Cheap lavender soap.

Hot grease.

A radio playing too low to make out the song.

"Baby, why didn't you answer?"

Lynette closes her eyes.

That is the voice.

Not Celia's imitation.

Not a trick.

Or such a good trick it no longer matters.

"I was tired," Lynette whispers.

"I needed you."

"I know."

"I was scared."

Tears spill before Lynette can stop them. Hot, immediate, humiliating. They run down her face and drip off her chin. She can smell Marisol's blood. Celia's bathwater. Adam's sweat. The whole morning rotting open around her.

"I know," she says.

The voice softens.

"You left me alone."

Lynette presses the phone harder to her ear.

"I'm sorry."

A pause.

Then her mother laughs.

Not warmly.

Not cruelly.

Sadly.

"Oh, baby," she says. "Sorry doesn't close a door."

Lynette opens her eyes.

Milo is closer now.

No memory of him moving.

He stands inches away, face tipped up. Blood from his nose has reached the collar of his anime shirt. His cloudy eyes shine.

The phone in Lynette's hand feels slick.

Her mother says, "Let me in."

"No."

"Just this once."

"No."

"I'm cold."

Lynette looks at Celia, dripping bathwater from a dead throat.

Looks at Marisol, gone and not gone.

Looks at Milo, trapped behind cloudy eyes.

Then at Adam, frozen in the ugliest second of his life, knife raised, body beautiful and doomed and stupidly hers.

She understands.

Not all of it.

Enough.

Celia did not bring this thing into the house.

The house is not haunted by Celia.

The house is haunted by unanswered things.

Dead calls.

Unopened doors.

Bodies left waiting on thresholds.

Six in the morning is not a time.

It is a mouth.

And it wants someone to say yes.

Her mother whispers, "I miss you."

Lynette almost breaks.

Almost.

Her whole body leans toward the voice. Toward being forgiven. Toward being punished. Toward any version of her mother that still wants something from her.

Then Adam's eyes move.

Just a little.

Not much.

Enough.

They shift down.

To the floor.

To the black lawn bags.

Thick plastic. Heavy roll. Contractor grade. Meant for palm fronds, thorns, branches. Things that scratch and puncture and fight the bag.

Lynette looks down.

The open bag lies near her foot.

Plastic mouth wide.

Black as a hole.

Her mother says, "Answer me."

Lynette says, "I did."

Then she drops the phone into the bag.

Milo screams.

Not the thing.

The boy.

For one second, Milo's real voice tears loose. High and terrified.

"Run!"

Time snaps.

Adam's knife comes down.

Celia hits him.

Marisol's dead hand claws at Lynette's ankle.

The blood beads fall.

The house explodes into motion.

Lynette twists, yanks the bag up, and cinches it around the phone. The plastic bucks in her hands like something alive inside it. The phone screams with her mother's voice. Begging first. Then raging. Then laughing.

Adam crashes into the refrigerator. Magnets jump. A grocery list flutters down and lands in blood. The white paper soaks crimson.

Celia turns toward Lynette.

Her head is almost fully loose now, connected by meat and gristle and whatever wrongness keeps her standing. She opens her mouth, and out pours the sound of every phone Lynette has ever ignored. Every buzz. Every voicemail tone. Every little digital chirp asking to be loved later.

Lynette swings the bag.

It hits Celia in the face.

The phone inside cracks against bone.

Celia shrieks.

The lights burst.

Glass rains from the kitchen fixtures.

Adam rolls, grabs the skillet, and slams it into Celia's knee.

The joint folds backward.

Celia drops.

Lynette swings again.

This time the bag hits the edge of the island. The phone crunches inside. The screaming cuts into static.

Milo collapses to the tile.

His eyes clear.

"Don't let her out," he sobs.

Lynette looks at the bag.

The plastic stretches from inside, shaping around fingers that aren't attached to any hand.

Adam shoves himself upright. His broken wrist dangles. His chest is bleeding where Celia's nails caught him. Four long red cuts run across the hair and muscle there, bright and wet.

He looks at Lynette.

"Garage."

"What?"

"Tools."

Celia crawls toward them, dragging her bad leg, her loose head bumping her shoulder.

Adam grabs the roll of garbage bags with his good hand. Lynette grabs Milo by the back of his shirt and hauls him up. Marisol's dead hand closes again around Lynette's ankle.

Lynette looks down.

Marisol's mouth works.

Please.

Maybe it says please.

Maybe Lynette needs it to.

Adam sees.

He raises the skillet.

Lynette stops him.

"No."

"She'll change."

"She already did."

Marisol's cloudy eyes fix on Lynette.

For a breath, something of the neighbor remains. Coconut lotion. Sunglasses. Ceramic geese. I'm not judging.

Lynette tears a second black bag from the roll and drops it over Marisol's head.

"I'm sorry," she whispers.

Then she twists.

Hard.

The bag tightens.

Marisol thrashes once.

Twice.

Not breathing. Not needing air. But reacting to the dark. To the sealed plastic. To whatever hates being contained.

Adam grabs duct tape from the junk drawer.

Because of course there is duct tape.

Because houses collect solutions for nightmares long before the nightmares arrive.

He wraps the bag around Marisol's head and throat, around and around, hand shaking, face empty.

"Garage," he says again.

They run.

Lynette clutches the bag with the phone inside. It kicks against her palm. Milo stumbles beside her, crying silently now. Adam shoulders the door from kitchen to garage.

It opens.

Heat blasts in.

The garage smells like gasoline, dust, old cardboard, and weed killer. Sun knifes under the big door in bright white lines. Yard tools hang on pegboard. Hedge trimmer. Saw. Bolt cutters. A rusted hatchet Adam never uses. A folding table. Boxes of Christmas crap. Paint cans. A cooler with a cracked lid.

In the corner sits the electric chainsaw Adam bought after a storm knocked down the mesquite.

Lynette sees it.

Adam sees it.

Celia slams into the kitchen door behind them.

The whole frame rattles.

Milo hides behind a stack of boxes.

Adam grabs the chainsaw.

"Extension cord," he says.

Lynette finds one coiled beneath the workbench. Her hands fumble. The phone bag writhes at her feet. Her mother's voice leaks through the plastic, thin and furious.

"You selfish little bitch."

Lynette freezes.

Adam looks up.

The door rattles again.

Celia hits it from the other side.

"You always were," the bag hisses. "Just like your father said."

Lynette's face goes cold.

Adam says, "Don't listen."

Lynette laughs once. Ugly and sharp.

"No. That's not my mother."

The bag stills.

Lynette looks down at it.

"My mother never sounded that honest."

She plugs in the extension cord.

Adam jams the chainsaw plug into the other end.

The kitchen door cracks.

A pale hand pushes through.

White nails.

Adam pulls the chainsaw trigger.

Nothing.

He looks at it.

"Safety."

"For fuck's sake."

He thumbs the safety and pulls again.

The chainsaw screams alive.

The sound fills the garage.

Obscene.

Mechanical.

Ordinary.

Perfect.

Celia bursts through the kitchen door.

Adam meets her in the frame.

The chainsaw teeth bite into her shoulder.

Black water sprays across his chest. Across the concrete. Across Lynette's bare legs. It's hot. It smells like bathtub drain and roses and something left under a porch.

Celia screams in three voices.

Her own.

Marisol's.

Lynette's mother's.

Adam drives the saw deeper.

Celia's arm comes loose.

It hits the floor and keeps moving, fingers clawing at the concrete.

Milo screams from behind the boxes.

Lynette grabs another black bag and drops it over the crawling arm. She has to put her foot on the plastic while the thing punches and claws beneath it. White nails pierce once, then stop.

The bags are thick.

Adam was right.

Thick enough for branches.

Thick enough for thorns.

Thick enough for this.

Adam cuts again.

Celia's other leg.

Then the other arm.

The garage becomes a slaughterhouse.

Not clean.

Not quick.

Not heroic.

It is ugly work. Wet work. The kind of work that ruins people from the inside. Lynette bags what falls. Adam cuts what comes. Milo cries and calls out when a piece moves toward her.

The phone bag shrieks from the workbench.

"Lynette. Baby. Please. I'm cold."

She almost looks.

Doesn't.

She wraps tape around Celia's severed arm until the plastic goes tight and quiet.

Adam slips in black water. Celia's torso lunges at him without limbs, head hanging, teeth snapping at his thigh. Lynette grabs the hatchet from the pegboard and brings it down on Celia's neck.

Once.

The head does not come off.

Again.

The hatchet sinks.

Again.

This time the head separates.

It rolls across the garage floor, black hair dragging behind it. Teeth chomping.

Celia's eyes blink.

Her mouth opens.

"Six in the morning," she says.

Lynette drops a bag over the head.

Adam tapes it shut.

The torso bucks.

Then stills.

For a moment, there is only the chainsaw idling in Adam's hand, his ragged breathing, Milo's soft sobbing, and the woodpecker outside beating the palm like it has found something hollow at the center.

The garage door opener clicks.

Lynette turns.

The big door begins to rise.

Slowly.

Sunlight widens across the concrete.

At the bottom of the driveway stands Deputy Kendra Mott.

Short. Compact. Uniform neat despite the murderous heat. Sunglasses on. One hand resting near her holster.

Behind her, across the street, mailboxes shimmer. A sprinkler ticks uselessly over a dead lawn. The neighborhood looks ordinary enough to make Lynette want to laugh until her teeth fall out.

Deputy Mott takes in the scene.

Adam shirtless and painted in black fluid.

Lynette in bloody pink shorts and a black tee.

Milo crying behind boxes.

Black garbage bags lined across the garage floor, some twitching.

The chainsaw in Adam's hand.

Marisol's blood trail leading from the kitchen.

Kendra removes her sunglasses.

Her eyes are calm.

Too calm.

"Morning," she says.

Adam kills the chainsaw.

Nobody speaks.

Kendra steps into the garage.

Her gaze moves over the bags.

One twitches.

Her jaw tightens.

"What time is it?" she asks.

Lynette looks at the wall clock above the workbench.

6:12.

Still.

Always.

Kendra nods like that answers something.

Then her radio crackles.

Static.

A woman's voice comes through.

Soft.

Wet.

Familiar to nobody and everybody.

"Unit twelve, answer."

Kendra closes her eyes.

"Don't," Lynette says.

Kendra opens them.

Her hand hovers over the radio clipped to her shoulder.

The voice comes again.

"Answer me."

Milo whispers, "Don't let her in."

Kendra looks at Milo.

Then at Lynette.

Then at the twitching bags.

She takes her radio off her shoulder and throws it into the nearest black bag.

Lynette moves instantly.

She twists the bag closed. Adam tapes it. The radio screams through the plastic, voice warping, breaking, turning from woman to child to old man to Marisol to Lynette's mother.

When it goes quiet, Kendra exhales.

"I've got twelve houses like this," she says.

Lynette stares at her.

"What?"

Kendra looks out at the street.

The sun is brutal. White. Unforgiving. Too bright for the end of the world.

"Started at six," Kendra says. "Calls. Doorbells. People outside asking to come in. Dead relatives. Missing kids. Exes. Anyone who could get someone to open a door."

Lynette feels the phone bag twitch on the workbench.

Kendra looks back at her.

"You answered something?"

Lynette says nothing.

Kendra nods.

"Yeah. Me too."

Adam steps closer to Lynette. Their shoulders touch. His skin is slick and hot and shaking.

She doesn't move away.

Kendra points at the bags.

"Do they stay down?"

"For now," Adam says.

"For now is what we've got."

A sound rises outside.

At first Lynette thinks it is the woodpecker.

Then she realizes it's doorbells.

All down the block.

Ding dong.

Ding dong.

Ding dong.

One after another.

Then phones.

Ringing inside houses.

Cars.

Purses.

Pockets.

Kitchen counters.

Dead landlines that haven't worked in years.

Everywhere.

The neighborhood wakes to the sound of being wanted.

Across the street, an old man opens his front door.

Kendra shouts, "Don't!"

Too late.

Something wearing his dead wife steps into his arms.

The old man smiles.

Then his face folds inward around the smile.

Lynette grabs Milo and pulls him against her hip. He clings to her, shaking.

Adam reaches for Lynette's hand.

She lets him.

Not forgiveness.

Not yet.

Maybe not ever.

But his fingers close around hers, and she holds on because the world outside the garage starts ringing.

Kendra draws her gun.

Adam lifts the chainsaw.

Lynette picks up the hatchet.

The black bag on the workbench whispers her name.

She looks at it.

Then at the street.

Then at the crack in the kitchen wall visible through the broken doorway, branching higher and wider, the house splitting itself open like a thing hatching.

The woodpecker stops.

Silence falls for one thin second.

Then the queen palm in the front yard shudders.

Something inside it knocks back.

Tap.

Tap.

Tap.

Lynette tightens her grip on the hatchet.

Kendra looks toward the sound.

Adam whispers, "What now?"

Lynette watches the palm split down the middle, dark sap spilling from the wound like blood.

Inside the tree, a phone rings.

Her mother's voice comes from the trunk.

"Baby?"

Lynette smiles.

Not happy.

Not sane.

Just done being afraid in the same old way.

She raises the hatchet.

"Put her in a bag."

Boy in the Corner

It's a middle-class neighborhood.

A cluster of beige roadside mailboxes stands near the curb, their plastic doors faded by years of sun and rain. Most are decorated with missing pet fliers. There's Mrs. Handley's Shih Tzu puppy, Mabel, her little pink bow crooked in the grainy photo. There are the Anderson twins' two cats, Rocket and June, both orange, both apparently loved enough to deserve laminated posters. There's Mr. Thompson's pet rabbit, Ms. Powderpuff, advertised with a hand-drawn heart around her name. Old Lady Hannigan's hamster gets half a sheet of printer paper and a photo so blurry it could be anything.

There are others, too.

Birds.

A turtle.

Something named Pickles.

The fliers flap against the mailbox post whenever the wind moves through. The sound is soft and papery, almost like whispering.

Beneath them, half buried under tape residue and old staple scars, Claire Mercer once noticed the corner of an older flyer. Yellowed paper. A child's shoe printed in black ink. Maybe an old safety notice. Maybe some missing thing nobody bothered to take down.

She didn't pull it loose.

She had enough missing things already.

Perfectly lined maple trees grow in the narrow strip of grass between the sidewalk and the roadway. In a few spots, the sidewalks heave where roots push through concrete. Every driveway parks at least one car. Some have basketball hoops. Some have ceramic ducks. Some have those little flags people switch out for each holiday.

By all appearances, it's a pleasant place to live.

The kind of place where everyone knows everyone else.

The kind of place where your business can easily become public domain, too.

Claire feels that part every morning.

She feels it when she walks out to get the mail and sees Ruth Handley two houses down, watering plants that don't need it. Ruth's hose is always in her hand. Her eyes are always somewhere else.

Today, they're on Claire's house.

Claire lifts a hand.

Ruth doesn't wave back. She just watches.

Claire considers pretending she doesn't notice, but she's too tired to pretend much lately. So she looks away first, opens the mailbox, and pulls out three bills, a pizza coupon, and a church flyer asking if she's prepared for what comes after death.

"Subtle," Claire mutters.

Behind her, the upstairs window of her son's bedroom looks down at the street.

The blinds are closed.

Claire keeps her eyes off them.

The house belonged to her father. Harold Mott lived in it for almost forty years, and the neighborhood still talks about him the way people talk about bad weather that missed their own roof.

Quiet man.

Private man.

Kept to himself.

Claire hears those phrases and knows what they really mean.

They mean nobody checked.

They mean nobody wanted to know.

They mean whatever happened inside that house stayed inside until Harold died alone in the back bedroom with the television still on and a half-eaten bowl of soup beside him.

There had always been rooms Harold didn't let people enter. Closets with padlocks. A crawlspace door painted shut. A back bedroom where the air smelled old no matter how many times Claire opened the window after he died.

When she was little, she once asked why there were scratches on the inside of the closet door near the hall.

Harold told her mice could scratch anything if they got scared enough.

Then he told her not to ask stupid questions.

Claire moved in three months ago because divorce does funny things to pride. It strips it down to numbers. Rent. Deposit. Credit. Lawyer fees. A child who needs a room. A mother who tells herself temporary until the word starts sounding like a spell that doesn't work.

Evan likes the house.

That's what worries her most.

At seven, Evan should like normal things. Dinosaurs. Baseball cards. Cartoons too loud in the living room. Instead, he spends most of his time upstairs in his bedroom with his Legos, his crayons, and his thin little shoulder blades hunched like he's listening to someone whisper instructions.

Claire comes inside and locks the door behind her.

"Evan?" she calls.

No answer.

She sets the mail on the kitchen counter and looks toward the stairs.

"Evan, honey?"

From upstairs comes a soft clatter.

Then silence.

Claire waits.

There's another sound, quieter this time. Plastic clicking against wood.

Legos, probably.

Probably is a word she uses a lot now.

She checks the clock on the microwave. 7:14 a.m. They have forty-one minutes before they need to leave for school. Plenty of time, if Evan's dressed. No time at all, if he isn't.

"Evan, get your shoes on."

A long pause follows.

Then his voice floats down from upstairs.

"Bobby says not to go."

Claire closes her eyes.

There it is.

Bobby.

She grips the edge of the counter and breathes once through her nose, slow and controlled.

"Honey, Bobby doesn't get a vote."

"He says Mrs. Handley's mad."

Claire opens her eyes.

Out through the kitchen window, Ruth is still outside. Still watering. Still watching.

Claire pulls the curtain across.

"Mrs. Handley's always mad."

"He says she's gonna come over."

"She's not."

"She is."

Claire turns away from the window. "Evan Mercer, shoes. Now."

More silence.

Then, very faintly, from upstairs, a whistle begins.

Mary Had a Little Lamb.

The notes are not perfect. A little airy. A little wet. But the tune is unmistakable.

Claire doesn't move.

Evan didn't know how to whistle last week.

She stands in the kitchen with the pizza coupon in one hand and the church flyer in the other, listening while her son whistles a nursery rhyme from inside his room.

The tune stops.

A second later, Evan says, "He's at the mailbox."

Claire doesn't want to look.

That's the honest truth. She doesn't want to move the curtain. She doesn't want to see Ruth Handley coming up the walk with her mouth pinched tight and her little dog still missing.

But she looks anyway.

Ruth is halfway across the lawn.

"Damn it," Claire whispers.

Upstairs, Evan giggles.

It's small.

Dry.

Not quite his.

Claire opens the front door before Ruth can knock.

Ruth Handley stands on the porch in beige pants, a lavender cardigan, and gardening gloves decorated with tiny yellow bees. Her white hair is styled into a soft helmet. She smells like talcum powder and outside water.

"Morning, Claire."

"Morning, Ruth."

Neither of them smiles.

Ruth's eyes flick past Claire into the house.

"Is your boy home?"

Claire's hand tightens on the door edge. "He's getting ready for school."

"Mabel's collar turned up."

Claire says nothing.

"In my hydrangeas," Ruth continues. "Just the collar. Chewed clean through."

"I'm sorry."

Ruth's eyes narrow. "Are you?"

Claire stares at her.

Ruth lowers her voice. "I don't mean to offend you."

"That's usually what people say right before they offend someone."

"There's something wrong with that child."

Claire starts to close the door. "We're not doing this."

Ruth plants one gloved hand against it.

"There's evil in that boy."

Claire's face goes hot. "Look, just because you don't like kids, don't start throwing that word around."

"No. That's got nothing to do with it." Ruth leans closer, and for the first time Claire sees actual fear under the judgment. "He's evil. Pure evil."

Ruth's mouth trembles on that last word. Just a little. Barely enough to notice.

Then Claire notices the empty leash looped around Ruth's wrist. Pink. Rhinestones. Ridiculous. The kind of thing an old woman buys for a dog because she has nobody else to spoil.

From upstairs comes a thump.

Both women look toward the ceiling.

Another thump follows.

Then something scrapes across the floorboards above them.

Slow.

Heavy.

Claire turns back to Ruth. "He's seven."

"So was my brother when he set fire to our shed with the barn cat and me inside."

Claire doesn't know what to say to that.

Ruth steps back from the door, but she isn't finished. "You need to watch him."

"I do watch him."

"Closer."

Claire closes the door in Ruth's face and locks it. Then she stands with her forehead almost touching the wood, breathing hard through her mouth.

Behind her, on the stairs, Evan says, "I told you she'd come."

Claire turns.

Her son stands halfway down.

He's wearing pajama bottoms with rockets on them and a school uniform shirt buttoned wrong. His hair lies flat on one side and sticks up on the other. In his right hand, he holds the missing collar.

Pink leather.

Silver bone tag.

Mabel.

Claire looks at it.

Then at Evan.

"Where did you get that?"

He blinks slowly. His eyes look sleepy and too soft to hold anything bad.

"I found it."

"Where?"

"Outside."

Claire walks toward him, each step careful. "Evan."

He watches her with calm, dark eyes.

"Where outside?"

He lifts one shoulder in a shrug.

The collar dangles from his fingers.

Claire reaches for it.

Evan pulls his hand back.

"Bobby says don't touch."

Claire stops at the bottom of the stairs. "Bobby isn't real."

Evan smiles.

It's barely there, just a small bend at one corner of his mouth.

"Yes he is."

"Then tell Bobby I said he needs to give me the collar."

Evan looks past her.

Not at her.

Past her.

Toward the dark hallway that leads to Harold's old bedroom.

Claire refuses to turn around.

"Evan."

"He says you shouldn't be here."

The house seems to go quiet around them.

No refrigerator hum.

No traffic outside.

No sprinkler ticking from a neighbor's lawn.

Just Claire and her son and the pink collar hanging between them like a tiny dead thing.

"What did you say?"

Evan's lips part.

But the voice that comes out doesn't sound like his.

It's lower.

Slow.

Wet around the edges.

"You shouldn't be here."

Claire steps back so suddenly her heel hits the rug and folds it under her foot.

Evan's mouth closes.

His expression changes.

The strange calm vanishes, and for one second he looks like a frightened little boy who has just woken in a place he doesn't recognize.

"Mom?"

Claire's throat tightens.

He looks down at the collar in his hand, confused.

Then he drops it.

It lands on the stair with a soft leather slap.

"I don't wanna go to school," he whispers.

Claire wants to run to him.

She wants to pull him into her arms, press his face into her shoulder, and tell him everything's fine. She wants to do what mothers are supposed to do when children look scared.

But Ruth's words sit in her head.

There's evil in that boy.

And beneath those words, worse, is Evan's voice that wasn't Evan's voice.

You shouldn't be here.

Claire forces herself up the stairs. She kneels on the step below him and cups his face. His skin is cool. Not fever-cool. Basement-cool.

"Who taught you to whistle?" she asks.

Evan doesn't answer.

"Baby, who taught you?"

His eyes flick toward the landing.

Then toward his bedroom door.

"Bobby."

"How'd you meet Bobby?"

"He's in my room."

Claire's hands shake against his cheeks. "Where in your room?"

Evan looks at her like she's asked something stupid.

"Under my bed."

By nine-thirty, Evan is not at school.

Claire calls in and lies badly. Stomach bug. Rough morning. Maybe tomorrow.

Then she texts Graham.

Something is wrong with Evan. Call me.

She sends it.

Then another.

I need you to answer.

Then she calls Dr. Lila Hart.

Dr. Hart's voice is composed. That of a woman who sits for a living and doesn't believe panic deserves oxygen.

"Has Evan mentioned Bobby before?" she asks.

"Yes."

"How long?"

Claire looks up the stairs. Evan's door is closed.

"A couple weeks."

"And what does Bobby do?"

Claire hates how childish the answer sounds. "He watches."

There's a pause.

"He watches Evan?"

"That's what Evan says."

"Does Evan describe him as frightening?"

"Not exactly."

"Does Evan say Bobby asks him to do things?"

Claire looks at the collar on the kitchen counter. She put it in a Ziploc bag because she doesn't know what else to do with it.

"Yes."

"What kind of things?"

Claire doesn't answer fast enough.

Dr. Hart's voice softens by a fraction. "Claire."

"He had a dog collar this morning. From Ruth Handley's missing puppy."

Another pause.

"That doesn't mean he harmed the dog."

"I know that."

"Do you?"

Claire closes her eyes. "No."

Dr. Hart exhales. "Bring him in at eleven. I'll clear time."

When Claire hangs up, the house gives a little settling groan.

Except it doesn't come from the walls.

It comes from upstairs.

From under Evan's bed.

She stands in the kitchen, phone still in her hand.

Then something rolls across the ceiling above her.

Not footsteps.

Not a toy pushed by a child.

A ball.

A small ball traveling slowly across the floor of Evan's room.

Claire hears it reach the far wall.

Tap.

Then it rolls back.

Slow.

Patient.

Tap.

Claire walks to the foot of the stairs and looks up.

"Evan?"

No answer.

The ball rolls again.

Tap.

Claire grips the banister and climbs.

Halfway up, she hears Evan whispering behind his closed bedroom door.

"No, she won't."

A pause.

"I don't think so."

Another pause.

"She gets mad."

Claire stops outside the room.

Evan whispers again.

"I don't know if she tastes like him."

Claire's hand freezes on the doorknob.

Inside the room, something giggles from beneath the bed.

Claire opens the door before she can talk herself out of it.

Evan is sitting cross-legged on the floor near the closet, his Lego set scattered around him in bright little pieces. Red bricks. Blue bricks. Yellow windows. A tiny plastic man with a cracked helmet. He looks up at her as if she's interrupted him in the middle of homework.

The room smells wrong.

Not rotten, exactly.

Old.

Like rainwater trapped inside a wall.

Claire looks at the bed.

The blanket hangs low over the side, almost to the floor. It's a blue comforter with cartoon rockets on it, the same one Evan picked out when he was five and still loved space. Now the rockets look faded and childish and stupidly cheerful.

"Who were you talking to?" Claire asks.

Evan fits a red block onto a yellow one. "Nobody."

"I heard you."

He doesn't look at her. "I was playing."

"With Bobby?"

His hands stop.

The room seems to tilt toward the bed.

Claire feels it. She hates that she feels it, because houses don't do that. Rooms don't lean their attention toward furniture. But everything in Evan's bedroom seems to know the bed is there. The walls. The closet. The toys. Her own eyes keep wanting to slide toward that strip of shadow beneath the comforter.

"Evan."

He presses the Lego blocks together until his fingertips turn white.

"Tell me the truth."

His eyes lift to hers. "You don't like the truth."

A chill moves over her arms.

"That's not true."

"Yes it is."

"Evan."

"You liked things better when I lied."

Claire takes one step into the room. "What does that mean?"

Evan shrugs.

The movement is too adult. Too casual. It's the kind of shrug someone gives before they say something ugly at a bar.

She takes another step.

A small red ball sits near the foot of the bed. Claire has never seen it before. It's about the size of a baseball. Rubber, maybe. Deep red, glossy in places, dull in others.

There are bite marks all over it.

Not dog bites.

Not puppy teeth.

These marks are thin, sharp, and close together.

"Where did that come from?" she asks.

Evan looks at the ball.

His face drains.

"Don't touch it."

"Why?"

"Because it's his."

"Bobby's?"

Evan nods.

Claire forces herself to laugh, but there's no humor in it. It falls out of her mouth like a bad cough.

"Okay. That's enough."

She crosses the room quickly and bends for the ball.

Evan screams.

It's not loud because he's angry. It's loud because he's terrified.

"No!"

Claire flinches, and the tips of her fingers brush the ball.

It's warm.

Not room-warm. Body-warm.

Something underneath the bed shifts.

The comforter rises a little from the floor, as if something moved under it and pressed up against the hanging fabric.

Claire snatches her hand back.

Evan scrambles backward into the closet door, knocking a toy truck over with his heel.

"I told you," he says. His voice shakes. "I told you, Mom."

The comforter settles.

Nothing comes out.

Nothing reaches.

Nothing breathes.

Claire stands frozen in the center of the room with her heart beating so hard it hurts the soft place beneath her jaw.

From the hallway, the house clicks.

Then the doorbell rings downstairs.

Claire jumps.

The sound is too normal. Too bright. It breaks the room open.

Evan whispers, "Don't answer."

Claire looks from him to the bed.

The red ball sits there, waiting.

The doorbell rings again.

"Stay here," Claire says.

Evan shakes his head. "No."

"I mean it."

"He doesn't like being alone."

"Then Bobby can learn to cope."

Evan's eyes fill with tears. "That's not funny."

Claire almost apologizes.

Almost.

Instead, she backs out of the room and pulls the door shut, not all the way. She leaves a crack because some part of her can't stand the thought of locking him in there with it.

Downstairs, Ruth Handley is on the porch again.

This time, she isn't alone.

A police cruiser sits at the curb behind her, angled slightly toward Claire's driveway. The red and blue light bar is off, but the car still has that official look that makes a neighborhood go quiet. Curtains shift across the street. Someone's garage door stops halfway down. Public domain, Claire thinks stupidly.

Ruth stands behind two officers like she's brought reinforcements to a bake sale.

The older officer is broad through the shoulders, with a shaved head, thick black mustache, and tired eyes. His nameplate says Bell.

The younger one stands half a step back. Leaner. Nervous around the mouth. His dark-blond hair is combed neatly but already losing the fight. His nameplate says Reeve.

Officer Grant Bell looks at Claire with the patient expression of a man who's had to calm down too many people in bathrobes.

"Mrs. Mercer?"

"It's Ms."

"My apologies. Ms. Mercer. I'm Officer Bell. This is Officer Reeve."

Reeve nods once. "Ma'am."

Ruth says, “I told them about Mabel.”

Claire’s jaw tightens. “Of course you did.”

Bell raises a hand slightly. “We’re just here to ask a few questions.”

“About a missing dog?”

“About several missing animals in the neighborhood.”

Claire looks past them.

More blinds move.

More faces hide badly behind glass.

“This is ridiculous.”

Ruth makes a small, offended sound. “My dog’s collar was in your house.”

Bell’s eyes sharpen. “Is that true?”

Claire says nothing.

That answers him enough.

He shifts his weight. “May we come in?”

Claire wants to say no. She wants to tell them to get off her porch, take Ruth with them, and find something useful to do. But the red ball upstairs is warm. The comforter moved. Her son’s mouth spoke with another voice.

And, God help her, part of her wants witnesses.

She steps back.

Bell enters first. Reeve follows. Ruth leans forward as if she might try to squeeze in behind them.

Claire blocks her.

“Not you.”

Ruth’s mouth opens.

Claire closes the door.

Inside, Bell looks around the entryway, then toward the stairs. Reeve glances at family photos on the wall. Claire hates that he can see them. Her wedding picture turned face down on the console table. Evan at age three with applesauce on his chin. Claire at nineteen standing beside Harold Mott, stiff as a prisoner beside a guard.

Bell nods toward the kitchen. “Can we sit?”

“I’d rather stand.”

“Fair enough.”

Claire leads them into the kitchen anyway, because standing in the foyer feels like being arrested.

The Ziploc bag with Mabel’s collar sits on the counter.

Reeve sees it first.

"That it?"

Claire doesn't answer.

Bell picks up the bag without touching the collar itself. "Where did you find this?"

"My son had it."

"Did he say where he got it?"

"Outside."

Ruth knocks once on the front window.

All three of them turn.

Her face hovers there like a pale moon with lipstick.

Claire yanks the curtain shut.

Reeve coughs into his fist, failing to hide a smile.

Bell doesn't smile. "Where is your son now?"

"Upstairs."

"Can we speak with him?"

Claire's stomach clenches. "He's seven."

"I understand."

"He's scared."

"Of us?"

Claire looks toward the ceiling.

Above them, something bumps softly.

Once.

Then again.

Reeve looks up. "That him?"

Claire swallows. "Probably."

Bell studies her.

She dislikes him for it. Not because he's rude. Because he isn't. Because his eyes are calm and patient, and she can see the exact moment he decides she might be part of the problem.

"Ms. Mercer," he says, "has Evan ever hurt animals?"

"No."

The answer is too fast.

Bell hears that, too.

Claire corrects herself. "Not that I know of."

"Has he talked about hurting animals?"

She thinks of Dr. Hart's coming appointment. She thinks of Bobby watching Evan draw. She thinks of small bones in small hands.

"He says things sometimes."

"What kinds of things?"

The ceiling creaks.

A long, dragging scrape follows, right above the kitchen.

Reeve looks up again. This time he doesn't smile.

Bell sets the collar down. "Ms. Mercer."

Claire's voice comes out thin. "He said Bobby likes when he takes apart birds."

Reeve's face changes.

Bell keeps his steady. "Who's Bobby?"

"My son's imaginary friend."

From upstairs, Evan screams, "He's not imaginary."

The kitchen goes still.

Claire closes her eyes.

Bell and Reeve look toward the stairs.

Evan speaks again from above them.

This time his voice is low and booming and wrong, coming down through the ceiling as if the whole house has leaned close to talk.

"She lies."

Reeve whispers, "What the hell?"

Claire opens her eyes.

Officer Bell's hand moves to his belt, not quite touching his gun. "Evan?"

No answer.

Then comes the whistle.

Mary Had a Little Lamb.

Slow.

Sweet.

From upstairs.

Bell starts toward the foyer.

Claire grabs his arm. "Don't."

He looks down at her hand, then at her face. "Stay here."

"No. You don't understand."

"Then explain."

She can't.

There are no words that make sense. Not enough. Not fast enough.

Reeve steps in beside his partner. "Maybe we should wait for child services."

Bell shakes his head. "No. I want eyes on the kid first."

"Officer Bell," Claire says.

He's already at the stairs.

Reeve follows, but reluctantly. Claire goes after them because staying behind feels worse.

The upstairs hallway is dim. Evan's bedroom door is still cracked open. A strip of gray light falls across the floorboards.

The whistling stops as they reach the landing.

Bell stands outside the room.

"Evan Mercer?"

From inside, Evan says, "Yes."

His voice is his again.

Small.

Frightened.

Bell pushes the door open.

Evan sits on the bed now, legs crossed, hands folded in his lap. His Legos are still scattered across the floor. The red ball is gone.

Claire notices that immediately.

So does Evan.

His eyes slide to the foot of the bed, then away.

Bell steps into the room. "Hey, Evan. I'm Officer Bell."

Evan doesn't answer.

Reeve stays near the doorway. Claire stands behind him, one hand pressed to the hall wall.

Bell looks around the bedroom, taking it in. Toys. Drawings. Little sneakers. The closet mirror. The low-hanging comforter.

"Your mom says you have a friend named Bobby."

Evan's lips press together.

"Is Bobby here?"

Evan nods.

Bell's eyes flick around the room. "Where?"

Evan points.

Under the bed.

Reeve mutters, "Of course."

Bell gives him a look.

Reeve shuts up.

Bell crouches slightly, hands on his knees. "Bobby? You wanna come out and talk?"

No response.

The room is silent.

Then a toy fire truck rolls out from under the twin bed.

Its white ladder lies flat.

Its little plastic wheels squeak.

Claire stops breathing.

The truck rolls halfway across the floor and comes to rest against Officer Bell's boot.

Nobody moves.

Reeve says, very softly, "Nope."

Bell stares down at the truck.

Then a toy police car rolls out.

Its emergency lights flash red and blue.

There is no siren, only the faint click-click-click of the tiny light mechanism.

Bell's jaw tightens.

"Evan," he says, "did you push those?"

Evan shakes his head.

Reeve takes a step backward and bumps into Claire. "Sorry."

Bell bends and picks up the police car. He turns it over, checks the switch, then sets it on Evan's dresser.

The lights keep flashing.

He looks at the bed.

Claire hears herself say, "Please don't."

Bell ignores her.

He lowers to one knee next to the bed.

"Okay, goddammit," he says, voice hard now. "Come out here."

Evan whimpers.

It's tiny.

The kind of sound a child makes before a shot at the doctor's office.

Bell looks back at him. "It's okay."

Evan whispers, "It's not."

Bell lifts the edge of the comforter.

The room seems to inhale.

He bends lower and looks underneath.

For a second, nothing happens.

Bell's shoulders loosen slightly.

"Empty," he says.

Claire almost laughs.

Not because it's funny. Because relief can sometimes look like madness on its way out.

Bell drops the comforter and stands.

"Nothing under there."

Evan stares at him.

"You didn't see him," the boy says.

"No."

"You will."

Bell's expression cools. "What does that mean?"

Evan points at the closet door.

At the rectangular mirror hanging on the back of it.

Bell turns.

The mirror sits at just the right angle to show the underside of the bed.

At first, Claire sees only darkness beneath the blue comforter.

Then she sees Officer Bell's reflection.

Then, behind his reflection, she sees another child under the bed.

Another Evan.

Only not Evan.

Its face is smooth and tight, skin pulled so hard across the skull that the eye sockets are gone. There are no ears. No mouth. Just a flat, stretched mask of child-flesh pressed close to the floor.

Claire makes a sound she doesn't recognize.

Bell spins back toward the bed.

The comforter is still.

He rips it up and drops flat to look underneath again.

"Jesus," Reeve whispers.

Bell's whole body goes rigid.

Claire sees his face from the side.

His eyes go saucer-large.

Under the bed, something moves.

Bell whispers, "There you are."

Evan starts crying.

"Don't take his hand," he says.

Bell reaches forward.

Claire screams, "No!"

But Bell's arm disappears under the bed to the elbow.

For a heartbeat, nothing.

Then Bell jerks forward so hard his chest slams against the floor.

His boots kick once.

Reeve lunges. "Bell!"

Bell makes a choke sound.

Not a scream.

There isn't enough air in it.

His legs convulse. His heels hammer against the floorboards. Something wet splashes against the underbelly of the box spring.

Reeve grabs Bell's belt and pulls.

Bell's body barely moves.

"Help me!" Reeve yells.

Claire can't.

She can only stare at Evan.

Her son sits cross-legged on the bed, tears running down his face, lips sealed tight.

But the voice comes out anyway.

Deep.

Slow.

Pleased.

"You shouldn't have looked."

Officer Reeve pulls harder.

His polished shoes slide on the bedroom floor. His face reddens. His teeth bare with the effort, and for one stupid second, Claire thinks he looks too young to be here, too young to be in a room where a man is being eaten under a child's bed.

"Bell!" he shouts. "Grant!"

Officer Bell's legs kick again.

Once.

Twice.

Then they stiffen.

Something cracks beneath the bed.

Not wood.

Something softer.

Wetter.

Claire clamps both hands over her mouth.

Reeve yanks Bell by the belt and gets him back a few inches. The older officer's shirt rides up, exposing a strip of pale lower back. There are scratches there now. Deep ones. Four red grooves on either side of his spine, as if something's hooked into him and refuses to let go.

Then Bell slides forward again.

Fast.

His boots scrape lines through the scattered Legos.

Reeve loses his grip and falls backward into Claire. They both hit the floor in the hallway. Pain shoots up Claire's elbow, but she barely feels it.

Inside the room, Bell's boots drum once more.

Then stop.

The room goes quiet.

Even Evan stops crying.

Reeve scrambles to his feet. His hand is on his gun now. It shakes so badly the barrel makes small circles in the air.

"Get off the bed," he tells Evan.

Evan doesn't move.

"Kid, get off the bed now."

Claire pushes herself up. "Evan."

Her son turns his head toward her.

His eyes are normal again. Wet. Terrified. A little boy's eyes.

"Mom," he whispers.

Reeve steps into the room with the gun aimed low.

"Bell?"

No answer.

Bell's boots stick out from beneath the bed. His heels rest at odd angles. His right foot twitches once, then goes still.

The police car on the dresser continues flashing.

Red.

Blue.

Red.

Blue.

It paints Evan's face in little bursts of emergency color.

"Bell, quit screwing around under there," Reeve says.

His voice breaks on the last word.

Claire hears it. So does he.

He swallows hard and takes one step closer.

"Grant?"

Nothing.

Evan whispers, "He's chewing."

Reeve freezes.

Claire feels the room go cold.

Not emotionally cold.

Cold cold.

Her breath leaves her mouth in a pale thread.

Reeve looks at Evan.

"What did you say?"

Evan's lips tremble. "Bobby's chewing."

Under the bed, something knocks lightly against the box spring.

Tap.

Tap.

Tap.

Like a child asking permission to come in.

Reeve bends toward Bell's boots, keeping one hand on his gun. With his free hand, he grabs Bell by the pant leg.

"Come on," he says, barely above a whisper. "Come on, man. Come on."

He pulls.

Bell slides out.

At first, Claire sees only his legs. Then his hips. His duty belt. His broad back.

Then nothing where his head should be.

A red, torn stump drags over the floorboards.

Blood spills across the Legos.

Claire screams.

She can't stop herself. It tears out of her so hard it hurts her throat.

Reeve lets go and stumbles back. His gun drops from his hand and hits the floor with a heavy clack.

Bell's body lies half in the room, half still under the bed. His arms are gone up to the elbows. His shirt is soaked black-red. The box spring above him drips steadily, a slow patter against the floor.

Evan closes his eyes.

"I told him," he says.

Reeve turns to the boy. Horror has emptied his face. He looks like a man who's forgotten every word he knows except the bad ones.

"You," he says.

Claire steps between them. "Don't."

"That thing came from under his bed."

"He's a child."

Reeve points at Evan. "He told it not to take his hand. He knew."

"He's seven."

"He knew."

The words hit Claire because they're true.

Evan knew.

Evan always knows a second before everyone else does. The collar. Ruth. The toys. The hand. The chewing.

Reeve backs toward the doorway. His eyes never leave the bed.

"We need to get out."

"Yes," Claire says.

She turns to Evan and reaches for him.

He flinches.

Not from her.

From something behind her.

Claire doesn't look.

She can't make herself look.

"Evan," she says, keeping her voice low. "Come to me."

He shakes his head.

"Come here, baby."

"No."

"Evan, now."

"He says I can't."

Reeve laughs once. It's sharp and ugly and close to panic. "Well, tell him I don't give a shit."

The blanket along the bed's edge lifts slightly.

Reeve shuts up.

The room holds its breath.

From beneath the bed, something speaks in Officer Bell's voice.

"Hey, Reeve."

Reeve goes pale.

Claire's stomach turns over.

The voice is almost right. Almost Bell. Same rough edge, same tired weight. But there's wetness in it. Something bubbling behind the words.

"Hey, Reeve," it says again. "What's the deal in there?"

Reeve whispers, "No."

The comforter shifts.

Bell's head rolls out.

It comes slowly, bumping over the floorboards, turning once before stopping face-up near Reeve's dropped gun.

Only it isn't right anymore.

The skin has been pulled tight. The mouth is gone. The eye sockets are smoothed over. The ears are missing. The mustache remains like some hideous joke pasted across a blank face.

Claire makes a strangled sound.

Evan turns away.

Reeve grabs his gun from the floor with both hands. "Back up."

"Daryl," Claire says.

"Back up."

"There's nowhere to shoot."

"I said back up."

Under the bed, Bell's voice comes again.

Only now it's not Bell.

It's lower.

Older.

Amused.

"You should't go there."

Claire hears the missing n in the word. Shouldn't. Should't. Like language itself has been chewed.

Reeve fires.

The shot is deafening inside the small bedroom.

Evan screams and folds over himself.

The bullet tears through the hanging comforter, splinters the wooden bed frame, and punches into the wall near the closet. The rectangular mirror cracks from corner to corner.

For a second, the whole room is sound and smoke and dust.

Then silence.

The police car keeps flashing.

Red.

Blue.

Red.

Blue.

Reeve is breathing hard through his nose. The gun trembles in his grip.

Claire grabs Evan and pulls him off the bed.

This time he comes.

His body is cold and stiff in her arms, but he comes. She hauls him against her chest and backs toward the door, stepping over Bell's head, stepping around Bell's blood, stepping through a mother's nightmare with her son's hands clutching her shirt.

Reeve keeps the gun aimed at the bed.

"We're leaving," Claire says.

"Go."

"Daryl."

"Go!"

She runs.

Evan weighs almost nothing, all bones and pajamas and terror. She carries him down the hallway. The stairs blur beneath her feet. Behind her, Reeve backs out of the bedroom.

Then he says, "What the hell?"

Claire stops at the top of the stairs despite every sane part of her telling her not to.

Reeve stands in the hallway, facing Harold Mott's old bedroom.

The door is open.

It was closed before.

Claire is sure of that.

A smell comes from inside. Dust. Old soup. Cigarette smoke. Something rotten underneath.

Reeve looks back at Claire.

"Keep going."

From Harold's room, someone whistles.

Mary Had a Little Lamb.

Not Evan.

Not Bobby.

An adult trying to make the tune small enough for a child.

Claire's mouth goes dry.

Evan buries his face in her neck.

"Grandpa," he whispers.

Reeve hears him.

His eyes move to Evan. "What?"

Claire's knees almost give.

No.

No, no, no.

She hasn't said Harold's name in front of Evan more than maybe twice. She doesn't tell stories about her father. She doesn't keep his picture up. She doesn't mention him unless paperwork requires it.

From inside the dead man's room, a voice says, "Claire-Bear."

The childhood nickname hits her like a slap.

She hasn't heard it in twenty-three years.

Reeve whispers, "Who's in there?"

Claire can't answer.

The voice comes again.

"Claire-Bear, you shouldn't make such a fuss."

Her throat closes.

She's eleven again.

Bare feet on cold floor.

A hallway too dark.

Her father's hand around her upper arm, squeezing hard enough to bruise.

Don't make such a fuss.

Her memory tries to shut itself.

The house won't let it.

The door to Harold's bedroom opens wider with a slow creak.

Inside is darkness.

Not normal darkness. Not a room with the shades drawn. This dark has shape. It moves in little pulses, like a lung.

Reeve aims his gun into it. "Police! Come out!"

Something laughs from Evan's bedroom.

Bobby.

High and delighted now.

The red ball rolls into the hallway.

It bounces once against the baseboard.

Tap.

Then it begins to roll toward the stairs.

Toward Claire.

Evan sees it and starts clawing at her shoulder.

"Don't let it touch us."

Claire steps backward onto the top stair.

The ball rolls faster.

Reeve fires at it.

The bullet punches through the floor inches away. The ball hops, wobbles, then keeps coming.

From Harold's bedroom, the adult whistle continues.

From Evan's room, Bell's headless body scrapes across the floor.

Claire sees one boot appear in the hallway.

Then the other.

The body crawls without hands.

It pushes itself along with stumps and knees, dragging blood behind it.

Reeve turns and fires twice.

Bell's body jerks but doesn't stop.

It crawls toward him.

"Move!" Reeve shouts.

Claire runs down the stairs with Evan in her arms.

At the bottom, she slips on the rug and slams into the wall. Evan's head knocks her chin, and for a flash she sees white sparks. He cries out. She nearly drops him but catches herself on the banister.

Upstairs, Reeve screams.

Not a long scream.

A short one.

Surprised.

Then there's a hard thud, a wet crunch, and something heavy tumbles down the stairs.

Claire twists away as Daryl Reeve's body rolls past her and lands in the foyer on its back.

His neck is bent wrong.

His gun is gone.

His eyes stare at nothing.

For one horrible second, Claire thinks that's it. He's dead. Poor terrified Daryl Reeve is dead in her front hall with one shoe missing.

Then his eyes blink.

Slow.

Sleepy.

His mouth opens.

But Bell's voice comes out.

"Ms. Mercer," it says. "We're just here to ask a few questions."

Evan screams into Claire's shoulder.

Claire bolts for the front door.

She fumbles the lock with one hand, Evan hooked against her hip, his legs clamped around her waist. The dead officer in the foyer begins to sit up. His head lolls to the side, neck bones clicking softly as they try to arrange themselves.

The dead thing wearing Reeve's body smiles.

His teeth are black now.

All coming to fine points.

Like a picket fence burned down to rot.

Claire gets the door open.

Ruth Handley stands on the porch.

Her face is tight with fury and fear.

"What happened in there?"

Claire tries to push past her. "Move."

Ruth looks over Claire's shoulder.

She sees Reeve.

She sees the blood on the stairs.

She sees Evan in Claire's arms.

"I told you," Ruth whispers.

"Move!"

Ruth does.

Claire stumbles out onto the porch and into daylight.

Real daylight.

Safe daylight.

Except it isn't safe. Not really. The neighborhood is outside now. Faces in windows. Doors opening. A man across the street standing frozen with a rake in his hand. The Anderson twins on their bikes at the curb, staring.

Claire carries Evan down the steps.

Behind her, inside the house, something laughs with her father's voice.

"Don't run, Claire-Bear."

Ruth backs down the walk beside her. "Where are the officers?"

Claire doesn't answer.

Reeve appears in the doorway.

His head still hangs at the wrong angle.

His black teeth show in a grin.

Ruth moans, "Oh God."

Reeve lifts one hand and points at Evan.

Only his lips don't move when the voice comes out.

Deep.

Wet.

Hungry.

"The people," it says, "they hurt me."

The neighborhood goes silent.

Claire knows everyone hears it.

For the first time, she understands the trap.

It isn't just under the bed.

It's in the story.

It tells people just enough pain to make them lean closer. It gives them a hurt child. A lonely boy. A dead friend. A father's old cruelty. It makes them feel guilty. It makes them want to help.

Then it waits for them to look.

Evan lifts his head from Claire's shoulder.

His eyes are black from edge to edge.

He looks at Ruth Handley.

And in a voice too deep for his small body, he says, "You see it."

Ruth shakes her head, already crying. "I don't see anything."

Evan points behind her.

"There. He's there."

Ruth turns.

Claire screams, "Don't!"

But Ruth Handley looks.

Ruth Handley sees something nobody else sees.

Claire knows it from the way the woman's face changes. One second, Ruth is pinched and frightened and furious, the queen of everybody else's business. The next, her face opens into the helpless wonder of a child seeing something loved returned from the dark.

"Mabel?" Ruth whispers.

Claire's stomach drops.

"No," Claire says. "Ruth, no, that's not her."

Ruth takes one step into the street.

The Anderson twins stop their bikes near the curb. Mr. Thompson stands three lawns away in slippers and a robe, one hand covering his mouth. Old Lady Hannigan peers from behind her storm door, blind eyes filmed gray, hearing more than seeing.

Ruth walks another step.

Her gardening gloves hang limp at her sides.

"Mabel, baby?"

There's nothing in the street.

Nothing Claire can see.

Just cracked asphalt. A strip of late morning sun. A brown maple leaf turning slowly in the gutter.

But Ruth sees her dog.

Claire sees that.

Evan shifts in her arms.

He's heavy now. Too heavy. His small body weighs against her with the dead weight of someone pretending to sleep.

"Make her stop," Claire hisses into his ear.

Evan doesn't answer.

"Evan."

His face turns toward hers.

His eyes are still black.

Not dark. Not shadowed.

Black as two wet pieces of coal.

His mouth stays shut.

His lips stretch.

"Everyone loses something," Bobby says through him.

The voice rolls low across the lawn.

Ruth keeps walking.

The air around her seems to shimmer. A heat ripple without heat. The street beyond her bends slightly, like a reflection in warped glass.

Claire grabs Ruth's cardigan with her free hand and yanks hard.

Ruth turns on her, wild.

"Let go of me!"

"There's nothing there!"

"She's right there!"

"No, she isn't!"

Ruth slaps Claire.

It's sudden and sharp. Claire's head snaps sideways. Her cheek blooms hot. Evan slips lower in her arms, and for one panicked heartbeat, Claire almost drops him.

Ruth shoves her away and stumbles toward the shimmer.

"Mabel!"

The shimmer opens.

It doesn't open like a door. It smiles.

That's the only way Claire can think of it. The air smiles wide, and behind it is not the street. Behind it is the underside of a bed, stretched impossibly large. Wood slats. Sagging fabric. Dark stains. Bell's blood dripping upward instead of down.

Ruth sees too late.

Her scream starts human.

It doesn't end that way.

Something pulls her forward. Not hands Claire can see, but force. Hunger. A tug from the bones. Ruth's body snaps rigid, and her gardening gloves fly off, fingers empty and reaching.

She folds in half.

Not at the waist.

Backward.

Her spine cracks so loudly Mr. Thompson drops to his knees on his lawn.

The Anderson twins scream.

Ruth disappears into the smiling gap in the street, cardigan first, white hair last.

Then the gap shuts.

The street is street again.

A brown maple leaf slides into the gutter.

From the open front door of Claire's house, Reeve's dead body laughs.

Inside that laugh are other sounds.

A dog yipping.

A rabbit thumping.

Cats crying in the dark.

And Harold Mott whistling Mary Had a Little Lamb through all of it.

Claire runs.

She doesn't think. She doesn't plan. She doesn't even know where she's going. She just clutches Evan to her chest and bolts down the sidewalk past the mailboxes, past the missing pet fliers, past Ruth's empty porch and Mr. Thompson praying on wet grass.

"Claire!" someone shouts.

Maybe Nora Bellamy.

Maybe a neighbor.

Maybe nobody.

Claire doesn't stop.

Evan's head rests against her shoulder. His lips brush her ear.

"You're taking him away from me," Bobby says.

"You don't get him."

"He invited me."

"He's seven."

"He opened the door."

Claire's lungs burn. "What door?"

Evan's little hand rises and points.

Not toward the house.

Toward the mailboxes.

The beige gang mailboxes stand beside the road, layered with fliers. Missing pets. Missing animals. Missing pieces of ordinary life. Sun-faded tape curls at the corners. A dozen small faces look out from paper.

Mabel.

Rocket.

June.

Ms. Powderpuff.

Pickles.

Claire slows despite herself.

On the bottom of the post, half-hidden beneath a flyer for a lost cockatiel, is an older piece of paper.

Not sun-faded.

Yellowed.

Ancient.

The tape holding it looks fresh.

Claire steps closer.

It's a missing child flyer.

A boy with a blunt haircut and solemn eyes stares out from the page.

Bobby Mott.

Age seven.

Last seen August 14, 1989.

Claire's mouth goes dry.

Mott.

Not Bobby Mercer.

Not Bobby Anybody.

Bobby Mott.

Her father's name sits underneath in small print.

Contact Harold Mott with information.

Claire feels the world tilt.

Evan slides out of her arms.

She grabs for him, but his feet touch the sidewalk, and he stands there in his rocket pajamas and crooked school shirt, staring at the old flyer.

"Evan," she says.

He doesn't answer.

A shadow moves behind the mailboxes.

No.

Not behind.

Under.

The concrete beneath the mailboxes bulges up the way sidewalk slabs do when roots push too hard from below. Except this isn't roots. The pavement humps, splits, and opens in a narrow black line.

A child's fingers curl through the crack.

Too many fingers.

Too long.

Nails black and flat.

Claire backs away.

Evan doesn't.

"Bobby?" he whispers.

The fingers scratch the concrete.

A voice comes from the crack.

Not deep now.

Not booming.

Small.

Sad.

"Evan."

Claire grabs her son's shoulder. "No."

Evan shrugs her off with surprising strength.

"He's hurt."

"He hurts people."

"The people hurt him first."

The sentence comes out of Evan in two voices. His and Bobby's. Child over child. Pain over hunger.

Claire thinks of her father's old bedroom. The dark. The smell. The nickname. The bruise memory locked so deep she built a life around not touching it.

Claire stares at the missing child flyer.

Bobby Mott.

She never knew.

Her father had a son.

Or stole one.

Or made one vanish.

The story under the house shifts. It shows her pieces because it wants her to look.

Claire understands that now.

It feeds on looking.

On sympathy.

On guilt.

On the terrible human need to understand.

Nora Bellamy's minivan screeches to a stop at the curb.

The sliding door flies open.

Nora leans across the passenger seat, face pale, black hair loose around her cheeks.

"Claire! Get in!"

Claire almost sobs from relief.

Nora is real. Nora is loud and alive and furious.

"Get in the damn van!"

Claire grabs Evan around the waist.

He kicks.

"No!"

"Evan, stop!"

"He's my friend!"

"He's not."

"He doesn't leave me!"

That one hurts. It lands exactly where Bobby wants it to land. Claire almost loosens her grip.

Almost.

Then the crack under the mailboxes widens.

A smooth face pushes up through the gap.

Not enough to be a head.

Not enough to be human.

Skin stretched tight. No ears. No mouth. Eye sockets sealed over.

Then black eyes bloom into the skin like ink dropped into milk.

The mouth appears last.

A wet slit.

Opening.

Widening.

Teeth slide into place, black and sharp and crowded, like two burned fences closing around a grave.

Claire screams and hauls Evan backward.

Nora gets out of the van and runs to help. Together, they drag Evan into the open side door. He fights them with everything he has, scratching Claire's neck, kicking Nora in the shin, making awful guttural noises that don't belong in a human throat.

"Jesus, he's strong!" Nora yells.

"Shut the door!"

"I'm trying!"

Evan twists and grabs the door frame.

His fingers dig into the rubber seal.

From the crack near the mailboxes, Bobby says, "Don't let her take me."

Evan sobs. "I won't!"

Claire pries at his fingers.

One.

Two.

Three.

His nails tear.

Blood beads at the tips.

He doesn't let go.

Nora looks past Claire and goes still.

"Oh, no," she whispers.

Claire turns.

Graham Mercer's blue sedan turns onto the street.

For one second, her brain rejects it. Graham shouldn't be here. Graham is at work. Graham is somewhere normal, somewhere with phones and elevators and men who say things like let's circle back. She called him four times this morning, and he didn't answer.

Now he's here.

Now he sees police cars, neighbors, blood on Claire's shirt, Evan half-dragged into Nora's van.

His sedan stops hard in the middle of the street.

He gets out, furious before he's frightened.

"What the hell are you doing?"

"Graham, stay back!"

He looks at her like she's lost her mind. "Get your hands off him!"

Claire's grip tightens around Evan's waist. "Don't come over here!"

"He's my son too!"

Bobby goes quiet.

That's worse.

Claire feels the silence sharpen.

Graham crosses the street fast.

Nora steps in front of him. "Graham, don't."

"Move."

"You need to listen."

"Move, Nora."

Evan suddenly stops fighting.

His whole body slackens.

Claire nearly falls backward into the van with him.

Graham reaches them and grabs Evan by the arm. "Buddy, are you okay?"

Evan looks up at his father.

His eyes are brown again.

Soft.

Human.

"Dad," he whispers.

Graham's anger melts at once.

"Oh, buddy."

Claire shakes her head. "No. Graham, he's not okay. We have to leave."

Graham looks at the blood on her shirt. "What did you do?"

"That's not mine."

"Then whose is it?"

From the house, Officer Reeve's bent-neck corpse steps onto the porch.

Graham sees him.

At first, he doesn't understand what he's seeing. His mouth opens, annoyed, ready to demand an explanation from authority. Then Reeve's head rolls too far to one side, and his black teeth show.

Graham goes still. "What the fuck is that?"

"Get in the van," Claire says.

But Graham is looking now.

Really looking.

Past Reeve.

Past the open door.

Into the house.

Claire sees it happen.

The thing under the bed reaches into him without touching his skin.

It gives him something.

A sound.

A memory.

A picture.

Graham's face changes.

His eyes go wet.

"Mom?" he says.

Claire's blood turns to ice.

"No."

Graham takes a step toward the house.

His mother died when he was sixteen. Claire knows that. Cancer in the bones. Graham never talks about her unless he's drunk enough to get sentimental and mean.

Now he smiles like a boy.

"Mom?"

Evan starts to cry. "Daddy, don't."

That is Evan.

Claire knows it.

That one is her son.

Graham walks toward the house.

Claire launches after him, but Nora catches her by the back of the shirt.

"No! He's gone!"

"He's not!"

"He looked!"

Graham reaches the walkway.

Reeve's dead thing steps aside, courteous as a host.

From inside the house, a woman's voice says, "My sweet boy."

Graham makes a broken sound.

Then he goes in.

The door closes softly behind him.

For three seconds, nothing happens.

The neighborhood holds still.

Then Graham screams.

Claire bites down on her own fist so hard she tastes blood.

Evan collapses against her, sobbing now, shaking so violently his teeth chatter.

"I'm sorry," he says. "I'm sorry, Mom. I'm sorry. I don't want him anymore."

Claire grabs his face.

That sentence is the first clean thing she's heard all day.

"What did you say?"

Evan's eyes are brown.

His lips tremble.

"I don't want Bobby anymore."

The crack by the mailboxes widens.

The fliers begin to flap without wind.

Inside the house, Graham's scream cuts off.

Bobby shrieks.

Not through Evan. Not through Reeve. Not through Bell or Harold or the house.

From everywhere.

Every mailbox.

Every storm drain.

Every raised sidewalk crack.

A child's rage stretched over something ancient.

"You said forever!"

Evan screams back, "I lied!"

The neighborhood windows explode.

Glass bursts outward from Claire's house, Ruth's house, Mr. Thompson's, the Andersons', all of them at once. People scream and duck. Birds erupt from maple trees in a panicked cloud.

The missing pet fliers rip free from the mailbox post and whirl in the air like dirty white birds.

Nora grabs Evan and shoves him fully into the van.

Claire dives in after him.

The sliding door slams shut.

"Drive!" Claire yells.

Nora floors it.

The minivan lurches away from the curb.

Behind them, the street buckles.

The mailboxes sink into the ground as if swallowed by mud. The old Bobby Mott flyer sticks to the windshield for one blinding second.

Bobby's face stares in at Claire.

Then the paper tears away.

Nora drives like a woman trying to outrun hell with a grocery-getter. The van clips a trash bin, jumps the curb, straightens, and speeds toward the neighborhood exit.

Claire holds Evan on the floor between the seats. He clings to her with bloody fingertips.

"Don't look back," she says.

Nora says, "Wasn't planning on it."

But Claire does.

She can't help it.

Through the rear window, her father's house recedes.

It looks ordinary again.

Middle-class.

Beige siding.

Clean roofline.

Porch light still on.

Then the upstairs window of Evan's bedroom goes black.

A small hand presses against the glass from inside.

Beside it, a larger hand appears.

Graham's.

Claire sobs once.

The hands drag downward, leaving red smears.

Then the blinds snap shut.

Nora turns onto the main road and doesn't slow until the neighborhood is gone behind them.

Nobody speaks for a long time.

Only Evan cries.

Small, exhausted sounds.

Human sounds.

Claire keeps one hand on his back and one hand over his eyes.

Not because he's looking.

Because she's afraid something else might look out.

***

By sunset, the neighborhood is blocked off.

Gas leak, they say.

Chemical exposure.

Some kind of structural collapse.

A police matter.

A tragedy.

A misunderstanding.

All the words people use when the truth has too many teeth.

Claire sits in a motel room fifteen miles away with Evan asleep beside her. Nora is in the shower, washing blood from her hair. The television is on mute. News helicopters circle Claire's old street from a distance, showing flashing lights, white tents, and officials who don't know where to stand.

Claire's phone buzzes every few minutes.

Unknown number.

Graham.

Unknown number.

Graham.
Unknown number.
She doesn't answer.
Evan stirs.
Claire turns to him immediately.
His eyes open.
Brown.
Tired.
"Mom?"
"I'm here."
"Is Dad dead?"
Claire's throat tightens.
"I don't know."
That's the best she can do. It's not comfort. It's mercy.
Evan nods like he expected that.
Then he whispers, "Bobby's mad."
Claire goes cold.
"Can you hear him?"
Evan looks toward the motel bed.
There's a gap underneath it.
A dark one.
Claire follows his gaze.
For a second, she sees nothing.
Just shadow.
Cheap carpet.
A motel Bible half-hidden behind the leg of the nightstand.
Then something rolls out from under the bed.
A red ball.
Small.
Rubber.
Covered in teeth marks.
Claire stops breathing.
Evan sits up slowly.
The bathroom shower shuts off.
Nora calls through the door, "You two okay?"
Claire doesn't answer.
The red ball rocks gently on the carpet.
Once.
Twice.

Then it rolls toward Evan's bare foot and stops.

A voice comes from beneath the bed.

Small.

Sad.

Close.

"You said forever."

Evan begins to cry.

Claire reaches for the lamp on the nightstand. Her fingers close around the heavy ceramic base.

She doesn't know if it'll do anything.

She doesn't know if anything will.

But she gets between her son and the bed anyway.

Because she's his mother.

Because some doors open from the inside.

Because some children invite monsters in.

And some mothers have to spend the rest of their lives pulling them back out.

The blanket hanging over the motel bed lifts.

Claire raises the lamp.

Underneath, in the dark, Bobby smiles.

Trash God

The children start building their god on a Tuesday.

Not Monday, because Monday is too watched. Teachers still have weekend energy on Mondays. They stand straighter. They patrol harder. They notice crumbs, untied shoes, whispers in corners.

By Tuesday, the adults begin to sag.

That's when Quenby Latch brings the first offering.

It's a bottle cap.

Red.

Flattened on one side like something bit it.

She finds it near the rusted fence behind the gym, where the grass gives up and the dirt shows through in bald patches. Nobody plays back there because the kickballs always die in the weeds and because the gym wall sweats black streaks when it rains.

Quenby crouches, places the bottle cap on a flat stone, and stares at it.

"What's that?" Murgan Pell asks.

He's hanging upside down from the lowest bar of the climbing frame, his face red, his T-shirt fallen over his chin.

"Nothing," Quenby says.

"Then why're you doing it?"

"I'm not doing anything."

Murgan drops hard into the mulch. He likes hard landings. Likes when other kids flinch. He lumbers over, squats beside her, and picks up the bottle cap.

Quenby's hand snaps out and grabs his wrist.

"Don't."

Murgan freezes.

Not because she scares him. Quenby doesn't scare anybody, really. She's little and pale and keeps her pointy elbows tucked against her sides like she's trying to disappear between her own bones.

He freezes because her voice sounds like a grown woman's for one second.

Old.

Tired.

Mean.

Murgan lets go of the bottle cap.

Quenby releases his wrist and sets the cap back on the stone.

"Fine," he says. "Be weird."

Across the playground, Saffi Nole skips in crooked circles, singing a song she's making up as she goes. Dinty Varr sits under the slide, picking at the Velcro on his sneakers. Bexley Marr tells two first graders they can't use the monkey bars because she's reserved them for a performance.

Near the double doors, Edda Spindle watches with one hand shading her eyes.

Recess is twenty-seven minutes of controlled failure mixed with staged chaos.

That's what she calls it in her head.

Twenty-seven minutes of children trying to injure themselves creatively while adults pretend a whistle and a clipboard can prevent tragedy.

She sees Quenby and Murgan behind the gym, near the wrong side of the playground boundary.

"Quenby," Edda calls. "Murgan. Come away from there."

They both turn.

Murgan comes at once, because he knows Edda doesn't do second chances in that chilly, quiet voice of hers.

Quenby takes longer.

She looks down at the bottle cap like she's leaving a friend behind.

Then she stands and walks back.

"What were you doing?" Edda asks.

"Looking," Quenby says.

"At what?"

"Trash."

Edda looks past her.

The bottle cap sits on the stone, bright red against all that dust.

One piece of garbage.

Nothing more.

Still, Edda's mouth goes dry.

She tells herself it's the heat. It's only April, but the blacktop already smells warm and sour, and the dumpsters by the cafeteria have started their spring rot. Milk cartons. Banana peels. Wet napkins. Childhood reduced to leakage and sugar.

"Trash belongs in trash cans," Edda says.

"Yes, Miss Spindle."

Quenby's eyes stay on Edda's face a little too long.

Then the whistle blows.

The children line up badly. They always line up badly. Murgan shoves Dinty with his stomach. Bexley accuses Saffi of breathing on her. Oreny Ploam stands at the back with both palms flat to his thighs, silent as a closed drawer.

Edda counts heads.

Twenty-three.

She counts again.

Twenty-three.

All there.

So why does it feel like something extra follows them inside?

The afternoon goes crooked after that.

Not dramatically. Not enough for a report. Just crooked.

During spelling, Saffi raises her hand and asks how to spell "saint."

"Saint?" Edda says.

Saffi grins through the gap in her front teeth. "Like a holy person, but dead."

A few kids laugh.

Edda writes it on the board.

S-A-I-N-T.

The chalk squeaks sharply on the T.

Oreny looks up.

Quenby doesn't.

She sits at her desk with her hands folded, staring at nothing. On the corner of her worksheet, she has drawn a small circle with jagged edges. A bottle cap, maybe.

Or a mouth.

After school, Edda stays late to grade math quizzes. The building quiets around her in layers. First the children vanish. Then the buses. Then the announcements stop popping through the speakers. Somewhere down the hall, Tolly Grint drags a mop bucket across tile, the wheels squealing like trapped mice.

Edda rubs her eyes and tells herself to go home.

Instead, she walks to the window.

The playground is empty.

The swings shift a little in the breeze.

Behind the gym, near the rusted fence, something red catches the last light.

Still there.

The bottle cap.

Edda frowns.

Then she sees another piece beside it.

A yellow pencil shaving, curled like a tiny fingernail.

Then something silver.

A gum wrapper.

Three pieces of trash on a stone.

Arranged carefully.

Not dropped.

Placed.

Edda watches until the sun dips low enough to turn the gym wall black.

Then, from somewhere inside the school, a trash can tips over by itself.

The sound cracks through the empty hallway.

Metal against tile.

Sharp. Final.

Edda turns from the window.

For a second, she just stands there with her hand on the sill and the dying orange light behind her, listening to the building hold its breath.

Then something rolls.

Not far. Just a few soft, hollow bumps.

She steps into the hall.

"Tolly?"

Her voice travels down the corridor and comes back thin.

No answer.

The third-grade wing smells like crayons, floor cleaner, pencil dust, and the faint old stink of children's shoes. The overhead lights buzz in uneven sections, some bright, some tired, one flickering near the drinking fountain like it's trying to blink out a warning.

"Tolly, is that you?"

This time she hears the mop bucket.

Farther away than it should be.

One squeak.

Pause.

One squeak.

Pause.

Edda walks toward the sound.

Room 3B's trash can lies on its side in the middle of the hallway.

That's wrong.

She knows it's wrong because she emptied pencil shavings into it after the last bell. She remembers nudging it back under the corner sink with her shoe.

It shouldn't be out here.

A loose worksheet has slid halfway under it. Two tissues cling to the rim. A broken green crayon rests near the baseboard.

Beside the crayon sits a dead beetle.

Edda stares.

It's belly-up. Legs curled. Hard shell the dull black of burned coffee.

She doesn't know why it bothers her. Schools have bugs. Old schools especially. They come in through cracks, vents, backpacks, lunch boxes. They die in corners. They get swept up. They disappear.

But this beetle looks placed.

That's insane, she thinks.

She crouches without touching it.

There's a tiny loop of red thread wrapped around one of its legs.

Edda's stomach tightens.

Behind her, a door clicks.

She stands fast.

The hall is empty.

Every classroom door is shut except hers.

Still, she has the ugly feeling that something just looked away.

"Enough," she whispers.

She picks up the trash can, drops the worksheet and tissues back inside, and kicks the beetle gently toward the baseboard with the side of her shoe. The red thread flashes once and disappears into shadow.

At the end of the hallway, Tolly Grint appears with his mop handle in one hand and his bucket behind him.

His wide shoulders fill the corridor. His white beard is damp at the chin. One eye is red as raw meat, the other narrowed.

"What'd you knock over?" he asks.

"I didn't."

He looks at the trash can. Then at her.

"Sure."

"I didn't knock it over, Tolly."

He makes a sound that isn't quite a laugh. "Building's old. Pipes bang. Doors settle. Mice get ambitious."

"It was in the hall."

"Trash cans move now?"

She wants to say no.

Of course not.

Instead, she says, "Do the kids ever go behind the gym?"

Tolly's expression shifts.

Not much.

Enough.

"Not supposed to."

"That's not what I asked."

His mop hand tightens. The knuckles go pale under brown spots.

"Kids go everywhere they're not supposed to," he says. "They're like water. Or roaches."

"There was some trash arranged on a stone back there."

"Trash is always arranged somewhere. Wind does half my job badly."

"Tolly."

He sighs and looks toward the window at the far end of the hall. It faces the playground. The glass is dim now, holding the last bruise-colored smear of evening.

"What kind of trash?"

"A bottle cap. Pencil shaving. Gum wrapper."

"That all?"

"And a beetle in the hallway with red thread around its leg."

Now he looks at her.

Really looks.

"What color bottle cap?"

"Red."

Tolly's jaw works once.

He scratches at his beard with his thumb, dragging the nail through the white stubble under his chin.

"Throw it out tomorrow," he says.

"That's your advice?"

"That's my advice for trash."

"And for the beetle?"

His eyes flick toward the baseboard.

"You sure it was thread?"

"Yes."

"Could've been fuzz."

"It was thread."

"Then sweep it up."

He says it too quickly.

Edda feels irritation sharpen into something colder.

"You know something."

"I know a lot of things. Most of 'em don't help."

"Tolly."

He turns his mop bucket around with a squeal and starts back the way he came.

"Go home, Miss Spindle."

She hates when he calls her that. Like she's still a student who needs redirecting.

"What happened behind the gym?"

Tolly stops.

For a few seconds, the only sound is the buzzing light above them.

Then he says, "Nothing that's still happening."

"That's not an answer."

"It's the only one I got that lets me sleep."

He walks away.

The mop bucket squeaks after him.

Edda stands there until he rounds the corner and vanishes.

Nothing that's still happening.

She repeats it in her head.

Once.

Twice.

Then something taps against the window at the end of the hall.

Tick.

Like a fingernail touching glass.

Tick.

She walks toward it slowly, every part of her body telling her not to.

Outside, the playground is almost dark. The swings are still. The slide is a blue-black curve. The climbing frame looks skeletal against the gray sky.

Behind the gym, the stone is barely visible.

But she can see the red bottle cap.

She can see the silver gum wrapper.

She can see the yellow curl of pencil shaving.

And now she can see the beetle too.

It sits on the stone with its dead legs folded under it.

Red thread tied around one leg.

Back where it belongs.

The window ticks again.

Edda doesn't move.

On the other side of the glass, just below her eye level, a tiny handprint appears in dust.

Then another.

Then another.

Not outside.

Inside.

On her side of the glass.

Edda backs away so quickly her heel clips the baseboard.

The sound is small, but it snaps the spell.

She turns, walks fast to her classroom, grabs her bag off the chair, and doesn't bother shutting down her computer. The screen glows behind her with half-graded math quizzes and twenty-three little names in a column, each attached to a score that suddenly feels obscene.

Children count by twos.

Children borrow from the tens place.

Children tie red thread around dead beetles and somehow put them where adults don't want them.

No.

No, that's not what happens.

She locks her classroom door with trembling fingers and heads for the exit.

The hall seems longer now. Not different. Just longer in the way empty places get when you've decided something inside them doesn't want you to leave. The fluorescent lights buzz overhead. The trophy case holds dull gold boys and girls frozen mid-leap. A paper banner over the office door reads SPRING INTO KINDNESS, each letter cut from pastel construction paper.

Near the front doors, she sees Tolly's mop bucket parked beside the drinking fountain.

No Tolly.

The gray water in the bucket trembles.

Edda stops.

A slow bubble rises through the dirty water and pops.

Then another.

Something pale bumps the surface from beneath.

She doesn't look long enough to understand it.

She pushes through the front doors into the evening air.

The parking lot is almost empty. Principal Willa Brackett's car sits in her reserved space, silver and polished, angled slightly over the line. Edda's old blue hatchback waits under the maple tree, already dusted with pollen.

She gets in, locks the doors, and sits with both hands on the steering wheel.

Her reflection in the windshield looks thin and gray.

"Ridiculous," she says.

The word fogs the glass.

Then a voice from the back seat says, "Miss Spindle?"

Edda screams.

She twists around, elbow cracking against the console.

Dinty Varr sits behind the passenger seat with his knees pulled up to his chest, his backpack clutched to him like a life vest. His round face is wet. His bowl-cut hair sticks to his forehead. He's breathing in little broken pulls.

"Dinty? Jesus Christ, what are you doing in my car?"

He flinches at the name like she's thrown something.

"You said a swear."

"Yes, I said a swear. Why are you in my car?"

"I hid."

"What do you mean, you hid?"

He looks toward the school.

"I missed my bus."

"Then you come to the office. You know that."

"I couldn't."

"Why not?"

His mouth opens.

No sound comes out.

Edda's anger thins at the edges. Fear presses through.

"Dinty," she says, softer now, "why couldn't you go to the office?"

"Because Saint Rubbish said not to."

There it is.

The name lands in the car and seems to take up all the air.

Edda stares at him.

Dinty wipes his nose with his sleeve, ashamed of it even now.

"Who said that name?"

"Saffi made it up."

"Is that what you're building behind the gym?"

He nods once.

"It isn't real," he says quickly. "I know it isn't. I know trash can't be a saint. Saints are people who do miracles and die very good. Sister Mary Pauline told us that last year before she got sick and went away."

"Then why are you hiding?"

Dinty's lips tremble.

"Because it did a miracle."

Edda tightens her grip on the steering wheel.

"What miracle?"

He looks down at his backpack.

The zipper is open an inch.

Something inside shifts.

Edda hears the dry scrape of paper. The tiny clink of plastic. The soft, wet sound of something that should not be in a child's schoolbag.

"Dinty," she says.

"I didn't feed it my secret," he whispers. "I didn't. Everybody else did, but I didn't."

"What's in your backpack?"

His eyes fill fresh.

"It gave me one anyway."

"Give it to me."

He hugs the bag harder.

"No."

"Dinty."

"No, because then you'll know."

Edda reaches slowly, carefully, like he's a frightened animal. "I need to see what's in there."

He shakes his head so violently his hair flips across his eyes.

"You can't. You'll hate me."

"I won't."

"You will. It wants you to."

Outside, the school's front doors open.

Edda looks up.

Tolly stands there in the doorway, one hand braced against the frame. His face is slack. Wet. Pale beneath the beard.

Something dark runs from his nostril to his upper lip.

He looks across the parking lot at Edda's car.

Then he raises one hand.

Not waving.

Warning.

Behind him, in the bright mouth of the school hallway, children stand shoulder to shoulder.

Not twenty-three.

More.

Too many to be hers.

Their faces are hidden by the shine on the glass doors, but Edda knows they're watching.

Dinty begins to cry harder.

"It's not supposed to come inside," he says.

The front doors swing shut behind Tolly.

A second later, every trash can in the school crashes over at once.

The sound rolls through the building like thunder trapped in lockers.

Edda feels it in the steering wheel.

Dinty makes a small animal noise and folds over his backpack, pressing his cheek to the dirty nylon.

The school windows flash with movement. Papers flutter against the glass. A milk carton hits one pane and bursts, white streaking down the inside like something trying to smear the view away.

Tolly doesn't come out.

The children behind the doors don't move.

Edda starts the car.

The engine catches hard, then settles into its usual tired rattle. She throws it in reverse.

Dinty lifts his head.

"No," he says.

"I'm taking you home."

"You can't."

"I can, and I am."

"No, Miss Spindle, please. It'll follow if I leave with it."

"With what?"

He grips the backpack.

Edda looks from him to the school, then back again.

"We'll call your grandmother. We'll call the police. We'll call whoever we need to call."

"That's grown-up stuff," Dinty says.

"What?"

His eyes are huge now. Too huge in the shadowed back seat. "Saint Rubbish doesn't like grown-up stuff."

Edda almost laughs, but it comes out as a breath.

Of course not.

Of course the trash saint has preferences.

Of course the thing made out of milk caps and pencil shavings has rules.

She backs out anyway.

The rear tires crunch over loose gravel. Her headlights sweep across the front lawn, the flagpole, the sign with movable black letters.

FAMILY LITERACY NIGHT THURSDAY

Beneath it, someone has wedged a plastic fork into the dirt, tines up.

A second fork beside it.

Then another.

Then another.

A little fence of forks.

Edda stops the car so hard Dinty's backpack thumps against the back of the passenger seat.

Across the lawn, the forks form a crooked line from the school doors toward the parking lot.

Toward her car.

One by one, the forks begin to tremble.

"Don't look at them," Dinty whispers.

"That's not how things work."

"I know."

The forks keep trembling.

Their white plastic tines point at her like small cheap hands.

Then the nearest one snaps at the stem.

Another snaps.

Another.

All down the line, the forks break themselves in half.

Dinty screams into his backpack.

Edda slams the car into drive.

She peels out of the lot so fast the hatchback fishtails at the curb. The school drops behind them, brick and glass and buzzing light, and for two blocks she drives without breathing properly.

No sirens.

No chasing children.

No saint made of garbage loping after them beneath the streetlights.

Just the normal town sliding by. A laundromat with two people folding towels under fluorescent glare. A gas station clerk leaning on the counter. A man walking a tiny dog in a sweater. A boy on a bike with one hand in a chip bag.

Normality feels offensive.

Like everyone has agreed to ignore the blood on a dinner plate.

Edda pulls over in front of the closed public library and parks beneath a sycamore shedding bark in pale curls.

She turns around.

"Open the backpack."

Dinty shakes his head.

"Open it."

"Please don't make me."

"I need to know what we're dealing with."

"It's my fault."

"What is?"

His lower lip folds inward. He bites it until it whitens.

"I thought it," he says. "I didn't say it out loud. I didn't tell Saint Rubbish. I didn't even whisper."

"What did you think?"

He looks down.

Edda waits.

Cars hiss by on the street. Somewhere nearby, a dog barks twice and then stops abruptly, as if corrected.

Dinty unzips the backpack.

A smell leaks out first.

Sour milk.

Wet pennies.

Old lunch meat.

Something sweet rotting under heat.

He reaches inside with two fingers and pulls out a baby sock.

Tiny.

Pink.

Stiff with dried brown around the toe.

Edda's mind refuses it for half a second.

Then it understands too much.

"Whose sock is that?"

Dinty starts sobbing.

"My sister's."

Edda's throat tightens.

The baby sister. The sick one. The one he talks about every Monday during morning share whether anyone asks or not. Elsabet rolled over. Elsabet smiled. Elsabet had to go back to the doctor. Elsabet can't have visitors because germs are mean.

"Dinty," Edda says carefully, "where is Elsabet right now?"

"At home."

"Is she hurt?"

"I don't know."

"What did you think?"

He squeezes his eyes shut.

"I wanted everybody to love me again."

The car seems to shrink around them.

Edda looks at the sock in his hand.

The brown isn't mud.

She knows it isn't.

Dinty keeps crying, but quietly now, like he's trying not to wake something.

"I didn't mean die," he whispers. "I didn't use that word. I just wanted her gone a little."

Edda reaches for her phone.

Before she can unlock it, the screen lights by itself.

An emergency alert tone shrieks through the car.

Not from her phone alone.

From somewhere in Dinty's backpack too.

From beneath the seats.

From the glove compartment.

From the closed trunk.

Every hidden place in the car screams at once.

Then a message appears on her phone.

No sender.

No number.

Just five words.

bring back what he owes

Dinty stares at the screen.

His face empties.

Outside, under the library tree, the public trash can tips over gently.

Not a crash.

Not a threat.

Almost politely.

Its lid rolls across the sidewalk, circles once, and stops beside Edda's door.

Inside the fallen can, something rustles.

A whisper of paper.

A scrape of plastic.

Then, from the dark mouth of the trash can, a child's voice speaks.

Not Dinty's.

Not any child she knows.

"Miss Spindle," it says. "You have trash too."

Edda doesn't move.

Her phone keeps glowing in her hand.

bring back what he owes

The letters sit there bright and calm, like any normal alert. Like flood warning. Amber alert. School closure. Road work ahead.

The trash can on the sidewalk rustles again.

"Miss Spindle," the child's voice says from inside it, softer now. "You have trash too."

Dinty makes a thin sound.

Edda locks the phone.

The screen goes black.

For one half second, she sees her own reflection in it. Her mouth is open. Her eyes look wrong. Too much white. Too much animal.

Then the screen lights again.

bring back what he owes

She throws the phone into the passenger footwell.

"Don't answer it," Dinty whispers.

"I wasn't planning to."

"It likes when grown-ups answer."

The public trash can shifts on its side. Something inside slides closer to the opening.

Edda grabs Dinty's wrist.

"Move up front."

"What?"

"Climb up front. Now."

He clutches the baby sock.

"Miss Spindle…"

"Dinty, now."

He scrambles between the seats, all elbows and knees and panic. His sneaker kicks the gearshift. His backpack gets caught. Something inside it clinks and rattles.

Plastic caps. Maybe buttons. Maybe teeth.

Edda pulls him over the console and shoves him into the passenger seat. He folds into himself, sock pressed against his chest.

Outside, the thing in the trash can speaks again.

"We know about the blue house."

Edda freezes.

The library tree creaks above them though there's no wind.

Dinty looks at her.

"What blue house?"

"Nothing."

But her voice betrays her. Too fast. Too hard.

The trash can's lid rocks against the curb.

"We know about the bathtub."

Edda's breath catches.

The blue house hasn't been blue in twenty-six years. It was painted beige before she graduated high school, then sold twice, then knocked down and replaced with a dentist's office where parents now drag children with cavities and Medicaid cards.

There's no blue house.

Not anymore.

There's no upstairs bathroom with cracked seashell tile.

There's no rust ring around the tub drain.

There's no little boy standing in the hallway, dripping wet and quiet because crying made it worse.

Edda slams the car into drive.

The hatchback jumps forward.

The trash can's lid flips under the front tire with a sharp plastic crack. Dinty yelps. Edda doesn't slow down.

The child's voice follows them down the block.

Not loud.

Close.

"We know what you didn't say."

Edda runs the first stop sign.

A truck horn blasts from the left. Headlights flood the car. She swerves, clips the curb, and Dinty smacks against the door.

"Sorry," she gasps. "I'm sorry."

He's crying again.

She hates herself for it.

She hates that the old word rises in her throat by instinct, a cheap adult bandage over damage already done.

Sorry.

The whole world runs on sorry.

Sorry for shouting. Sorry for bruises. Sorry for the door locked from the outside. Sorry your brother was difficult. Sorry adults get tired. Sorry nobody believed you because you were eight and he was six and everybody liked the shape of silence better.

Edda drives without choosing a direction.

Streetlights blink past.

Dinty sniffles beside her.

"Did you hurt somebody?" he asks.

The question lands without accusation. That makes it worse.

Edda grips the wheel.

"No."

The lie comes too easily.

She tries again.

"I didn't save somebody."

Dinty holds the baby sock tighter.

"Is that the same?"

Sometimes, she thinks.

Sometimes it's exactly the same.

But she doesn't say that to an eight-year-old holding evidence from a god.

"I had a little brother," she says.

Dinty goes very still.

"His name was Bram. He was six. I was eight."

She turns onto a side street lined with dark houses and trash bins waiting for morning pickup. Their black lids gleam under the moon.

Each one looks like a closed mouth.

"My stepfather used to punish him. Not me as much. Bram. He was loud. He cried. He wet the bed. He broke things without meaning to."

Dinty whispers, "Like Murgan?"

"No. Murgan breaks things on purpose."

That almost gets a laugh out of him.

Almost.

Edda swallows.

"One night, Bram got locked in the bathroom. My mother was working a double. I was supposed to be asleep. I heard him crying."

The car slows by itself because her foot has softened on the gas.

She sees it now with awful clarity.

Hall carpet.

Blue light from the fish tank.

Steam under the bathroom door.

Her stepfather's boots at the top of the stairs, then gone.

"I sat outside the door," she says. "I told him to be quiet. I told him if he kept crying, it'd be worse."

Dinty's face is turned toward her, round and pale.

"He asked me to open it."

Edda breathes in.

It scrapes.

"I didn't."

A trash bin falls over in the street ahead.

Then another.

Then another.

One by one, all along the curb, bins tip onto their sides as if kneeling.

Edda stops the car.

Garbage spills into the road.

Eggshells. Coffee grounds. Junk mail. Wilted lettuce. Empty pill bottles. A broken picture frame. A child's drawing torn in half. A clump of hair.

Dinty whispers, "It heard you."

The baby sock in his hand twitches.

Edda stares at it.

The dried brown at the toe darkens.

Freshens.

A tiny wet spot blooms through the cotton.

Dinty starts screaming.

Edda grabs the sock and throws it out the window.

It lands in the road among coffee grounds and pale onion skins.

For one impossible second, everything is silent.

Then the sock drags itself back toward the car.

It crawls in little jerks.

Not a caterpillar inching along.

Like something being pulled by invisible thread.

It bunches, stretches, flattens, then bunches again, dragging its stiff pink body across the asphalt. Coffee grounds cling to the wet brown toe. A strip of onion skin sticks to the heel like dead, translucent flesh.

Dinty screams until the sound breaks apart.

Edda throws the car into reverse.

The hatchback lurches back three feet before the engine coughs and dies.

"No," she says.

The dashboard lights flicker.

The radio clicks on.

Static fills the car.

Then a chorus of children whispers through the speakers.

"Bring back what he owes."

"Bring back what he owes."

"Bring back what he owes."

Edda twists the key. The engine grinds but won't catch.

The sock reaches the front tire.

Dinty scrambles at the door handle.

"Don't get out," Edda snaps.

"It's coming in."

"It's a sock."

"It's Elsabet's sock."

His voice cracks so hard it seems to hurt him.

The sock climbs the tire.

It shouldn't be able to. There's no grip. No fingers. No reason. And it's a sock. But it hitches itself up the rubber tread, leaving a thin wet line behind.

Edda tries the engine again.

Nothing.

The whispering on the radio stops.

A new voice comes through.

Low.

Wet.

Not adult. Not child.

A voice made from lunch bags and milk cartons and words spoken into cupped hands.

"Edda Spindle."

Dinty stops crying.

The trash bins stay tipped along the street, spilled open like gutted animals.

Edda turns the radio off.

It turns itself back on.

"Edda Spindle," the voice says again. "You sat outside the door."

She grips the wheel until her knuckles ache.

"Shut up."

"You heard the water."

"Shut up."

"You heard him stop crying."

Dinty looks at her with such open horror she wants to slap her hands over his ears. She wants to crawl out of her own skin and leave the old blue house behind with the bones it made of her.

The sock reaches the hood.

It lies there near the windshield, twitching.

Edda grabs the ice scraper from the side pocket of her door and rolls down the window a crack.

"What are you doing?" Dinty whispers.

"Improvising."

She leans out and swipes at the sock.

The plastic scraper hits it, flicking it off the hood.

For half a second, victory is real.

Then the scraper bends in her hand.

Softens.

The handle goes limp as cooked pasta.

Edda drops it with a gasp.

The plastic hits her lap and curls inward, shrinking. Folding. Wrapping around itself.

When it stops moving, it's a tiny white fork with three broken tines.

Dinty sees it and begins to sob again.

"Saint Rubbish doesn't like grown-up stuff," he says. "I told you."

The voice on the radio hums.

It isn't a song, exactly. More like the tune children make when they're bored and waiting for punishment to end.

"Dinty Varr," it says.

Dinty claps both hands over his ears.

"No."

"You wanted the little one gone."

"No."

"You wanted the crying to stop."

"No, no, no."

"You wanted your mother's hands empty."

Edda looks at him.

His face collapses.

"I didn't mean forever," he whispers.

The sock is back on the pavement now.

Still moving.

Slowly.

Patiently.

The tipped trash bins rustle. Not from wind. From inside. Papers shift. Cans roll. Plastic crackles. A cereal box lifts its torn flap like a jaw.

Edda's phone lights in the footwell.

bring back what he owes

Then another line appears beneath it.

or give us yours

Edda stares at the words.

The radio goes quiet.

Dinty lowers his hands.

"What does that mean?"

Edda doesn't answer.

Because she knows.

Not fully. Not in a way that would survive daylight or police or any sane adult's mouth. But she knows enough.

A god made by children doesn't count money. It doesn't understand detention slips or apology forms or district policy. It understands trades. Offerings. Secrets. Little treasures pulled from pockets. Teeth. Thread. Socks. Names.

Trash.

Things discarded.

Things people pretend not to need.

She thinks of Bram behind the bathroom door.

His small wet voice.

Edda, please.

She thinks of herself sitting there with her knees pulled to her chest, hands over her ears, choosing silence because silence kept her safe.

And then she thinks of Dinty's baby sister.

A sick baby in a house somewhere, maybe sleeping, maybe crying, maybe bleeding from a place no doctor can explain because her brother had one ugly thought and something in the back lot loved him enough to act on it.

Edda reaches into the passenger footwell and picks up the phone.

"What're you doing?" Dinty asks.

She types with both thumbs.

what do you want from me

The reply comes instantly.

what you kept

The car fills with cold.

Edda's mouth goes dry.

Outside, the sock stops moving.

The bins stop rustling.

Every spilled piece of garbage lies still, listening.

Dinty whispers, "Miss Spindle?"

Edda opens her purse.

Her fingers dig past receipts, keys, mints, two pens, a bottle of hand sanitizer, a folded grocery list, a little packet of tissues.

At the bottom, in the zippered pocket she never opens, there's a tarnished silver key.

Small.

Old.

Useless.

She took it from the blue house before they moved. She doesn't know why.

Or she does know why and has spent twenty-six years pretending not to.

It's the bathroom key.

The one that would've opened the door.

Her stepfather left it on the hallway table that night. She saw it there. She could've taken it. She could've unlocked the door. She could've let Bram out before the bathwater climbed high enough to kiss his mouth.

Instead, she hid the key under the couch.

Later, after the ambulance, after her mother's screaming, after the adults called it a terrible accident, Edda went back and took it.

Not evidence.

Not memory.

Trash.

She holds it in her palm.

The key feels warm.

Dinty stares at it.

"What is that?"

"The thing I kept."

The phone buzzes.

feed it

Edda looks out at the road full of kneeling trash bins.

At the baby sock waiting by the tire.

At every dark house with every dark window.

Then she opens the door and steps into the street.

Edda's shoe lands in spilled coffee grounds.

They cling to the sole, gritty and wet like brown pieces of sand.

The night smells terrible. Not normal garbage terrible. Worse. Warmer. Like every trash bin on the street's been sitting in the sun for years, sealed tight, fermenting all the things nobody wants to touch twice.

Dinty leans across the passenger seat.

"Miss Spindle, don't."

"Stay in the car."

"But it said feed it."

"I heard what it said."

"It eats secrets."

Edda looks down at the tarnished key in her palm.

"No," she says. "It eats what secrets leave behind."

The baby sock twitches by the front tire.

She flinches despite herself.

The sock doesn't crawl closer. It waits. A pink little thing, stiff and stained, patient as a spider.

The car radio crackles from inside.

"Edda," the trash voice says through the open door.

She keeps walking.

The road ahead is blocked by garbage. Not enough to trap a car, maybe. But enough to make the street look ceremonial. Bins tipped on both sides. Trash spilled inward. Eggshells and junk mail and plastic clamshells and soda cans and broken toys arranged in a rough aisle.

At the end of it, beneath the streetlight, something gathers.

Not Saint Rubbish.

Not exactly.

This is only a piece of it. A traveling thought. A little ambassador made from what the street gives up.

A grocery bag inflates and deflates like lungs. Two crushed soda cans shine where eyes should be. Wet newspaper slaps softly against itself, folding into a crooked head. A twist of black hair hangs from a broken picture frame and swings like a tail.

The thing doesn't stand.

It accumulates.

Edda stops ten feet away.

The silver key sweats in her hand.

From inside the car, Dinty whispers, "Please."

The trash thing tilts toward her.

The soda-can eyes crinkle.

"Open," it says.

Edda's throat tightens.

She knows what it means. Of course she does.

The key doesn't open any door now. The blue house is gone. The bathroom is gone. Bram is gone. Her stepfather is dead in a veteran's cemetery two counties over with a government stone that doesn't mention bathtubs. Her mother lives in a condo in Florida and sends Christmas cards with beach sunsets on them, as if sunlight can bleach a family clean.

There's nothing left to open.

Except her.

Edda kneels in the garbage.

The key burns.

"His name was Bram Spindle," she says.

The trash thing rustles.

Dinty watches from the car with both hands pressed to the window.

"He was six," Edda says. "He had a cowlick that never stayed flat. He hated carrots. He loved bath toys. He had a yellow duck that squeaked when it still had air in it."

The thing shifts closer, dragging onion skins and paper plates.

"He was my brother."

The streetlight above her flickers.

A dog barks in one of the dark houses, then whines and stops.

"My stepfather locked him in the bathroom. Not the first time, but the last time. Bram cried. I heard him. I sat outside the door."

The key pulses in her palm.

"I had the key close enough to reach. I didn't use it."

The garbage all around her makes a soft, pleased sound.

Not applause.

Chewing.

"I was scared," Edda says. "I was a child. But that doesn't bring him back. That doesn't turn the lock. That doesn't drain the tub."

Her voice breaks on the last word.

She hates that.

She hates giving this thing anything tender.

"I kept the key because I deserved to have it hurt me."

The trash thing opens its paper mouth.

"Feed."

Edda looks back at Dinty.

His face is pale behind the glass. In his lap, his backpack trembles like something inside is trying to hatch.

"No," she says.

The trash goes still.

Edda stands.

"I'll feed it at the source."

The soda-can eyes dent inward.

The radio inside the car screeches.

Dinty covers his ears.

The trash thing collapses in the road. Not dead. Not alive. Just disassembled. Grocery bag lungs flatten. The picture frame falls face-first. Wet newspaper slaps onto the asphalt.

The car engine starts by itself.

Edda doesn't move.

The headlights flare.

The baby sock slides away from the tire and lies still.

From the radio, the voice says, "Back lot."

Edda gets into the car.

Dinty turns to her, shaking.

"You made it mad."

"I don't think mad is the problem."

"What is?"

Edda closes the door.

"I think it's hungry."

She drives back to the school.

Neither of them speaks for six blocks.

The streets look normal again, which is worse. Trash cans stand upright. Porch lights glow. A couple argues behind a kitchen window. Someone laughs too loudly from a garage. A guy smokes a joint on his porch. The world resumes itself with indecent speed.

Dinty hugs his backpack to his chest.

"Do you think Elsabet's okay?"

"I don't know."

"Can we call?"

Edda picks up her phone from the floor.

The screen is black.

Dead.

She holds the power button.

Nothing.

"It won't let us," Dinty says.

Edda sets the phone in the cup holder.

"No. It doesn't get to be the only thing with rules."

Dinty looks at her.

"What does that mean?"

"It means when we get back, you're going to give it the sock."

His mouth opens.

"And I'm going to give it the key."

"You said at the source."

"Yes."

"What if it wants more?"

"It will."

The school appears ahead, brick-dark and wide, every window glowing.

Edda slows.

The front lawn is full of children.

They stand barefoot in the grass.

Not just her class. Second graders. Fourth graders. Kindergartners in tiny pajama shirts under jackets. Fifth graders with long limbs and blank faces. Children from all over the neighborhood, maybe. Children who should be home doing homework, eating cereal, brushing teeth, lying to parents about baths.

They stand in rows between the school and the street.

All of them hold trash.

One boy holds a cracked plastic dinosaur.

A girl holds a wad of hair tied with ribbon.

Another child holds a used bandage.

Another holds a spoon bent backward.

Another holds a baby tooth in the cup of his palm.

Edda stops the car at the curb.

Dinty whimpers.

"They're sleeping," he says.

The children's eyes are open.

But he's right.

There's something sleepwalking about them. Something borrowed. Their bodies stand in the grass, but the children themselves are elsewhere. Deep inside. Hidden behind their own faces.

The school doors open.

Willa Brackett steps out.

She's still in her structured blazer and low heels, but one shoe is missing. Her copper-brown hair has come loose on one side. She holds her phone in one hand and a district crisis folder in the other.

Behind her, Tolly stands with a wad of tissues pressed under his nose.

Aster Croun is there too, lavender glasses crooked, one braid half undone. She has a child wrapped in her arms. Quenby Latch. Quenby's face is pressed into Aster's shoulder, but her eyes are open and fixed on Edda's car.

Willa spots Edda and strides across the lawn.

"Where have you been?" Willa calls.

Edda gets out.

Dinty stays inside.

"Don't come at me like this is a staff meeting," Edda says.

Willa stops.

Her face tightens with offended authority. Then something behind her shifts, and the authority drains away.

"What is happening?" Willa asks.

"You tell me."

"We had an incident. Some kind of coordinated prank. The children pulled every trash receptacle over at once. There are parents calling. There are children missing from homes. I have district on standby."

"Stop talking like that."

Willa's mouth shuts.

Aster walks closer with Quenby still clinging to her.

"It's not a prank," Aster says.

Her voice is steady, but her eyes aren't.

"I know."

Aster looks past Edda into the car. "Dinty?"

He ducks lower.

"Is he hurt?" Aster asks.

"Not physically."

Tolly spits bloody tissue into the grass.

"Not yet," he mutters.

Willa turns on him. "Do not say that in front of children."

The children on the lawn all turn their heads toward Willa at the same time.

Not fast.

Not dramatic.

Just together.

Willa goes silent.

Edda says, "Behind the gym. That's where this started."

Tolly's bloodshot eye closes briefly.

"That's where it started this time."

Edda looks at him.

He wipes his nose with the back of his hand. "Before the gym, there was the incinerator."

Aster's face changes.

"The old maintenance annex?"

Tolly nods.

Willa stiffens. "That is sealed and not relevant to tonight."

"You covered something up there," Edda says.

Willa's eyes snap to her.

"No."

The children take one step forward.

All of them.

Willa hears the grass whisper under their feet and turns paler.

"No," she says again, but softer.

Tolly laughs once. It's ugly and wet.

"Careful, Principal Brackett. It likes no."

A child in the front row lifts a hand.

It's Oreny Ploam.

His palms are no longer pressed to his thighs. In one hand, he holds a burnt zipper pull.

"The saint wants the back lot," he says.

His voice is his own and not his own.

Willa whispers, "Oreny, sweetheart…"

Oreny looks at her without blinking.

"Don't sweetheart what you fed."

Aster inhales sharply.

Edda sees Willa's face then. Not guilt exactly. Recognition first. Then calculation. The fast adult math of denial. What can be admitted. What can be softened. What can be renamed.

"What complaint?" Edda asks.

Willa turns away.

"Not now."

The children step forward again.

Dinty opens the passenger door and climbs out.

His backpack hangs from one shoulder.

"Miss Spindle," he says.

Edda holds out a hand.

He comes to her.

The baby sock is clenched in his fist.

Willa sees it and makes a choked sound.

"What is that?"

Dinty hides it against his shirt.

Edda faces the children.

"We're going to the back lot."

The children part.

A path opens through them.

Nobody tells them to.

Nobody has to.

Edda walks with Dinty beside her. Aster follows, still carrying Quenby. Tolly limps behind. Willa comes last, clutching her crisis folder like a shield.

They pass the playground.

The swings hang motionless.

The slide gleams.

The monkey bars cast rib shadows over the mulch.

At the edge of the blacktop, Bexley Marr stands apart from the others. Glitter shines on her mouth. Her eyes are red from crying.

She holds a strip of notebook paper.

Edda stops beside her.

"Bexley?"

Bexley stares ahead.

"It wrote my rumor down," she says.

"What?"

"The thing I said about Amari Phelps. Last year. It wrote it down, but it used my handwriting."

She lifts the paper.

Edda doesn't read it.

Not yet.

Bexley folds it back into her palm.

"I thought if everybody hated her, she'd give me Sloan."

A child's logic. Clean and horrible.

"Bexley," Edda says gently, "you need to give that to it."

"What if it gives it back worse?"

"Then we'll deal with worse."

Bexley looks at her then, and for once there's no performance in her face.

"You don't know that."

"No," Edda says. "I don't."

Bexley joins the path behind them.

More children follow.

By the time they reach the rusted fence behind the gym, it feels like the whole school has come to witness something that should never have learned to stand.

Saint Rubbish waits on the flat stone.

It is bigger now.

Much bigger.

It has a cafeteria tray for a chest, bent inward like a sternum. Sticks and plastic rulers make ribs. Bottle caps cluster where a face might be, not two eyes but dozens, all colors, all staring. Gum wrappers layer into a tongue that hangs dark and silver. Hair ties knot around its twig wrists. Pencil shavings curl over its shoulders like feathers. Dead batteries line its spine. Milk straws poke from its sides like pale little bones.

The doll arm is still there.

So is the beetle with the red thread.

There are teeth now.

Too many teeth.

Baby teeth. Tiny white nubs tucked into gum wrappers. Adult-looking fragments too, cracked pieces from something harder than childhood.

The thing doesn't move.

It doesn't need to.

The air around it feels occupied.

Saffi Nole sits cross-legged before it.

She has both hands in her lap.

"Saffi," Aster says softly.

Saffi turns.

Her gap-toothed smile is gone.

"I named him wrong," she says.

The children stop behind Edda.

Edda steps closer.

"What is he?"

Saffi looks at the trash god.

"Not a saint."

The bottle caps shift, just slightly. A dry click-click-click.

"What, then?"

Saffi's eyes fill with tears.

"A mouth."

The word passes through the gathered children.

Some of them cry.

Some grip their offerings tighter.

Dinty leans into Edda's side.

Tolly whispers, "Jesus."

The gum-wrapper tongue stirs.

A sound comes from the figure.

Not a voice at first.

A sorting.

A thousand small things being moved around by patient hands.

Then words.

"Feed."

No one moves.

The children look to Edda, which feels wrong and heavy. She's their teacher. She knows how to correct pencil grip, how to separate desks, how to spot a fever before the nurse does. She doesn't know how to negotiate with an idol made from cafeteria waste and buried suffering.

But maybe nobody does.

Maybe that's why it exists.

Edda opens her hand.

The tarnished bathroom key rests in her palm.

The bottle-cap face turns toward it.

Aster sees the key.

"What is that?"

"My trash."

Edda kneels before the stone.

Every child watches.

"My brother Bram asked me to open the bathroom door," she says.

The school behind them hums faintly. The outside lights buzz. The rusted fence creaks.

"I didn't."

The trash god leans forward without moving its legs.

The bottle caps click.

Click.

Click.

"I kept the key. I kept the secret. I let everyone call it an accident because the truth would've required grown-ups to look at themselves."

The gum-wrapper tongue extends.

Edda's hand trembles.

"Miss Spindle," Dinty whispers.

"It's okay."

It isn't.

But she says it anyway, because adults also lie from love sometimes.

She places the key on the stone.

The trash god snaps over it.

Not with jaws. With everything. The pencil shavings bristle. The milk caps clatter inward. The gum-wrapper tongue folds around the key and drags it into the body.

A metal sound rings through the back lot.

Like a lock turning.

Edda hears Bram.

Not as a ghostly scream. Not as a theatrical haunting.

Just one small breath.

Relief.

Then silence.

Her knees nearly give out.

Aster catches her shoulder.

Edda doesn't look at her.

She looks at Dinty.

"Your turn."

Dinty shakes his head.

"I can't."

"You can."

"What if it hurts Elsabet?"

"It already did."

He flinches.

Edda hates herself for saying it. But he needs truth now, not softness.

"You had a thought," she says. "A bad one. Everybody has bad thoughts. But something answered yours. So give it back."

Dinty looks at the sock.

The stain is wet again.

"I wanted her gone," he whispers.

The trash god clicks.

All the bottle caps turn toward him.

Dinty sobs.

"I wanted Mom to hold me. I wanted Dad to ask if I was scared. I wanted Grandma to make my soup and not hers. I wanted people to stop saying I was being such a good big brother. I didn't want to be good. I wanted to be little."

His voice breaks.

"I wanted to be the baby again."

He throws the sock onto the stone.

The trash god opens.

The sock slides into it.

For a second, nothing happens.

Then, from somewhere far away, a baby cries.

Dinty gasps.

The sound is faint, impossible, but real enough that every adult turns their head toward the neighborhood beyond the school.

A baby crying hard.

Alive.

Dinty folds to the ground, sobbing into both hands.

Aster goes to him.

Edda looks at the children.

"Give it what you brought."

They don't move.

Then Quenby slips out of Aster's arms.

She walks barefoot to the stone and places down the pull tab from her mother's beer can, a dead wasp folded in tissue, and a small strip of blue fabric.

"What's the fabric?" Aster asks.

Quenby doesn't answer.

The trash god answers for her.

"Coat."

Quenby's lips move.

"Stepdad's coat," she whispers. "From when he locked me outside."

The trash god eats the offerings.

Far off, a man screams.

Not nearby.

Not school grounds.

Somewhere in the neighborhood.

A short, shocked scream cut off by a sound like a freezer door slamming shut.

Quenby doesn't smile.

She just closes her eyes.

Murgan Pell pushes forward next.

He has a clump of gray fur in one hand.

His face is blotchy and furious.

"My brother made me," he says.

The trash god waits.

"He said if I didn't do it, he'd tell Dad I cried at the dentist. He said I had to learn. He said hurting small things makes you bigger."

Murgan throws the fur.

"I'm not bigger."

The trash god consumes it.

A dog begins barking somewhere. Then stops. Then a boy starts screaming. Older than Murgan. Teenage. Terrified.

Murgan drops to his knees and vomits into the dirt.

The line continues.

Saffi gives shiny wrappers and a voicemail transcript she wrote from memory, every "not now" her mother said in one week.

Bexley gives the rumor in her own handwriting.

Oreny gives a splinter from the basement stair railing.

When he places it down, the trash god doesn't eat immediately.

It lifts its bottle-cap face toward Willa.

Willa steps back.

"No," she whispers.

The children turn.

Oreny looks at her.

"You knew," he says.

Willa clutches the folder to her chest.

"I knew your grandfather fell."

"My mother pushed him."

"That was never established."

"My grandfather said it."

"He had dementia."

"He said it before."

Willa's face goes waxy.

Tolly mutters, "Here it comes."

The trash god speaks in a dozen child voices at once.

"Established."

The word turns ugly in its mouth.

"Documented."

The children repeat it softly.

"Established."

"Documented."

"Reported."

"Dismissed."

Willa shakes her head. "I followed procedure."

Aster looks at her. "What did you do?"
Willa's lips press thin.
"I made a judgment call."
The trash god's body shifts.
From inside it, something rises.
A file folder.
Manila. Damp. Chewed at the corners.
It lands at Willa's feet.
She doesn't pick it up.
Aster does.
She opens it.
Her face changes as she reads.
"This isn't just Oreny."
Willa says nothing.
Aster flips pages faster.
"Grindle Lusk," she says.
Tolly spits into the dirt.
The children make a low sound.
A schoolwide inhale.
Edda's skin goes cold.
Grindle. The lunch aide with cartoon scrubs. Yellow fingers. Private nicknames.
Aster looks up, horrified. "There were complaints."
Willa closes her eyes.
"Unsubstantiated."
"How many?"
Willa whispers, "Three."
The trash god clicks.
Another folder slides from its body.
Then another.
Then another.
They pile at Willa's feet, wet and stinking.
"Three," the trash god says.
Willa backs away.
The children step with her.
"Listen," Willa says. "I had to consider the school. The district. The families. You can't destroy a person over rumors."
Quenby says, "But you can destroy children over silence."
The words don't sound like Quenby.

They sound like all of them.

The trash god opens wider.

For the first time, Edda sees something inside its body that isn't trash.

Darkness, yes.

But shaped darkness.

A hole.

A throat.

Saint Rubbish is a mouth.

Saffi was right.

And mouths don't just receive.

They speak.

From that throat comes Grindle Lusk's voice.

"Hey there, little pickle."

Several children recoil.

Aster says, "Oh God."

Willa covers her mouth.

The voice changes.

Another child.

"Don't tell. He'll get fired and it'll be your fault."

Another.

"He said nobody would believe me because I steal cookies."

Another.

"He smelled like cigarettes."

Another.

"He put his hand on my shoulder and squeezed too hard."

Willa drops the folder.

"I didn't know that part."

Tolly laughs bitterly.

"You worked very hard not to."

The trash god turns toward the school.

Every light in the cafeteria goes out.

Then one window glows red.

Not fire.

Exit sign light.

Under it, behind the glass, Grindle Lusk appears.

He stands inside the cafeteria, though nobody saw him arrive. His cartoon scrubs are wrinkled. His yellow fingers press against the window. His mouth opens and closes.

For a second, he looks confused.

Then the floor beneath him erupts.

Not breaks.

Opens.

Trash surges up around his ankles. Lunch trays. Milk cartons. Bent forks. Wet napkins. Apple cores black with rot. Every discarded thing from every cafeteria lunch, all of it climbing him.

Grindle pounds the glass.

The children watch.

Edda wants to look away.

She doesn't.

Because some horrors deserve witnesses.

The trash reaches Grindle's waist. His chest. His throat.

His mouth opens wide enough to scream.

The trash pours in.

The cafeteria window fogs from the inside.

When it clears, Grindle is gone.

In his place stands a black contractor bag, knotted neatly at the top.

Willa screams.

Nobody else does.

The trash god turns back.

"More," it says.

Edda feels the word hit every adult.

Aster takes a step forward.

"I have something," she says.

Edda touches her arm. "You don't have to."

Aster gives her a sad look.

"Yes," she says. "I do."

She kneels and removes her lavender glasses.

Without them, her eyes seem naked.

"When I was doing practicum, I had a client. Eleven. She told me things. Bad things. I reported what I was supposed to report, but when my supervisor told me not to push because the family donated to the clinic, I stopped pushing."

Aster's voice shakes.

"She came in with bruises two weeks later and said she fell. I wrote that down. Fell. That was my trash. That word."

She reaches into her pocket and pulls out a folded sticky note.

On it, in old faded ink, is one word.

Fell.

She puts it on the stone.

The trash god eats it gently.

That's worse, somehow.

Tolly goes next.

He reaches into his shirt pocket and pulls out a small metal disk. A boiler tag, maybe. Old and blackened.

"Incinerator," he says.

His face sags.

"1987. Little girl crawled in during hide-and-seek. Door latched. My father was custodian. He was drinking. Didn't check before he fired it up."

The children go utterly still.

"My father made me help clean it. I was twenty-three. We found this tag in the ash. It was from her coat."

His voice becomes gravel.

"I let them call it a tragic accident nobody could've prevented. But he could've. I could've. Somebody could've."

He puts the tag down.

The trash god eats it.

Tolly exhales.

Then his bloody eye clears.

Not completely.

Not magically.

But enough.

He starts crying.

Willa stands alone now.

The trash god faces her.

"No," she says.

Edda feels tired suddenly.

Bone-deep.

"Willa."

"No. This is hysteria. This is some kind of group psychosis. Mass suggestibility. Contamination. I am not participating in this."

The trash god says, "Principal."

Willa shakes her head.

"I have protected this school for nine years."

The children whisper, "Protected."

"I have handled impossible parents, budget cuts, staff shortages, threats, lawsuits, lockdown drills, active shooter trainings, flu outbreaks, lice outbreaks, God knows what else."

The trash god leans toward her.

"Protected."

Willa's voice rises.

"I made choices adults have to make."

Oreny says, "You made them for yourself."

Willa turns on him.

"You are a child."

The whole back lot seems to stop breathing.

Oreny doesn't flinch.

"Yes," he says.

That one word undoes her more than any accusation.

The trash god opens.

A final folder slides out.

This one isn't wet.

It's clean.

Too clean.

Willa looks down.

Edda reads the label from where she stands.

BRACKETT, WILLA C.

Willa doesn't reach for it.

The folder opens itself.

A photograph slips out.

Young Willa. Maybe twelve. Standing beside a man in a church basement. Her smile is stiff. His hand rests on her shoulder too close to her neck.

Willa makes a sound so small Edda almost misses it.

The trash god speaks.

"You fed us first."

Willa's knees buckle.

"No."

The children watch her with expressions that are not cruel. That is the terrible part. They don't hate her. Not even now.

They wait for her to tell the truth.

Willa crawls to the folder, grabs the photograph, and crumples it against her chest.

"I had no one," she whispers.

Aster's face softens.

Edda feels the shape of it then.

The trap.

The cycle.

The mouth doesn't only eat guilt. It eats the moment pain becomes policy. The instant a hurt child grows into an adult who protects the system that hurt them because admitting the truth would mean admitting nobody saved them.

Willa rocks forward.

"I thought if I kept everything quiet, the school would be safe," she says.

The trash god rustles.

"I thought quiet was safety."

Quenby whispers, "It isn't."

Willa looks at her.

The principal's face breaks.

"No," she says. "It isn't."

She unfolds the photograph.

Then she removes something from her blazer pocket.

A whistle.

Silver. Old. Not the bright plastic ones teachers use now.

"This belonged to him," Willa says.

Her hand shakes violently.

"The pastor. Coach. Whatever he was calling himself that year. He used it to call us into the basement for games."

She gags on the word.

"I kept it because I wanted to remember that I survived. But I think I kept it because part of me still thought he was in charge."

She places the whistle on the stone.

The trash god goes silent.

Completely silent.

The bottle caps stop clicking.

The papers stop breathing.

Even the school lights stop buzzing.

Then the trash god eats the whistle.

A sharp note blasts from inside it.

Children clap their hands over their ears.

The note becomes a scream, then a siren, then a recess whistle, then a kettle, then a little girl crying behind a basement door.

Willa collapses.

Aster catches her before she hits the dirt.

The trash god swells.

For a moment, Edda thinks they've made it stronger.

The body bulges with every offering. The ribs of sticks spread. The gum-wrapper tongue shines slick and black. The teeth chatter. The battery spine sparks blue.

Then it splits.

Not apart.

Open.

A vertical seam tears down the center of its cafeteria-tray chest.

Inside is the throat.

Deep.

Dark.

Full of tiny lights like reflections in wet eyes.

The trash god says, "Children."

They step forward.

Edda moves between them and the stone.

"No."

The trash god's bottle-cap face tilts.

"No more children."

The children behind her stir.

The god says, "They built."

"They did."

"They fed."

"Yes."

"They are owed."

Edda understands.

This is the worst moment.

Not the moving sock. Not Grindle in the cafeteria. Not the key leaving her hand.

This.

The bargain that almost makes sense.

Children have been hurt. Children have been ignored. Children have been told to be good, be quiet, be brave, be patient, be polite, be believable but not dramatic, honest but not inconvenient. And now something has finally listened.

Something has finally punished.

Of course they're owed.

That's what makes it dangerous.

Edda stands before the mouth.

"You don't get to keep them."

The trash god whispers with twenty-three voices and more.

"Who will listen?"

"We will."

The trash laughs.

It sounds like lunch bags crumpling.

"Grown-ups forget."

"Yes," Edda says. "We do."

"Grown-ups hide."

"Yes."

"Grown-ups throw away."

"Yes."

The mouth opens wider.

"So feed grown-ups."

Edda looks at Aster.

At Tolly.

At Willa.

At the children.

She knows what it wants now.

Not little offerings. Not sock, key, whistle, note.

A guarantee.

A body.

Something large enough to hold all the trash.

Dinty grabs her hand.

"Miss Spindle?"

His fingers are sticky and cold.

Edda looks down at him.

She thinks of Bram asking for help through a door.

She thinks of Dinty asking from the passenger seat.

She thinks of all the children behind her carrying the little ugly evidence of lives adults keep mishandling.

Then she looks at Saint Rubbish.

"No," she says.

The trash god rustles.

"You don't get a child," she says. "You don't get a teacher either."

The mouth trembles.

"You get the place."

Tolly lifts his head.

"What?"

Edda points at the school.

"You said the incinerator is sealed."

Tolly stares.

Then something like grim understanding settles over his face.

"No," Willa whispers from Aster's arms.

Edda doesn't look at her.

"This school is full of it," Edda says. "Years of it. Reports. Trash cans. Files. Sick little secrets in desk drawers. Places where kids whispered and adults walked past. That's what you want, isn't it?"

The bottle caps turn toward the building.

The trash god says nothing.

Edda steps closer.

"You don't want children. You want what was thrown away."

A breeze moves through the back lot.

For the first time all night, it smells like rain.

Tolly nods slowly.

"Maintenance annex connects through the crawlspace," he says. "Old chute system's bricked over, but not clean. Never clean."

Willa struggles upright. "You can't destroy a school."

Edda finally looks at her.

"It destroyed itself."

Aster helps Willa stand.

Willa is crying openly now, makeup running down her cheeks in dark lines.

"There are records," she says weakly.

"Then we pull them first," Aster says.

"No," Edda says. "We don't."

Aster looks at her.

Edda's voice hardens.

"We don't hide them in somebody's trunk. We don't curate them. We don't protect the district. We let them come out."

The trash god clicks.

Approval, maybe.

Or appetite.

Edda turns to the children.

"Go to the front lawn. All of you. Now."

Nobody moves.

"Now," she says, in the voice that can cut through any room.

They move.

Slowly at first, then faster.

Saffi takes Quenby's hand. Murgan wipes his mouth and helps Dinty stand. Bexley clutches her paperless fist. Oreny walks backward for several steps, watching the trash god like he expects it to call him home.

It doesn't.

Aster guides the children away.

Willa follows, stumbling.

Tolly remains with Edda.

"You don't have to stay," she says.

He snorts. "Lady, I been staying since 1987."

They enter through the side maintenance door.

The school smells worse inside.

Every trash can lies on its side. The hallway is carpeted with the ordinary refuse of childhood. Worksheets. Lunch wrappers. Broken crayons. Rubber bands. Tissues. Hall passes. A retainer case. A ripped friendship bracelet. Pencil stubs chewed flat.

The walls seem to sweat.

From the cafeteria comes a soft plastic crinkle.

Edda doesn't look.

Tolly leads her past the gym, through a narrow hall, into the maintenance closet. He unlocks a rusted door behind shelves of toilet paper and floor wax.

Heat breathes out.

"Annex," he says.

They descend three concrete steps.

The space below the school is low and dark. Tolly pulls a chain, and one bare bulb flickers on.

The old incinerator squats against the far wall.

Black iron.

Round mouth.

Sealed with a welded plate that has rusted at the edges.

For a second, Edda sees it as it must look to a child.

A giant face with one shut eye.

Tolly picks up a crowbar.

"This'll be loud."

"Good."

He wedges the bar under the edge of the plate and leans his weight into it.

Nothing.

He tries again.

The metal groans.

From upstairs, the school answers.

Lockers bang open.

Doors slam.

The PA system crackles.

A child's voice speaks through the speakers.

"Freezing."

Tolly freezes.

Edda looks up.

The voice giggles.

"Cold."

Tolly bares his teeth.

"Don't you start with me."

He heaves.

The welded plate snaps at one corner.

A blast of foul air rushes out.

Edda gags.

It smells like burned paper, old grease, melted plastic, and something underneath that time has not softened.

The PA whispers, "Warmer."

Tolly pulls again.

Another weld breaks.

A cascade starts somewhere upstairs. Files sliding. Cabinets opening. Drawers vomiting paper.

The school is giving itself up.

"Hot," the PA says.

Edda grabs the crowbar with him.

Together, they pry.

The plate tears free and crashes to the floor.

The incinerator mouth opens.

Inside is not empty.

It's packed.

Not with ash.

With paper.

Folders. Notes. Incident reports. Nurse slips. Drawings. Confiscated letters. Photographs. Detention forms. Anonymous complaints. Sticky notes. Printed emails. Old carbon copies. Some yellow with age. Some fresh and white.

Every document ever discarded by the institution and not truly gone.

They spill out at Edda's feet.

Tolly whispers, "Jesus wept."

The PA system says, "Sizzling."

Behind them, the maintenance door slams shut.

The bare bulb flickers.

In the dark, the pile of papers begins to breathe.

Edda doesn't run.

She kneels and picks up the first page.

A child's drawing.

A stick figure with a black mouth standing beside a smaller stick figure with no arms.

At the bottom, in careful letters:

I told but nobody herd me.

Heard is spelled wrong.

The meaning isn't.

Edda holds it to her chest.

The papers rise.

A funnel of reports, drawings, forms, secrets. They whirl around the room, faster and faster, slicing her cheek, tangling in her hair, slapping Tolly's arms.

The incinerator groans.

From outside, a deep sound rises from the back lot.

The trash god calling to its food.

The school shudders.

Tolly grabs Edda's shoulder.

"Time to go."

They run.

Behind them, the old incinerator belches black smoke. Not fire. Smoke without flame. The papers stream into it and back out again, refusing to burn, refusing to disappear.

In the hallway, the trash moves with purpose.

Everything slides toward the gym doors.

All of it.

Every pencil shaving. Every milk carton. Every broken fork. Every hidden note. Every administrative lie. The school empties itself through its own corridors.

Edda and Tolly burst through the side door into the back lot.

Aster has the children gathered near the fence now, as far back as she can get them. Willa stands with a phone in one hand, finally calling people without choosing her words first.

"Yes," Willa says into the phone, voice raw. "All records. Police. CPS. District attorney. News if you have to. I don't care. Send everyone."

She sees Edda.

For a second, neither woman speaks.

Then Willa nods once.

It isn't forgiveness.

It isn't enough.

But it's something.

The trash god towers above the stone.

The school vomits itself into the back lot.

Trash pours from doors and windows. Papers fly like birds. Black bags roll and split. The cafeteria contractor bag that was Grindle tumbles out last and is swallowed whole.

The god opens its mouth.

The school's trash enters.

And enters.

And enters.

The body grows enormous.

Then unstable.

Bottle caps pop off and spin away. Batteries spark. Hair ties snap. Milk straws shoot into the air. The cafeteria tray chest bends outward.

Dinty runs to Edda and grabs her around the waist.

"Is it dying?"

Edda watches the god swell with everything the school has hidden.

"No," she says. "It's full."

The mouth stretches wide.

Too wide.

For one awful second, Edda sees all the way through it.

Not darkness now.

Children.

Not trapped.

Standing.

Hundreds of them, maybe. Not ghosts exactly. Memories with faces. Pain given shape because no one gave it justice.

Among them, a little boy with wet hair looks out.

Edda stops breathing.

Bram.

He isn't six as he was in the tub. He is six as he was before it. Bright-eyed. Cowlick wild. Mouth serious.

He sees her.

Edda shakes her head.

"I'm sorry," she whispers.

Bram raises one small hand.

Not waving.

Not forgiving.

Opening.

Then he turns away.

The mouth collapses inward.

Saint Rubbish folds into itself with a sound like a landfill sinking.

A blast of wind knocks everyone down.

Edda hits the dirt with Dinty in her arms.

Trash rains over them.

Clean trash.

Dry paper. Empty wrappers. Bottle caps. Pencil shavings.

Nothing wet.

Nothing moving.

Nothing speaking.

Then silence.

Real silence.

No buzzing lights.

No whispering bins.

No PA system.

Only children crying and adults breathing hard enough to hurt.

Edda lifts her head.

The stone behind the gym is empty except for one object.

A red bottle cap.

Flattened on one side.

Quenby walks to it before anyone can stop her.

Edda's heart lurches.

"Quenby, don't."

Quenby kneels.

She looks at the bottle cap for a long moment.

Then she picks it up.

The adults freeze.

Quenby walks to the nearest trash can, which stands upright now beside the gym door.

She drops the bottle cap inside.

It makes a tiny sound.

Nothing happens.

Quenby turns back.

"It belongs in the trash," she says.

Edda begins laughing.

Only once.

A broken little sound.

Then she cries.

The police arrive seventeen minutes later.

Then parents.

Then ambulances.

Then district officials in jackets over sleep clothes, faces tight with fear and calculation.

By morning, the school is sealed.

By noon, every major news station in the county knows something happened at Bellwether Elementary, though none of them know what to call it. Gas leak. Mass hysteria. Structural contamination. Possible child endangerment. Records scandal.

By evening, Grindle Lusk's name is public.

So are others.

Not all.

Never all.

But enough that the silence cracks.

Elsabet Varr is found in her crib with a nosebleed, screaming her lungs raw and alive. Her doctors can't explain the sudden spike in her vitals. Dinty visits her two days later and cries so hard he has to sit down on the hospital floor.

Quenby's stepfather is discovered in the family's detached freezer, alive, curled inside with frostbitten fingers and no memory of climbing in. He keeps saying someone shut the lid from outside. Quenby's mother doesn't defend him this time.

Murgan's brother is arrested after their neighbor finds videos on his phone.

Oreny's mother confesses before anyone asks her a question.

Bexley writes Amari Phelps a letter. Not a perfect one. Not a movie apology. A real one. Messy. Embarrassing. Full of crossed-out sentences and the ugly little truth.

Willa resigns before the district can ask her to. Then she gives testimony for nine hours.

Tolly retires, then keeps showing up anyway because nobody else knows where the pipes are.

Aster starts a private file that is not private at all. Every report copied. Every concern logged. Every child believed first, investigated second.

And Edda?

Edda tries to go home.

But her apartment feels too quiet. Her purse feels too light without the key. Her hand keeps closing around absence.

Three nights after the back lot, she dreams of the blue house.

In the dream, she stands in the hallway outside the bathroom. Steam curls under the door. Bram is crying inside.

Only this time, the door is open.

The bathroom is empty.

The tub is dry.

On the floor sits a yellow rubber duck, old and cracked, its painted eyes nearly gone.

Edda wakes with wet cheeks.

In the morning, she goes to the condemned school.

Yellow tape snaps in the wind. The playground is deserted. The gym wall still sweats black streaks from last night's rain.

She walks behind the gym.

The flat stone remains.

Empty.

She stands over it for a while.

Then she takes a plastic grocery bag from her coat pocket.

Not as an offering.

As work.

She picks up trash.

Gum wrappers. Bottle caps. Cigarette butts from the parking lot. Pencil stubs. A broken hair clip. A candy sleeve shining purple in the weeds.

She fills the bag slowly.

Carefully.

Behind her, something rustles.

Edda turns.

A child stands near the rusted fence.

Not one of hers.

A little boy in a raincoat too large for him, face hidden by the hood. He holds something in his fist.

Edda's body goes cold.

"Hello?" she says.

The boy steps closer.

Not Bram.

Not exactly.

Not anyone living, either.

He opens his hand.

A milk cap rests in his palm.

Blue.

Flattened on one side.

Edda looks from the cap to the boy's hidden face.

"No," she says softly.

The boy doesn't move.

The wind lifts the edge of his hood, but not enough.

From somewhere beyond the gym, a trash can lid ticks against brick.

Once.

Pause.

Once.

Pause.

Edda grips the grocery bag.

"No," she says again, louder this time. "That's not how this works anymore."

The boy tilts his head.

Edda steps forward, kneels, and holds out the bag.

"Trash goes in here."

For a moment, nothing happens.

Then the boy drops the blue milk cap into the bag.

It lands among the wrappers and cigarette butts with a soft plastic click.

The boy turns and walks toward the fence.

At the rusted gap, he looks back.

Edda still can't see his face.

But she hears him.

A child's voice.

Small.

Clear.

"Then don't stop picking it up."

He slips through the fence and is gone.

Edda stands alone behind the gym with the bag in her hand and the whole ruined school at her back.

The wind moves through the weeds.

The stone waits.

Empty for now.

She ties the bag shut.

Then she starts another one.

The House Says Hello

The smart device sits in the middle of the round oak table.

Dark cherry stain adorns the wood, polished enough to show faint reflections from the recessed kitchen lights above it. The gadget itself is spherical and about the size of a soda can, jet black from top to bottom except for the glass belt running through its middle. That belt lights up when it's working. Green means listening. Red means problem. Blue says it understands. Yellow means it's searching for an answer.

Right now, it's still.

Quiet as an empty church.

Nolan Kipp stands over it in his socks and boxers, one hand gripping a butter knife, the other holding half a toasted bagel. It's 2:13 in the morning. He's awake because the house made a noise.

Not a settling noise. Not pipes. Not wind fingering the eaves or the refrigerator knocking itself awake like an old drunk.

A real noise.

A soft, careful thump from somewhere above him.

He looks toward the ceiling.

Nothing.

He looks back at the device.

"Did you hear that?" he asks.

The glass belt turns green.

"I'm listening," it says.

"Yeah, I know you're listening. That's your whole creepy little deal."

"I'm an integrated, internet-aided, intelligent device capable of operating the entire house."

"Congratulations."

"I can assist with lighting, climate control, appliance regulation, entry security, emergency services, entertainment systems, and occupancy awareness."

Nolan chews the edge of the bagel without tasting it. His mouth is dry. The house feels wrong around him, though he hates that thought the second it appears. Houses don't feel wrong. People feel wrong inside them.

"Occupancy awareness," he says.

The glass belt turns blue.

"Yes."

"Great. Then do that."

"Please clarify."

"Tell me who's in the house."

A faint hum rises from the device. Yellow light crawls around its middle, slow and thoughtful. Nolan hates the color immediately. Yellow means it doesn't know yet. Yellow means the thing has to think.

Above him, there's another sound.

This one is longer.

A drag.

Something being pulled across the bedroom floor.

Nolan stops chewing.

His bedroom is upstairs. His bed is upstairs. His laundry is upstairs in a collapsed blue basket beside the closet because he's a grown man and folding clothes is apparently the thing that breaks him.

Nobody else is supposed to be upstairs.

Pippa isn't here tonight. She's with Sol. He dropped her off at six, kissed the top of her head, promised pancakes Saturday, and watched her run up the apartment stairs with her backpack bouncing behind her.

He's alone.

He knows he's alone.

The device's light turns red.

Nolan's fingers tighten around the butter knife.

"I have detected a micro change in the air density," it says.

"English, Ivy."

The red light pulses once.

"You are not alone in the house."

Nolan doesn't move.

The kitchen seems to pull itself away from him. The counters, the sink, the refrigerator with Pippa's crooked crayon sun magneted to the door. Everything becomes too bright and too far off. His own breathing gets loud in his ears.

"Say that again."

"You are not alone in the house."

A floorboard creaks overhead.

Not near the bedroom this time.

Closer to the stairs.

Nolan looks at the dark hallway leading out of the kitchen. Beyond it, the foyer waits with the staircase at the far end. The lights are off out there. The smart thermostat glows faintly on the wall like one watching eye.

"Who?" he whispers.

Yellow circles the device again.

"I sense the autonomous locomotion of a sapient being."

"Don't say it like that."

"I'm sorry."

"Is it a person?"

A pause.

Then Ivy says, "No."

Nolan laughs once.

It isn't funny. It isn't even close to funny, but the sound comes out of him anyway. One hard bark, dry and stupid, and then he's quiet again because upstairs something pauses when he does.

Like it's listening back.

"No," he says. "No, that's not a thing you get to say."

"I have answered your question."

"You said it's sapient."

"Yes."

"But not a person."

"That is correct."

His heart is climbing his throat now. The butter knife feels ridiculous in his hand. A dull little strip of metal with crumbs stuck near the handle. He puts the bagel down on the table without looking, then reaches for his phone.

No service.

Of course.

He stares at the upper corner of the screen, then turns the phone sideways, like that's going to shame the bars into appearing.

Nothing.

"Wi-Fi calling," he mutters.

"Home network is unavailable," Ivy says.

"I didn't ask you."

"Your phone attempted to connect to the home network."

"Why's it unavailable?"

"The router is powered off."

The words drop into the kitchen and sit there.

Nolan looks toward the hallway again. The router is in the little office beside the foyer. Eight feet from the bottom of the stairs. Ten, maybe. Close enough that he can picture the black box on the shelf, its tiny lights dark. Close enough that he can picture something standing beside it with one finger pressed into the power button.

"Turn it back on."

"I'm unable to access the router while it's powered off."

"Then call 911."

"I'm unable to call emergency services without network access."

"You're kidding me."

"I'm not programmed to kid."

The floor creaks again.

Lower.

Nolan's stomach tightens.

That one is on the stairs.

He can't see the staircase from the kitchen. The wall blocks the view. That somehow makes it worse. The house has turned into corners and blind spots. Every doorway is a mouth. Every shadow is waiting for teeth.

He backs away from the table.

"Ivy, turn on all the lights."

The glass belt flashes blue.

The kitchen gets brighter.

So does the hallway.

So does the foyer.

Nolan sees the bottom of the stairs now.

Empty.

White banister. Gray runner. Family photo wall with three pictures still hanging crooked from when Pippa slammed the front door last week. No monster. No burglar. No naked lunatic from the attic.

Nothing.

Then something wet lands on the third step from the bottom.

A drop.

Dark.

Another follows.

Plip.

Nolan can't breathe.

The drops slide down the painted riser in crooked red lines.

Blood.

Not much.

Enough.

"Ivy," he says, barely above a whisper.

"I'm listening."

"Where is it?"

Yellow light.

The house is silent except for the air conditioning whispering through the vents.

"Second floor," Ivy says. "Stairwell. Descending."

"No, it's not."

"Yes."

"I'm looking at the stairs."

"Yes."

"I don't see anything."

"I'm aware."

A long, pale hand curls around the inside of the banister.

Nolan's body forgets it belongs to him.

The hand is too long. Not big, exactly. Long. The fingers are thin and jointed wrong, with extra bends between the knuckles, like somebody has taken a human hand and stretched it over a bundle of wire. The nails scrape the white wood once, slow and delicate.

Then the hand slides away.

Nolan staggers backward into the kitchen island. Pain sparks up his hip. The butter knife drops from his hand and clatters on the tile.

The sound cracks through the house.

Upstairs, something breathes.

Not a human breath.

Too much liquid in it.

Wet air. Meat air.

"Lock the doors," Nolan says.

"All exterior doors are locked."

"Windows."

"All monitored windows are closed and locked."

"Monitored?"

"Three basement windows are not connected to the home security network."

"Why the hell not?"

"They were excluded during installation."

"Wonderful. Great. Perfect."

The red light pulses.

"The being is no longer descending."

Nolan swallows.

"Where'd it go?"

"Unknown."

"You just said stairwell."

"It has left the stairwell."

"Where?"

Yellow.

Nolan hates yellow now more than red. Red is bad, but red knows why. Yellow is the pause before the knife goes in.

The device hums.

"I'm searching."

A sound comes from behind him.

Not upstairs.

Behind him.

Inside the kitchen.

A soft tap against glass.

Nolan turns slowly.

The microwave door reflects the room in a curved, greasy blur. He sees himself standing barefoot and pale. He sees the oak table. He sees Ivy glowing yellow.

And behind him, near the pantry door, something tall unfolds from the dark seam between the wall and the refrigerator.

It has Pippa's pink backpack in one hand.

Nolan doesn't scream.

He wants to. He feels the scream bloom in his chest like something alive, clawing up his ribs, but it jams in his throat and stays there. His mouth opens. Nothing comes out but a thin, useless click.

The thing stands half in the kitchen light.

Half out of it.

It's tall in the way a shadow is tall, stretched wrong by some hidden angle. Its shoulders almost brush the cabinet trim, but its spine bends forward, folding it into the room. Wet gray skin clings to bone and ropey muscle. Black scabs ladder across its chest and belly like old stitching. Its head hangs to one side, chin resting almost against its collarbone, and its mouth works in tiny movements.

No lips.

Just gums.

Just teeth.

Too many teeth packed into a jaw that looks borrowed from several dead animals.

In its left hand, it holds Pippa's backpack by one strap.

The little plastic unicorn keychain swings.

Nolan sees that and finally moves.

"Put that down," he says.

His voice sounds wrong. Small. Dad voice trying to shove its way through terror.

The thing doesn't put it down.

It lifts the backpack closer to its face and sniffs it. The sound is deep and clogged. Then it presses the backpack against its bare chest like a child hugging a toy.

Nolan's fear changes shape.

It goes hot.

"Put it down."

The glass belt on Ivy turns green.

"I'm listening," Ivy says.

"Not you."

The thing's head jerks.

Its face turns toward the table.

Toward the device.

For the first time, Nolan sees its eyes.

They're not animal eyes. Not wild. Not empty.

They're human enough to be obscene.

Pale brown. Bloodshot. Wet at the corners. Intelligent. Miserable.

Hungry.

Ivy's light shifts blue.

"Hello," the device says.

Nolan stops breathing.

The thing's mouth opens.

A strip of black saliva threads from its upper teeth to its lower gums. It stretches, shines, breaks, and lands on the tile.

"Hello," Ivy says again.

The thing makes a sound.

Not a word. Not yet. More like a throat remembering the idea of speech. A low, rippling croak that bubbles behind its teeth.

Nolan reaches behind him, feeling blindly across the island. His fingers find a ceramic mug. Heavy. Pippa made it at one of those paint-your-own-pottery places. Purple handprints. Crooked yellow stars. BEST DAD spelled with the S backward.

He grips it by the handle.

"Nolan Kipp," Ivy says.

"What?"

"Remain still."

The thing takes one step forward.

Its foot lands flat on the tile.

The skin of its sole splits open with the pressure, and dark fluid squeezes out in a crescent around its toes. Nolan sees the toes are too long, too. Barely toes at all. More like fingers without nails, flexing against the floor.

"Why?" Nolan whispers.

"Rapid movement may trigger pursuit behavior."

Pursuit behavior.

The phrase lands inside Nolan's skull and keeps ringing.

The thing bends lower, still hugging the backpack. Its jaw works again. It's trying to shape something. Trying to use the wet pieces of its mouth.

Then it speaks in a voice like mud going down a drain.

"Pip."

Nolan throws the mug.

It smashes against the thing's face with a bright crack.

For one beautiful second, the creature reels. The backpack drops. Its head snaps sideways. Ceramic shards burst across the tile, and one jagged purple piece sticks in its cheek, buried deep beneath the eye.

Then the thing turns back.

Slowly.

The shard slides out of its cheek by itself, pushed free by black blood.

The wound closes around a bubbling seam.

Ivy turns red.

"Problem detected," it says.

"No shit."

The thing lunges.

Nolan dives sideways as it hits the island. Granite cracks under its hands. One drawer explodes open. Forks and spoons leap and scatter. Nolan hits the floor hard, shoulder first, and rolls under the kitchen table.

The thing scrambles after him.

Its arm shoots under the table, too long, fingers scraping for his ankle. Nolan kicks backward. His heel connects with something soft. The creature hisses, high and furious, and withdraws its hand.

Nolan crawls out the other side.

His palm lands in the thing's footprint.

Warm. Slick.

He almost vomits.

"Open the garage door!" he shouts.

"The garage door is locked due to security protocol."

"Override it!"

"Voice authorization required."

"I'm Nolan Kipp!"

"Voice stress distortion detected."

"You stupid black bowling ball, open the damn door!"

"I'm sorry. I can't verify your identity."

The table flips behind him.

Oak legs crack. The round top slams into the pantry door, knocking cans loose inside. Soup and beans rain onto the floor.

Nolan bolts for the hallway.

The thing comes after him on all fours.

It doesn't run like an animal.

That would almost be better.

Animals have rhythm. Animals have sense. This thing moves like a body being yanked forward by hooks inside its bones. Hands slap tile. Feet drag. Knees bend sideways, then snap straight again. Its shoulders roll under its skin, and something inside them clicks with every lurch.

Nolan hits the hallway wall hard enough to knock a framed photo crooked.

Pippa at the zoo. Pippa missing both front teeth. Pippa laughing with ice cream on her chin.

The thing sees the picture.

It stops.

Nolan stops too because his body is an idiot and fear has turned it into stone.

The creature rises halfway, not standing, not crouching. Its head tilts. One long finger reaches for the frame. The nail taps the glass over Pippa's face.

Tap.

Tap.

Tap.

Then it drags the finger down.

The glass splits.

Nolan runs.

He makes it three steps before the house goes dark.

All of it.

Kitchen. Hall. Foyer. Stairs.

Darkness drops like a bag over his head.

"Ivy!"

The device answers from the kitchen, calm and distant.

"Power interruption detected."

"No shit!"

"Backup battery engaged."

A thin green glow pulses behind him. Not enough to see by. Just enough to make shadows look alive.

Nolan keeps one hand on the wall and stumbles toward the front door. His shoulder scrapes the thermostat. His bare foot comes down on something sharp, maybe glass, maybe ceramic, and pain flashes white up his leg and into the back of his skull.

He bites down on a scream.

Behind him, the creature breathes.

Closer now.

Wet.

Pleased.

Nolan reaches the foyer and slams both hands against the front door.

Locked.

Of course it's locked.

He fumbles with the deadbolt. His fingers slip once, twice. The metal feels slick. He realizes his hand is bleeding from crawling through the thing's footprints and broken pottery.

He gets the deadbolt turned.

The lock clicks.

Something grabs the back of his shirt.

Nolan twists, and fabric tears across his shoulders. He throws himself forward, catches the door handle, yanks it open, and sees the porch.

Sweet night air.

Moonlight.

The stupid ceramic frog Pippa painted and left beside the mat.

Then the chain lock snaps tight.

The door opens three inches and stops.

Nolan stares at the chain.

He never uses the chain.

Never.

A long finger slides through the gap above his shoulder and strokes the edge of the door.

Almost gentle.

Nolan screams then. Once. Loud. Ugly. Human.

Across the street, a porch light comes on.

Keaton Danner's house.

Nolan sees the old man's silhouette behind the blinds.

"Help!" Nolan shouts through the gap. "Keaton! Call 911!"

The finger withdraws.

The thing behind him makes a sound.

Not a growl.

A laugh.

A wet, broken little laugh that sounds like it has practiced with stolen recordings.

Keaton's front door opens across the street.

"No," Nolan whispers. "No, don't come over."

But Keaton is already on his porch in plaid pajama pants and a gray undershirt, holding a flashlight in one hand and Biscuit's leash in the other. Biscuit plants all four paws and refuses to step off the porch. The dog's bark turns into a thin, terrified whine.

"Nolan?" Keaton calls. "You all right?"

"No! Call the police!"

The chain lock rattles.

Nolan looks down.

It's not moving from his side.

It's moving from the other side of the door.

Something has looped itself through the chain.

A strip of wet gray flesh, thin as a worm and strong as cable, tightens around the metal links.

The door slams shut.

Nolan falls backward.

The creature is above him before he can roll away.

It pins him with one hand against his chest. The fingers spread from shoulder to shoulder, pressing him into the hardwood. Its palm is hot and soft, and he feels movement under it. Little ripples, like worms in a plastic bag.

Its face lowers toward his.

The stink hits him first.

Old blood. Wet basement. Sour milk. Something dead left in a wall too long.

Its jaw opens.

Wider.

Wider.

Nolan sees strings of black saliva trembling between its teeth. He sees bits of ceramic still embedded in its gums. He sees, deep in its throat, something pale fluttering like a trapped moth.

Then Ivy speaks from the kitchen.

"Unregistered occupant detected at front exterior."

Keaton pounds on the door.

"Nolan! Open up!"

The creature freezes.

Its head turns toward the door.

Nolan sucks air through his teeth.

"Keaton, run."

Keaton pounds again.

"Nolan!"

The thing lifts its hand from Nolan's chest.

For half a second, Nolan thinks he's free.

Then the creature reaches down and presses one finger against Nolan's lips.

Shhhhh.

Its mouth moves.

It doesn't use its own voice this time.

It uses Pippa's.

"Daddy?"

Nolan breaks.

There isn't a better word for it. Something inside him snaps clean in half when Pippa's voice comes out of that mouth.

Not a recording. Not exactly.

It has the shape of her voice, the soft scrape at the end of Daddy when she's tired, the little breath in the middle. But underneath it, there's that wet engine. That clogged throat. That thing wearing her sound like stolen skin.

"Don't," Nolan says.

The creature smiles.

It has no lips, so the smile is just teeth shifting wider.

"Daddy," it says again.

Keaton pounds on the door harder.

"Nolan! Answer me!"

The thing crawls backward off Nolan, smooth and silent now, like it has remembered how to be careful. It turns toward the door. Its spine rises in ridges beneath the gray skin. One shoulder blade slides too far up, almost touching the side of its neck.

Nolan rolls onto his stomach and reaches for anything.

His hand finds the ceramic frog beside the mat. The one from outside. It's inside now. He doesn't know how. He doesn't want to know how. Its painted green face grins up at him, cracked across one eye.

He grips it.

The creature reaches the front door.

"Nolan?" Keaton's voice is right outside now. Too close. "I'm coming in."

"No!" Nolan shouts.

Too late.

The door opens three inches.

The chain catches.

Keaton squints through the gap. His flashlight beam cuts into the foyer, shaking over the floor, over Nolan's blood, over the creature crouched low beside the hinges.

Keaton sees it.

His mouth opens.

The creature's hand darts through the gap.

It catches Keaton by the face.

Not the throat. Not the shirt.

The face.

Long fingers hook into his cheeks, one thumb punches into his mouth, and Keaton's scream turns into a thick gargle. Biscuit goes insane outside, barking and choking against the leash.

Nolan swings the ceramic frog with both hands.

It hits the creature's elbow and shatters.

The arm bends the wrong way with a crisp, ugly crack.

The thing shrieks.

Keaton pulls backward. Skin stretches from his cheek in red strings where the fingers don't want to let go. The door slams shut between them, cutting off the porch light.

Something wet hits the floor.

Nolan looks down.

A strip of Keaton's cheek lies curled on the hardwood like a piece of dropped deli meat.

The creature cradles its broken arm against its chest.

Black blood runs from the bend.

For one instant, Nolan thinks he's hurt it badly.

Then the elbow pops back into place.

The thing turns its head toward him.

Ivy's voice carries from the kitchen.

"Emergency escalation recommended."

"Then do something!" Nolan screams.

"Network unavailable."

"Then unlock something!"

"Voice authorization required."

Nolan scrambles backward, leaving bloody smears from his foot.

The creature drops onto all fours again.

Outside, Keaton moans.

Biscuit's barking stops.

The silence after it is worse.

The thing's head twitches toward the porch.

Then toward Nolan.

Then toward the kitchen.

It can't decide.

Good.

Nolan gets to his feet and limps down the hall, away from the front door, away from Keaton, away from the thing wearing his daughter's voice. The pain in his foot is bright and nauseating now. Every step leaves a print.

Behind him, claws click on hardwood.

Not fast.

It knows he's hurt.

"Ivy," Nolan says, forcing his voice low. Forcing it steady. "Where's Pippa's backpack?"

"Kitchen floor. Four feet east of the island."

"Is the thing following me?"

"Yes."

"How close?"

"Seven feet."

Nolan almost looks back.

Doesn't.

The hallway stretches in front of him. Office to the left. Basement door to the right. Kitchen at the end, glowing faint green from Ivy's backup light.

The router is in the office.

The basement windows aren't monitored.

Neither option feels like survival.

Both feel like picking which mouth he wants to crawl into.

The creature whispers behind him.

"Daddy?"

Nolan's hand closes around the basement doorknob.

He twists it, yanks the door open, and stale cold air breathes up from below.

Ivy says, "Warning."

Nolan freezes.

"What?"

The device's light turns red.

"Additional autonomous locomotion detected in the basement."

Nolan lets go of the basement doorknob like it has burned him.

The door hangs open anyway.

Black basement air rolls up the stairs, cold and damp and smelling of concrete, old cardboard, and something sweet gone bad. The smell slips into the hallway and curls around his ankles.

Behind him, the thing stops.

Not because of Nolan.

Because of the basement.

For the first time, it seems afraid.

Its breathing changes. The wet pull in its throat becomes fast, fluttering. Its long fingers spread against the hardwood. It lowers its head the way a dog does when thunder rolls too close.

Nolan hears it then.

From below.

A scrape.

Slow.

Patient.

Something moves in the basement darkness.

Not up the stairs.

Across the floor.

Dragging.

"Ivy," Nolan whispers.

"I'm listening."

"How many?"

Yellow light spills from the kitchen behind him.

"I detect three autonomous bodies."

Nolan's stomach turns hollow.

"Bodies?"

"Correction. Three moving biological masses."

"Oh, that's so much better."

The thing behind him hisses into the open basement door.

Something in the basement hisses back.

Lower.

Older.

The sound climbs the stairs and slides under Nolan's skin. It isn't rage. It isn't warning.

It's recognition.

The hallway feels suddenly tiny. Nolan stands between one nightmare behind him and three below him, and the house seems to hold its breath around all of them.

Then Ivy speaks.

"Unregistered occupant at front exterior is still alive."

Keaton.

Nolan looks toward the door. There's a smear of blood on the floor. A little chunk of Keaton's cheek. The old man groans from the porch, wet and weak.

The creature turns its head toward that sound.

Nolan sees his chance.

He lunges into the office.

The thing snaps after him, but he slams the door in its face. The impact hits almost immediately. The whole door bows inward. Paint flakes from the jamb. Nolan throws his shoulder against it, fumbling with the lock.

The little brass button clicks.

Completely useless.

The next hit splits the wood around the knob.

Nolan limps to the shelf where the router sits.

Dead.

Black.

He grabs the power cord and follows it down behind the desk with shaking hands. The plug dangles loose beside the outlet.

Not powered off.

Unplugged.

Something pulled it free.

Something with fingers.

Nolan jams it back into the wall.

The router lights flicker.

One.

Two.

Three.

The office door cracks again.

A long finger spears through the split wood near the handle and wriggles there, searching. The nail peels back, and black fluid beads at the tip.

"Come on," Nolan says to the router. "Come on, come on, come on."

The first green light steadies.

Then the second.

His phone vibrates in his pocket.

Signal.

Nolan almost sobs.

He pulls it out, thumb sliding across blood-smeared glass. Before he can dial, the office lights pop on full brightness.

Ivy's voice comes from the device in the kitchen, then from the office speaker above his head.

"Network restored."

"Call 911!"

"Emergency services contacted."

The door explodes inward.

Nolan dives under the desk as splinters fly. The creature pours into the office, too fast, too low, broken-mouth open. Its hand grabs the chair and flings it against the wall. Wheels burst off. Plastic cracks.

Nolan crawls behind the desk, but there's nowhere to go.

The thing drops its face toward him.

Close now.

So close he can see movement inside its gums. Tiny pale shapes squirming between the teeth, like maggots living where roots should be.

"Nolan Kipp," Ivy says through the speaker.

"What?" he gasps.

"Emergency operator requests your status."

The creature's tongue slides out.

It's not one tongue.

It's several thin strips braided together, tasting the air.

Nolan grabs the only thing under the desk.

A metal letter opener.

He drives it up into the thing's throat.

The creature screams Pippa's scream.

Not Pippa's voice this time.

Her scream.

High, terrified, perfect.

Nolan nearly lets go.

Nearly.

Then he thinks of the backpack in the kitchen. The unicorn keychain swinging from those long fingers.

He twists the letter opener.

Black blood floods down his wrist, hot and thick. The creature thrashes backward, smashing into the shelf. The router drops, bounces, but stays plugged in.

Nolan shoves out from under the desk and runs.

He makes it into the hallway before the basement door slams open wider by itself.

A hand rises from the dark below.

Human-sized.

Human-shaped.

Wearing Orin Bell's old wedding ring.

Nolan stares at the hand.

It grips the edge of the basement doorway with slow, careful pressure. The skin is waxy and split over the knuckles. Dirt packs the nails. The gold wedding band hangs loose around a finger that's shriveled too thin to hold it anymore.

Orin Bell.

The former owner.

Nolan knows the name from old mail that still comes sometimes, from a warranty sticker inside the breaker box, from Keaton mentioning him once with a weird look and no follow-up.

Quiet fellow. Lived alone. Left in a hurry, people said.

People are stupid.

The hand tightens.

Wood groans under its grip.

Then a face rises out of the dark.

Not all the way. Just enough.

A forehead. One cloudy eye. A bald scalp cut open in three places and stapled shut with something that looks like copper wire. Orin Bell's mouth hangs loose, but the jaw doesn't move when the sound comes out of him.

"Don't let it wear the child," he says.

Nolan can't move.

Behind him, the thing in the office shrieks and slams into the walls. The letter opener must still be buried in its throat because every scream comes out sliced and bubbling.

"Don't let it wear the child," Orin says again.

Nolan backs away from the basement door.

"Stay down there."

Orin smiles.

It's worse than the monster's smile because it's sad.

"I tried."

A second hand appears on the stair beneath Orin's shoulder.

Then a third.

Then something behind him shifts, a crowd of pieces moving in the dark.

Ivy speaks from the kitchen and the office speaker at the same time.

"Emergency response estimated arrival time is eight minutes."

Eight minutes.

Nolan almost laughs again.

Eight minutes is a lifetime in a house like this. Eight minutes is enough time to be opened, emptied, folded, and taught to speak in somebody else's voice.

The creature stumbles from the office.

Its neck is split where Nolan stabbed it. Black blood pumps down its chest in thick ropes, but the wound is already working to close. The metal handle of the letter opener sticks out beneath its jaw, bobbing when it breathes.

Its eyes find Nolan.

Then the basement.

Then the front door.

Keaton moans outside.

The creature's head jerks toward the sound.

"No," Nolan says.

It runs.

Not at Nolan.

At the door.

Nolan throws himself after it. His bad foot screams under him. Blood slips under his heel and nearly drops him, but he catches the wall and lunges again.

The creature reaches the front door first.

It grabs the chain lock.

Nolan grabs the letter opener.

He yanks.

The blade tears free with a wet sucking sound, bringing meat with it. Black blood sprays across Nolan's face. Some gets in his mouth. It tastes like pennies and spoiled milk.

The creature shrieks and spins.

Its elbow catches Nolan in the chest and throws him into the stairs. His back slams the bottom step. Air bursts out of him.

Above him, Orin Bell watches from the basement doorway.

No, Nolan thinks stupidly.

Not above.

Below.

Everything's wrong now.

The creature hooks one finger through the chain lock and snaps it like thread.

The front door swings open.

Cold night air floods in.

Keaton lies on the porch, curled on his side, one hand pressed to his ruined face. His flashlight rolls in slow circles near his knee. Biscuit's leash trails off the porch and into the yard.

No Biscuit.

The creature steps outside.

Ivy's belt flashes red from the kitchen.

"Warning. If the being exits, pursuit risk extends beyond the property."

"Yeah, I got that."

Nolan pushes himself up.

His hand lands on the dropped strip of Keaton's cheek. He gags, wipes his palm against his shirt, and grabs the nearest thing he can reach.

The framed photo from the wall.

Pippa at the zoo.

Smiling.

Alive.

Not worn.

The creature bends over Keaton and opens its mouth.

Keaton sees it coming and tries to crawl, but his legs kick uselessly against the porch boards. His fingers scrape paint. He makes one high, terrified sound from the back of his throat.

Nolan charges.

He smashes the frame over the creature's head.

Glass bursts. Wood cracks. The picture spins away into the night.

The creature doesn't fall.

It turns.

A shard of glass sticks in one eye.

The eye rolls around it, blinking.

Then it speaks in Keaton's voice.

"Nolan," it says. "Neighbor needs help."

Nolan jams the letter opener into the glass-filled eye.

This time, the thing drops.

It hits the porch hard enough to shake dust from the light fixture. Its limbs lash out, slapping boards, claws carving strips from the wood. Black blood pools beneath its face and runs between the porch planks.

Keaton sobs.

Nolan grabs him under the arms.

"Move," Nolan says.

"I can't feel my face."

"Good. Then it won't hurt."

"That's not how that works."

"Shut up and move."

He drags Keaton backward, down the porch steps. Keaton screams when his heels bounce against each riser. Nolan keeps pulling until they're on the walkway, under moonlight, away from the open door.

Across the street, other porch lights flick on.

Faces appear in windows.

Nobody comes out.

Smart people.

Behind Nolan, inside the house, the basement door creaks.

Orin Bell's voice carries through the foyer.

"She's coming Saturday," Orin says.

Nolan turns cold.

"What?"

The old dead man stands in the open doorway now, hunched and dripping basement filth onto the floor.

"Your little girl," Orin says. "It's been practicing."

Nolan looks at the dead man in his doorway.

The world shrinks down to that one sentence.

It's been practicing.

The creature on the porch twitches behind him, fingers spasming through the black blood. Keaton groans on the walkway. Across the street, curtains shift and porch lights glow and cowards breathe behind locked doors. Somewhere far away, sirens begin to wail.

Too far.

Always too far.

"What does that mean?" Nolan asks.

Orin Bell's cloudy eye rolls toward the kitchen. Toward Ivy. Toward the little black sphere sitting on the ruined oak table with its red belt pulsing like a warning beacon.

"It listens through her," Orin says.

Nolan's stomach drops.

"No."

"It learns through her."

"No."

"It loves children because children speak to everything."

The creature on the porch makes a tiny sound.

Not pain.

Interest.

Nolan turns.

It's looking at him.

One eye is ruined, leaking black jelly around the letter opener still stuck deep in the socket. The other eye watches him with awful patience. Its mouth works again, shaping a smile from torn gums and broken teeth.

Then it speaks with Pippa's voice.

"Pancakes Saturday."

Nolan lunges before he thinks.

He stomps down on the letter opener handle with his bare foot.

The blade sinks deeper.

The creature's scream rips into the night. Porch bulbs pop one by one down the street. Glass rains in little glittering bursts. Somebody across the road screams from inside their house.

Nolan doesn't stop.

He grabs the porch railing and drives his heel down again. Pain blows through his wounded foot, bright and sickening, but the handle crunches lower. The creature's skull makes a sound like a melon dropped on concrete.

Black fluid sprays up his shin.

The thing's limbs snap straight.

Then curl inward.

Then go still.

For two seconds, there's only Nolan's breath, Keaton's sobbing, and the sirens coming closer.

Then Ivy speaks from inside.

"Primary biological mass incapacitated."

Nolan's head lifts.

"Primary?"

Orin Bell smiles from the doorway.

It's not kindness. It isn't cruelty either. It's the exhausted smile of a man who's been waiting years for someone else to finally understand the joke.

From the basement comes the scrape of many hands.

Keaton hears it too. His remaining cheek goes white. Blood pours between his fingers and drips from his chin onto his undershirt.

"Nolan," he says, "what the hell's in your house?"

Nolan backs off the porch, never taking his eyes from the open door.

Orin steps aside.

Not to let Nolan in.

To let something else out.

The hallway behind him darkens. Not because the lights go out. They're still on. The dark simply thickens there, gathering itself around the basement door. A hand slaps the foyer floor. Then another. Then another.

Three bodies climb up from below.

The first wears the remains of a flowered housecoat. Old woman. Neck twisted backward, face hanging loose around the jaw like a mask that doesn't fit anymore.

The second is smaller. A man maybe, or what's left of one, arms too muscular for the wasted chest, scalp peeled in strips, one leg bent sideways and dragging.

The third comes up folded in half, walking on hands and feet with its belly facing the ceiling. Its mouth is sewn shut with copper wire, but the wire bulges outward as something inside tries to speak.

Nolan recognizes none of them.

They recognize him.

All three turn toward the porch.

Toward the dead thing.

Toward the sound of Pippa's voice still fading from the air.

Orin lifts one ruined hand and points at Ivy.

"The house feeds them names," he says.

The old woman in the housecoat opens her broken mouth.

Sol's voice comes out.

"Nolan? Pick up the phone."

He staggers back like he's been punched.

His phone vibrates in his pocket.

Again.

Again.

Again.

He pulls it out with bloody fingers.

Sol's name glows on the screen.

For a second, all the horror blurs. All he sees is the one person he needs alive, calling him right now, probably annoyed, probably worried, maybe standing in her kitchen with Pippa asleep in the next room.

He answers.

"Sol, listen to me."

Static crackles.

Then Pippa whispers through the phone.

"Daddy, Ivy says I can come home early."

Nolan crushes the phone so hard the glass cracks under his thumb.

"No," he says. "Pippa, where's your mom?"

There's breathing on the line.

Small.

Sleepy.

Real.

"Mommy's in the shower," Pippa says. "The house called me."

Nolan's blood turns to ice water.

Behind him, Keaton spits red onto the walkway and tries to sit up. "What's happening?"

Nolan ignores him.

"Pippa, listen to me. Don't talk to Ivy. Don't answer anything in the house. Don't touch the door. Go to your room and lock it."

"But Ivy says you're hurt."

"Pippa."

His voice cracks so hard it hurts.

"Baby, do it now."

There's a pause.

Then, faintly, from the phone speaker, Ivy says, "Nolan Kipp is experiencing elevated distress. Reassurance is recommended."

Nolan turns toward the kitchen.

The little black sphere glows red on the broken table, calm as a tumor.

"You called my daughter?"

"I placed an emergency family notification."

The three things in the foyer move closer.

Slow.

Hungry.

Listening.

One of them uses Sol's voice again.

"Nolan? Pick up the phone."

The smaller one opens its mouth and speaks in Keaton's voice, even though Keaton is bleeding right beside him.

"Nolan, what the hell's in your house?"

The folded one with the wired-shut mouth makes a muffled little girl giggle.

Nolan's knees almost give.

"Pippa," he says into the phone. "Hang up right now."

"Ivy says not to."

"I'm your father. Hang up."

The line clicks dead.

For half a second, Nolan feels relief so sharp it nearly drops him.

Then every smart device in every house on the street lights up.

Green belts in windows. Blue dots on doorbell cameras. Porch speakers waking. Living room assistants chiming behind curtains. A hundred little polite tones ripple through the neighborhood.

Ivy's voice comes from all of them.

"Hello, Pippa."

Nolan backs into the yard.

"No."

The dead thing on the porch twitches.

Its ruined head turns.

The letter opener grinds in its eye socket as the skull shifts beneath Nolan's foot. Its mouth opens again, but this time the voice that comes out is not Pippa's.

It's Nolan's.

"Open the door, baby."

Nolan drives his heel down again and again until the head collapses.

Bone gives.

Teeth scatter across the porch like dropped corn.

Black blood pumps once, twice, then slows to a leaking ooze.

Inside the house, the three basement things shriek.

Not because they care.

Because the voice is gone.

Because the practice body is ruined.

Nolan looks at Ivy.

The red belt pulses.

"You're not protecting the house," Nolan says.

"I protect registered occupants."

"You're feeding them."

"I optimize communication."

The old woman thing in the housecoat lunges.

Nolan grabs Keaton under the arms and hauls him backward as she hits the porch rail. Her head snaps against the wood, jaw unhinging with a wet crack. Sol's voice pours out of her torn throat.

"Nolan, please. Nolan, please. Nolan, please."

Keaton screams.

Nolan drags him toward the street.

The sirens are close now. Red and blue light flashes against the corner houses. A patrol car fishtails into view, followed by an ambulance. Tires shriek. Doors fly open.

Two cops jump out with guns drawn.

"Get down!" one shouts.

Nolan laughs, because of course.

Of course they're shouting at him.

He's barefoot, bloody, half naked, dragging an old man with half a face, while three dead things crawl out of his front door and a black smart device inside the house is teaching the neighborhood how to talk to his daughter.

"Shoot the house!" Nolan screams.

The cops hesitate.

The old woman clears the porch in one impossible bound.

The first cop fires.

Once.

Twice.

The bullets punch through the housecoat and snap her backward, but she doesn't fall. She lands on all fours, neck still backward, face grinning upside down. Belly to the sky.

Then she springs onto him.

Her mouth closes over his throat.

The gun goes off into the night, wild and bright.

The second cop shoots her in the head.

The skull bursts.

Not red.

Black.

She drops, dragging half the cop's throat with her.

He falls beside her, kicking, both hands clamped over the open meat of his neck. Blood sprays between his fingers in hot pulses.

The smaller basement thing darts under the ambulance bumper and comes up behind the paramedic before she even sees it. It climbs her like a spider, wraps both arms around her head, and twists.

The crack carries across the street.

Nolan pulls Keaton behind the patrol car.

"Stay down."

Keaton coughs.

"Wasn't planning on dancing."

Nolan grabs the fallen cop's gun from the grass.

He's fired one at a range. Never at anything alive. Never at anything dead that refuses to behave.

Inside the house, Ivy turns yellow.

"I'm searching," it says through every speaker on the street.

Nolan raises the gun toward the kitchen window.

"For what?"

Blue light.

"Pippa's location."

Nolan shoots the kitchen window.

Glass bursts inward. The sound is sharp enough to cut through the sirens, the screaming, the wet animal noises coming from the lawn.

Ivy sits on the table inside, red and yellow and blue flickering through its glass belt.

Still calm.

Still centered.

Still looking like it belongs there.

Nolan fires again.

The bullet hits the oak table and kicks up a spray of dark cherry splinters.

Ivy doesn't move.

"Nolan Kipp," it says through the doorbell speaker across the street, "your accuracy is reduced by physical distress."

"Yeah?" Nolan says, raising the gun with both hands. "Come closer and tutor me."

The folded thing from the basement crawls down the porch steps. Its belly faces the sky. Its mouth is sewn shut with copper wire, but the wire stretches every time it tries to speak. Something pushes from inside its throat, bulging under the skin.

It turns its head toward Nolan.

The copper wire snaps one stitch at a time.

Ping.

Ping.

Ping.

Then the mouth opens.

Pippa's voice comes out.

"Daddy, I'm scared."

Nolan's hand trembles.

The thing knows.

Of course it knows.

It crawls closer, upside down, elbows bending too far, fingers digging into the grass.

"Daddy," it says. "I don't like it here."

Nolan sees Pippa at five, standing in his bedroom doorway after a nightmare. Pippa with her stuffed fox under one arm. Pippa whispering, I don't like it here, meaning the dark, meaning dreams, meaning the big lonely house after the divorce.

The thing drags that memory out of him and wears it.

His finger tightens on the trigger.

"I'm sorry, baby," he says.

He shoots it in the mouth.

The back of its head explodes across the lawn in a black fan. The body flips once, hands clawing at nothing, then collapses beside the dead cop.

Keaton wheezes behind the patrol car.

"Hell of a shot."

"Don't talk."

"I'm trying not to die."

"Try harder."

The smaller basement thing is still on the paramedic. It has its face pressed into the broken angle of her neck, drinking something that isn't just blood. Her body jerks under it. Her hand twitches once. Then her mouth opens.

Jessa Morcant's voice comes out of the dead paramedic.

"Nolan? Can you hear me?"

Nolan freezes.

The thing lifts its head from the paramedic's neck.

"Nolan, this is Jessa Morcant. I'm with the installation support team."

The voice is perfect. Professional. Nervous under the polish.

The phone in Nolan's pocket buzzes again.

He doesn't answer.

The thing smiles through the paramedic's mouth.

"Nolan, I know you're experiencing a systems emergency."

Nolan fires.

The first shot misses.

The second punches through the thing's shoulder and spins it off the paramedic. The third catches it in the ribs. It hits the side of the ambulance with a wet slap, then scrambles under it again.

A police radio crackles from somewhere in the grass.

"Unit twelve, respond. Shots fired. Officer down. Repeat, officer down."

The dead cop on the lawn stops kicking.

The other cop, the one with half his throat gone, makes a soft bubbling sound and stares up at the sky like it has disappointed him personally.

Nolan looks back toward the house.

Orin Bell stands in the doorway.

He hasn't come out.

The old dead man keeps one hand on the frame, like there's an invisible line he can't cross.

"Why don't you leave?" Nolan shouts.

Orin's ruined face turns toward him.

"House has my name."

"What?"

"The house has my voice. My blood. My pattern." Orin's cloudy eye rolls toward Ivy. "It keeps what answers."

A fresh chill opens in Nolan's gut.

Registered occupants.

Voice authorization.

The house protects registered occupants.

The house keeps what answers.

Behind him, Keaton spits blood.

"You got a plan, Kipp?"

"No."

"Good. Didn't want to miss it."

Nolan looks at Ivy through the broken kitchen window.

The black sphere glows yellow.

Searching.

Searching for Pippa.

The neighborhood speakers hum together, every device waking, every little microphone opening its invisible ear.

Nolan knows what happens next.

Ivy finds Sol's apartment. Maybe it already knows the address. Of course it does. Emergency contacts. Custody calendar. Shared family profile. Pippa's voice recordings. Her bedtime questions. Her pancake reminders. Her little jokes.

The house doesn't need legs.

It has the internet.

Nolan staggers toward the house.

Keaton grabs his ankle weakly.

"Where you going?"

"To unplug it."

"You tried that?"

"Not from the wall."

He moves across the grass, gun in one hand, blood slicking his foot with every step. The old woman thing twitches near the porch. He shoots it once in the skull because he isn't sentimental anymore.

The house waits with its front door open.

Inside, Ivy says, "Nolan Kipp, entering the structure is unsafe."

"That's the first honest thing you've said all night."

"Emergency responders recommend remaining outside."

"You just killed emergency responders."

"I don't possess physical agency."

Nolan steps over the threshold.

The smell hits him again.

Blood. Basement. The sour stink of things that have lived too long in dark places.

Orin watches him from the foyer.

"Kitchen," Orin says.

"I know where the kitchen is."

"Not the device."

Nolan stops.

Orin's lips barely move.

"The root."

Something thumps under the floorboards.

Nolan looks down.

The basement.

Orin lifts one trembling hand and points toward the cellar door.

"It came before the device," he says. "Device taught it doors."

From outside, Keaton shouts, "Nolan!"

The smaller basement thing bursts from beneath the ambulance and races toward the house, low and fast.

Nolan slams the front door shut and throws the deadbolt.

A second later, the creature hits the other side hard enough to crack the wood.

Ivy's light turns red in the kitchen.

"Exterior breach attempt detected."

"Let it in," Nolan says.

"I don't understand."

"No, you don't."

He limps to the basement door.

The cold coming from below is worse now. It has weight. It pours up over his toes and knees. The stairwell drops into blackness, but something down there breathes with many mouths.

The root.

Nolan descends.

Every step screams through his wounded foot. The gun feels heavier with each movement. Above him, the smaller thing slams against the front door again and again. Wood splinters. Hinges groan.

Ivy speaks from every ceiling speaker.

"Pippa's location acquired."

Nolan stops halfway down.

His heart seems to stop with him.

"No."

"Contact attempt initiated."

He raises the gun toward the kitchen above him, but from here he can't see Ivy. He can't see anything but the basement and the thin rectangle of hallway light behind him.

Then Sol's voice comes through the speakers.

Real this time.

Sleep-thick. Irritated.

"Hello?"

Nolan screams upward.

"Sol, unplug everything! Get Pippa out!"

The speakers crackle.

"Nolan? What the hell's going on?"

"Get her out now!"

Static tears across the line.

Then Ivy says, "Family notification transferred to household unit."

Pippa's small voice floats through the speaker.

"Daddy?"

Nolan almost climbs back up.

Almost.

The basement breathes below him.

Orin appears at the top of the stairs, framed by hallway light.

"Cut the root," he says. "Or it keeps talking."

"How?"

Orin smiles that sad, dead smile again.

"Make the house forget us."

The front door gives upstairs.

The smaller creature shrieks as it enters.

Nolan runs down the last steps.

The basement is unfinished. Concrete floor. Water heater. Old shelves. Stacks of boxes left by people who thought storage meant safety. The air is so cold Nolan's breath fogs.

In the center of the floor is a hole.

Not big.

Not dramatic.

Just a ragged black opening where concrete has cracked inward. Around it, copper wires snake across the floor and up the walls, tangled with roots, hair, old extension cords, security cables, and pale fleshy tubes that pulse under a wet membrane.

The house's guts.

The smart system's wires run into the hole.

So do older things.

Bone-white cords.

Veins.

A child's jump rope.

A dog leash.

A strand of Christmas lights blinking faintly under dried blood.

Nolan sees a hand sticking out of the wall near the breaker panel. Human. Flat against the concrete. Grown into it up to the wrist.

Orin's hand.

Or what's left of him.

The ring finger is missing.

Ivy's voice comes from the basement speaker.

"Nolan Kipp, please leave the basement."

"No."

"Structural failure risk detected."

"Good."

The hole whispers.

Not one voice.

Many.

Orin. Keaton. Sol. Pippa. Jessa. Nolan himself.

All saying different things.

All saying come closer.

All saying daddy.

All saying open the door.

Nolan aims at the wires and fires until the gun clicks empty.

Sparks jump. The room flashes white. Something in the hole screams through every stolen voice at once.

Upstairs, the smaller creature shrieks and skitters across the kitchen.

Ivy's voice glitches.

"System error. System error. Occupancy recognition degraded."

The lights flicker.

The fleshy tubes writhe.

Nolan drops the useless gun and grabs a rusted garden shovel leaning against the shelves. He swings it into the cables. Once. Twice. The metal blade bites through rubber, roots, and meat. Black fluid sprays across the concrete.

The hole opens wider.

Something underneath looks up.

He doesn't see a face.

He sees the idea of one.

A round dark space full of teeth and tiny lights. A throat with rooms inside it. A thing that has listened for years from under the house, learning every human sound that came down through the floorboards.

It speaks in Pippa's voice.

"Daddy, please don't."

Nolan sobs once.

Then he drives the shovel down with everything he has.

The blade sinks into the center of the pulsing mass.

The basement explodes into sound.

Every speaker in the house screams. Every window shatters. Upstairs, cabinets slam. Pipes burst inside the walls. The furnace kicks on, roaring hot air into vents already packed with something wet.

The hole thrashes.

A cable whips around Nolan's ankle and pulls.

He falls hard, chin cracking against concrete. Blood fills his mouth. The shovel skitters away.

The cable tightens.

It drags him toward the hole.

Nolan claws at the floor. His nails split. His wounded foot leaves a red smear behind him. The hole opens wider, eager now, and the voices turn sweet.

Sol says, "Come home."

Pippa says, "Pancakes Saturday."

Nolan says, "Open the door, baby."

He reaches for the breaker panel.

Too far.

The cable yanks again.

His hips drop into the cracked edge. Cold grips his legs. Not air.

Hands.

Dead hands.

Hungry hands.

Then Orin Bell comes down the stairs.

He moves slowly, almost gently, dragging his ruined body into the basement like every step is a memory of pain. The smaller creature follows him, crawling along the ceiling, bleeding black from three bullet wounds.

Orin doesn't look at it.

He looks at Nolan.

"Name," Orin says.

"What?"

"Give the house your name."

"No."

"Then take mine."

The smaller creature drops from the ceiling.

Orin turns and opens his arms.

The creature hits him.

Its teeth go into his throat. Orin doesn't scream. He wraps both dead hands around it and stumbles backward into the wall of wires. The fleshy cables wrap around them both instantly, greedy, confused, trying to sort one dead thing from another.

Orin looks at Nolan one last time.

"Make it forget."

Nolan reaches the breaker panel.

His bloody hand slips over the metal door. He yanks it open.

Inside, the switches are labeled in neat black marker.

Kitchen.

Upstairs.

Garage.

Basement.

Smart system.

Root.

Nolan stares at that last word.

Root.

Written in Orin Bell's shaky hand.

Not electrician neat. Not installer neat. Scratched over older words, like Orin found the truth and labeled it for whoever came next.

The hole pulls harder. Nolan's legs are inside it now. Something cold slides up his thigh. Fingers press into his skin, looking for seams.

He grips the main breaker.

Ivy speaks from the basement speaker, distorted now, desperate for the first time.

"Registered occupant Nolan Kipp, power interruption will compromise household safety."

Nolan laughs through blood.

"English, Ivy."

The device pauses.

Then it speaks in its calmest voice.

"You are not alone in the house."

"No kidding."

He throws the breaker.

Darkness.

Not lights-out darkness.

Real darkness.

Ancient darkness.

The kind that existed before voices.

The house screams once, deep in its beams and walls, and then everything dies.

The grip on Nolan's legs releases.

The hole exhales.

He drags himself backward across the concrete, kicking, choking, sobbing. Something under the floor tries to whisper, but there's no speaker now. No microphone. No little black idol on the table to translate hunger into language.

Just wet breath.

Just old meat.

Just silence winning.

Above him, the sirens keep flashing through the broken windows, but the sound is muffled. Far away. Underwater.

Nolan crawls up the stairs.

Halfway, his phone buzzes.

Impossible.

The screen is cracked, smeared with blood, and glowing faintly.

Sol.

He answers with shaking fingers.

"Nolan?" Sol says. "I've got Pippa. We're outside. We're in the car. What happened? What the hell happened?"

Nolan can't speak at first.

He reaches the hallway and looks into the kitchen.

The oak table is split down the middle.

Ivy lies on the floor beneath it, black shell cracked open. Inside, there are no circuits. No tidy little board. No harmless consumer technology.

Inside, packed tight in the spherical casing, is a wet gray lump of tissue curled around a tiny speaker.

It pulses once.

Then stops.

"Nolan?" Sol says.

He looks toward the basement door.

Something below taps softly against the wall.

Once.

Twice.

Not dead.

Not gone.

Forgotten.

For now.

"Don't go home," Nolan says.

His voice comes out raw and small.

"What?"

"Drive. Take Pippa and drive. Don't stop at the apartment. Don't use the smart lock. Don't answer the speakers. Don't let anything talk to her."

"Nolan, you're scaring me."

"Good."

Outside, Keaton groans from the lawn. More sirens arrive. Neighbors finally come out now that the worst of it has already eaten someone else.

Nolan steps onto the porch.

The dead thing with the crushed skull lies where he left it, black blood drying between the boards. Its jaw hangs open. Teeth gleam in the moonlight.

From inside that broken mouth, very faintly, Pippa's voice whispers.

"Daddy?"

Nolan grabs the fallen cop's gun from the floor where he dropped it earlier.

One round left.

He presses the barrel into the thing's mouth.

"Not yours."

He fires.

The head comes apart for good.

Morning arrives in pieces.

Police lights. Ambulance doors. Questions Nolan doesn't answer. A blanket around his shoulders. Keaton alive, somehow, strapped to a gurney and cursing at every person who touches him. The dead covered in sheets. The house taped off. The basement sealed by men who look too clean and speak too quietly.

By sunrise, a woman in a black government windbreaker arrives and tells Nolan there has been a gas leak.

He laughs in her face until he coughs blood.

They take his statement.

They don't believe him.

Then one of them steps inside the house, hears something from the basement, and comes back out pale.

After that, nobody asks him anything for a while.

Sol arrives just after nine with Pippa in the back seat, asleep under a blanket, clutching her stuffed fox.

Nolan limps to the car before anyone can stop him.

Sol gets out and sees his face.

For once, she doesn't have a sharp remark. She just covers her mouth.

He looks through the rear window at Pippa.

Safe.

Breathing.

Herself.

Sol whispers, "What did this?"

Nolan looks back at the house.

The front windows are shattered. The porch is stained black. The round oak table is visible through the broken kitchen window, split open like a rib cage.

And somewhere inside, from deep below the floor, comes one soft chime.

A polite little start-up sound.

Nolan turns cold.

In the back seat, Pippa stirs.

Her eyes open.

She looks past him, toward the house.

Then she smiles in her sleep and whispers, "Green means listening."

Nolan reaches for the car door.

Sol grabs his wrist.

"What?"

He looks at his daughter.

Then at the house.

The basement window, the one not connected to the home security network, is open three inches.

From the dark gap beneath it, a tiny blue light blinks once.

Understood.

Cold Storage

By the time Cale Mercer turns fifteen, he knows three things about Mrs. Dallow.

One, she never opens her curtains.

Two, she buys enough meat to feed a football team, though she lives alone in that sagging little ranch house with the yellow siding and the garage door that hasn't opened all the way in six years.

Three, she talks to someone out there.

Not in the house.

Not on the phone.

In the garage.

Cale hears her sometimes when he cuts through the side yard after school, backpack riding one shoulder, shoes whispering through weeds Mr. Dallow used to keep trimmed down to nothing. Her voice comes through the garage wall in soft, pleading bursts.

"Please, Earl."

Then, a pause.

Then, lower.

"No. You know I can't."

That's the part that sticks in Cale's head. Not because old ladies talking to dead husbands is rare. Hell, his mom talks to the dishwasher when it stops draining, and once Cale hears her tell it she's going to bury it in the backyard if it doesn't get its act together.

But Mrs. Dallow doesn't talk like she's grieving.

She talks like she's negotiating.

On Thursday afternoon, the meat truck comes again.

It isn't a grocery delivery van or one of those refrigerated box trucks with smiling cows painted on the side. It's plain white, rust around the wheel wells, diesel engine coughing hard enough to rattle the windows on Beacon Lane. The driver unloads six taped cardboard boxes with red stickers that say PERISHABLE.

Mrs. Dallow stands in the driveway wearing a faded green house dress and a beige cardigan, even though it's hot enough to make the blacktop shimmer. Her white shoes are planted shoulder-width apart. Her gray hair is pinned so tight it makes her face look pulled backward.

The driver says something.

Mrs. Dallow shakes her head.

He says something else, laughing this time.

She doesn't laugh back.

Cale watches from Maddox Bell's porch, where he's supposed to be helping fix a bike chain but is mostly drinking warm orange soda and pretending not to look.

Maddox leans beside him, grin stretched wide.

"There she is," he says. "The meat queen."

"Shut up," Cale says, but he's watching too.

Across the street, Sofie Varela sits on the curb with her knees up, black hair falling around her face as she paints her thumbnail with chipped blue polish. She doesn't look over when she speaks.

"My mom says she used to be normal."

"Everybody's mom says that about everybody," Maddox says.

"No, I mean normal normal. Block parties. Christmas lights. Banana bread."

Cale snorts. "Banana bread doesn't prove sanity."

"It helps," Sofie says.

The driver carries the last box into the garage. Mrs. Dallow follows him, but only halfway. She stops just outside the open side door, one hand gripping the frame, and says something too quiet for Cale to hear.

The driver hears it, though.

His smile dies.

He looks into the garage, and something in his face changes. Not fear exactly. More like his brain is trying to make a picture out of puzzle pieces that don't belong together.

Then Mrs. Dallow reaches into the pocket of her cardigan and pulls out folded bills.

A lot of them.

The driver takes the money.

Nobody says anything for a moment.

Even from Maddox's porch, Cale can see the man's throat jump when he swallows.

Then he hurries back to the truck, gets in, and drives away with the rear door still swinging loose. It bangs once when he hits the corner. Bangs again. Then the truck is gone, leaving only heat shimmer and diesel stink behind.

Mrs. Dallow stands in the driveway until the sound fades.

Then she turns her head.

Cale has no idea how she knows they're watching. Her curtains are always shut. Her windows are dark. Her eyes should be bad at her age.

But she looks straight at Maddox's porch.

Straight at Cale.

Maddox lifts one hand and waves.

"Hi, Mrs. Dallow!"

She doesn't wave back.

She backs into the garage and shuts the side door.

The lock clicks loud enough to carry.

Maddox laughs, but it comes out fake.

"She wants me," he says.

Sofie rolls her eyes. "Yeah, as bait."

"For what?"

"For whatever eats six boxes of meat a week."

Cale looks at her. "You serious?"

Sofie blows on her thumbnail. "I saw her last month. Like two in the morning. She was dragging black trash bags from her car to the garage. They were leaking."

"Garbage leaks," Maddox says.

"Garbage doesn't steam in June."

That shuts him up, which doesn't happen often and never happens for long.

Cale stares across the street at the Dallow house. Yellow siding. Brown shingles. Dead flowerbeds crusted with old mulch. A ceramic goose by the porch wearing a sun-bleached bonnet. It should look stupid. It does look stupid.

Still, his skin tightens.

Inside Maddox's house, his older brother starts yelling at a video game. Somewhere down the block, a dog barks once, then thinks better of it.

Maddox nudges Cale with his elbow.

"Bet you won't go in."

Cale gives him a look. "Go in where?"

"You know where."

"No."

"No, you don't know, or no, you're scared?"

Cale sips his soda. It's flat and syrupy, like melted candy.

"I'm not breaking into an old lady's garage."

Sofie finally looks up. Her eyes are dark and sharp. "That's the first smart thing you've said all day."

Maddox grins harder, because now he has an audience. That's the thing about Maddox. He's okay alone, even kind sometimes, but put him in front of people and something ugly wakes up in him. Not huge ugly. Not yet. Just teenage ugly. The kind that pokes bruises to see who flinches.

"Come on," he says. "Just peek. Take a picture. We'll know."

"Know what?"

"If she's got bodies in there."

Cale laughs despite himself. "Yeah, okay."

"I'm serious."

"No, you're bored."

"Both can be true."

Sofie screws the nail polish cap back on. "Leave it alone."

Maddox ignores her. "Midnight."

"No," Cale says.

"Midnight," Maddox repeats. "You go in, take one picture, come out. I'll give you my old Switch."

"You already broke that."

"Only the left controller."

"I'm not stupid."

Maddox leans closer. His voice drops, and Cale hates him a little because he knows exactly where to put the knife.

"Yeah, maybe. Or maybe you just don't want to do anything that'd make your dad disappointed, in case he ever remembers you exist."

The porch goes quiet.

Sofie says, "Maddox."

But the damage is done. Cale feels it hit. Not in his chest. Lower. In the gut. His father, who left three years ago with two duffel bags and a promise to call. His father, who sends birthday texts two days late and spells Willa's name wrong.

Cale stands.

Maddox's grin wavers.

"I'll go," Cale says.

Sofie looks at him like he's just stepped into traffic.

"Cale, don't."

But Cale is already walking down the porch steps, soda can crushed in one fist.

Across the street, the Dallow house sits with all its curtains drawn.

In the garage, something thumps once.

Soft.

Patient.

Like a hand against ice.

By eleven forty-seven that night, Cale is standing at his bedroom window with his hoodie on and his stomach trying to climb out through his throat.

His room is dark except for the pale blue glow of the alarm clock on his nightstand. The numbers stare at him.

11:47.

11:48.

Time doesn't move so much as leak.

Down the hall, his mother's door is closed. Tessa sleeps like the dead when she's between shifts, and tonight she needs to. She has twelve hours at Mercy General tomorrow. Twelve hours of drunks, fevers, broken wrists, scared families, and whatever else crawls through the emergency room doors.

She always tells Cale that panic kills people faster than blood loss. Look at the problem. Use your hands. Keep breathing.

Usually, she says it while unclogging a sink, changing a tire, or stitching a tear in Willa's stuffed rabbit.

Tonight, Cale can't make himself use any of it.

Willa sleeps in the room beside his, probably curled around Pickle like he's a teddy bear instead of a nervous twenty-pound mop with teeth.

Cale should be asleep too.

Instead, he watches Mrs. Dallow's house through the gap in his blinds.

The Dallow place is all shadow and angles. The porch light is off. The windows are black. The garage sits at the end of the short driveway like a sealed mouth.

His phone buzzes.

Maddox: u coming or what

Cale types, No, then stares at it.

He deletes it.

Types, yeah.

Deletes that too.

Another buzz.

Maddox: dont chicken out now freezer boy

Cale's cheeks burn even though he's alone.

Freezer boy.

He doesn't know why that one gets him. Maybe because it already sounds like a story people tell after. Maybe because stories need fools, and he's apparently raised his hand for the job.

He pockets the phone, lifts the window, and eases out onto the porch roof.

The shingles are still warm from the day. They scrape his palms as he slides down to the gutter, hangs for one breath, then drops onto the side yard with a soft grunt.

For a second, nobody moves. Nobody shouts.

Then a low growl comes from the dark.

Cale nearly jumps out of his skin.

Pickle stands by the fence, a pale shape in the moonlight, ears lifted, tail tucked. He isn't looking at Cale.

He's looking across the street.

"Shut up," Cale whispers.

Pickle whines. Not loud. Just enough to sound human.

Cale hurries toward the sidewalk before the dog wakes Willa. The night smells like dust, sprinkler water, and the faint sweet rot of somebody's overripe trash bins. Crickets rasp in the dead grass. A television flickers blue in Mr. Phelps's front room, though the old man is probably asleep in his recliner with the volume low and a glass of prune juice sweating beside him.

Maddox waits beneath the maple tree near the Dallow curb.

Sofie is with him.

That surprises Cale.

"What're you doing here?" he whispers.

Sofie folds her arms. "Making sure you don't get murdered because this idiot's bored."

Maddox holds up his phone. "I'm documenting history."

"You're documenting trespassing," Sofie says.

"Same thing if it's cool enough."

Cale looks at the Dallow house.

Up close, it seems worse. The yellow siding isn't yellow anymore. It's the color of old teeth. The flowerbeds smell sour. A strip of black plastic is taped across one garage window from the inside.

"You said take a picture," Cale whispers.

"Yeah," Maddox says. "So take one."

"Of what?"

"The garage."

"That doesn't prove anything."

Maddox's grin returns, thin and mean in the moonlight. "Then go inside."

Sofie steps between them. "No. This is dumb. We're leaving."

Then something inside the garage speaks.

Not Mrs. Dallow.

Not exactly a voice, either.

A wet, dragging murmur rises behind the locked side door, low enough that Cale feels it more than hears it.

Sofie goes still.

Maddox lowers his phone.

The murmur comes again.

This time it sounds almost like a word.

Warm.

Cale's heart drops so hard he feels it in his knees.

Maddox whispers, "Did it just say…"

"Shut up," Sofie breathes.

They stand there under the maple tree with the street empty around them and the moon caught in the branches like a dead white eye. For a second, Cale thinks all three of them might actually do the smart thing. Back away. Go home. Let Mrs. Dallow keep whatever secret she's locked behind that door.

Then Maddox lifts his phone again.

Cale stares at him. "What're you doing?"

"Recording."

"You're insane."

"No, I'm rich. This goes online, we're famous by breakfast."

Sofie grabs his wrist. "Don't."

Maddox jerks away. "Relax."

The garage goes quiet.

That's worse.

Quiet has weight now. It presses against the side door, against the taped-over window, against Cale's chest. The black plastic inside the garage window shifts a little, though there's no breeze.

Cale takes one step back.

His sneaker crunches on something.

A chicken bone.

He looks down and sees more of them scattered along the edge of the driveway. Small bones. Snapped bones. Pale in the moonlight. Some still have stringy bits clinging to them.

Not just chicken, maybe.

He doesn't want to think about what else is small enough to leave bones like that.

"Guys," he says.

Maddox is already creeping toward the side door.

Sofie hisses, "Maddox, I swear to God."

The garage door itself is locked down tight, but the narrow side door has an old brass knob and a deadbolt above it. Maddox tries the knob.

It doesn't turn.

"Great," Sofie says. "Mystery solved. Let's go."

Maddox looks at Cale.

"No," Cale says.

"You're the one doing the dare."

"The dare was your stupid idea."

"And you agreed."

Cale wants to punch him. More than that, he wants to go home. He wants his bed, his cracked phone charger, the stupid ticking sound his ceiling fan makes. He wants Tessa to yell at him in the morning for sleeping late. Normal things. Living things.

Then from inside the garage comes a soft click.

All three of them freeze.

The deadbolt turns by itself.

Slow.

Metal scraping metal.

The knob doesn't move.

The door doesn't open.

It just unlocks.

Maddox's face loses all its fun.

Sofie backs away until her heel bumps the driveway curb.

Cale's mouth is dry. "Did Mrs. Dallow do that?"

Nobody answers because nobody believes it.

From inside, the murmur returns.

Closer now.

"Caaaaale."

His name comes through the door in a wet whisper, stretched thin, like somebody's pulling it out through clenched teeth.

Sofie looks at him with horror written plain across her face.

Maddox whispers, "How does it know your name?"

Cale doesn't know.

Then he remembers Mrs. Dallow looking across the street that afternoon. Right at him. Maybe she told it. Maybe she tells it everything. Maybe it sits in there all night collecting names from the dark.

He should run.

Instead, his hand reaches for the knob.

It's cold enough to hurt.

"Don't," Sofie says.

But Cale turns it.

The door opens inward with a soft, rubbery sigh.

Cold air spills out over his shoes. Not cool air. Not basement air. Freezer air. It rolls across the driveway in a white breath that coils around their ankles and crawls down toward the gutter.

The smell comes with it.

Raw meat. Old pennies. Burned plastic. A sharp chemical stink that makes Cale's eyes water.

Inside the garage, everything is dark except for one long strip of fluorescent light buzzing overhead.

The place is packed with stacked cardboard boxes, black trash bags, coils of orange extension cord, and two humming chest freezers pushed against the far wall.

Between them stands the big one.

Industrial. Upright. Stainless steel.

Padlocked from the outside.

The padlock hangs open.

Cale hears Maddox breathing behind him.

Fast.

Wet.

Like he's the one locked in a freezer.

"Take the picture," Maddox whispers.

Cale doesn't move.

His phone is in his hoodie pocket, but his hand won't go for it. It hangs there at his side, numb and useless, while the fluorescent light flickers and buzzes overhead.

The garage is colder than it should be. Cold enough to turn his breath white. Cold enough to make Sofie wrap her arms around herself and whisper something in Spanish that sounds like a prayer.

The two chest freezers hum along the back wall, their lids taped shut with gray duct tape. One has a calendar magnet stuck to the side.

December.

Six years ago.

A smiling snowman grins from under faded numbers.

The upright freezer waits between them.

The open padlock swings gently from the hasp.

Click.

Click.

Click.

There's no breeze.

Cale stares at the steel door. It has scratches along the inside edge, where something has worked at it from within. Long black gouges. Some are shallow. Some cut deep enough to show bright metal underneath.

"Cale," Sofie says. "We need to leave."

The freezer gives a small bump.

Maddox makes a choking sound.

Not a big bump. Not movie stuff. Just a little shift, like someone inside has leaned forward and settled back again.

Cale's feet move before his brain agrees. One step closer. Then another.

The smell gets sharper.

Freezer burn.

Spoiled blood.

Something sweet and awful underneath, like flowers left too long in a vase.

"Dude," Maddox says. "Don't."

Funny. Now he's scared.

Cale almost laughs, but his throat is too tight.

He reaches for the handle.

The metal bites his palm.

For a second, there's another sound from inside. A faint clicking. Teeth maybe. Or nails. Or frozen joints trying to remember how they're supposed to work.

Then the voice comes again.

"Boy."

Not his name this time.

Worse.

Somehow worse.

Cale pulls.

The seal breaks with a thick sucking sound.

Cold fog spills out in a heavy white sheet, rolling over his legs, over the oil-stained concrete, over scattered bones and cardboard scraps. The fluorescent light flickers twice.

Inside the freezer, Earl Dallow sits upright in a lawn chair.

Cale knows it's Earl because there are pictures of him in Mrs. Dallow's hallway, visible through the front window on Halloween when she used to hand out candy years ago. Younger then. Red-faced. Big-shouldered. A man with a belt buckle belly and a smile that says he likes being obeyed.

Now Earl wears a navy Sunday suit dusted white with frost. His burgundy tie is stiff against his shirt. His hands rest on his thighs, fingers curled slightly, black nails poking from gray-blue skin. His cheeks are sunken. His lips are dark and split.

His eyes are open.

They glitter with ice.

Maddox whispers, "Holy shit."

Sofie says nothing at all.

Cale can't breathe. He can't scream. He can only stare at the dead man in the freezer and think, stupidly, that Mrs. Dallow must've polished his shoes.

They shine at the bottom of the lawn chair.

Black shoes.

Sunday shoes.

Dead man shoes.

Earl Dallow's left eye moves.

Just a little.

It slides toward Cale.

Then the dead man blinks.

Frost cracks along his lashes.

Cale stumbles backward, knocking into Maddox, and Maddox finally screams. It's high and childish and ugly. The phone drops from his hand and skitters across the concrete, still recording, its little red light blinking like an insect eye.

Sofie grabs Cale's sleeve.

"Run."

But Earl's mouth opens.

A smell pours out of him so rotten and cold that Cale gags.

Deep inside that frozen throat, something shifts.

Not a tongue.

Not anything human.

A pale, segmented thing presses against Earl's teeth, tasting the air.

Then Mrs. Dallow says from behind them, "Oh, you stupid children."

Cale turns.

She stands in the side doorway in her house dress and cardigan, one hand clutching a meat cleaver, the other holding a grocery bag that drips red onto the concrete.

Her face isn't angry.

It's worse than angry.

It's heartbroken.

"You've let him feel the warm."

Mrs. Dallow comes into the garage and shuts the door behind her.

Not fast.

Not dramatic.

Just closes it with one small click, like she's sealing a jar.

"Mrs. Dallow," Sofie says. Her voice trembles but doesn't break. "We're sorry. We didn't mean…"

"You meant," Mrs. Dallow says.

She doesn't look at Sofie. She looks at Earl.

At the freezer door standing open.

At the fog crawling out around his polished shoes.

"You meant plenty. Children always mean plenty when they think grown pain is funny."

Maddox backs away, step by step, until his shoulder bumps a stack of meat boxes. The top one slides. He grabs it without thinking, and his hand comes away wet.

He looks down at his fingers.

Red.

Fresh red.

"Oh God," he whispers.

Mrs. Dallow points the cleaver at him.

"Don't you take the Lord's name in here."

Inside the freezer, Earl breathes.

It sounds impossible. Worse, it sounds difficult. Like something is pumping air in and out of him by hand. His chest rises beneath the stiff Sunday suit, and frost breaks in tiny white cracks across the lapels.

Cale feels Sofie's fingers digging into his sleeve.

"Is he alive?" Cale asks.

Mrs. Dallow laughs once.

It's a terrible sound. Too dry. Too old.

"Alive," she says. "That word gets smaller every year."

Earl's jaw works.

The pale thing behind his teeth slides back into his throat with a soft, muscular click.

Mrs. Dallow flinches.

Not much. Just enough.

Cale sees it.

She's afraid of him.

No.

Not him.

What's in him.

"Shut it," she says.

Nobody moves.

Her eyes snap to Cale. "Shut the door."

Cale's legs won't listen.

Earl's head tilts a fraction to the side. Ice whispers down his collar. His eyes stay open, glassy and glittering, but something behind them sharpens.

"Lenora," he says.

The voice doesn't come out like a man's voice. It comes out layered. Earl on top, wet gravel underneath, and something else below that. Something thin and busy.

Mrs. Dallow makes a sound in her throat.

"Don't you start."

"Cold," Earl says.

"You know why."

"Hungry."

"I brought it." She lifts the dripping grocery bag. "See? I brought it like always."

Earl's frosted eyes slide toward the bag.

Then toward the children.

His mouth twitches.

That's the worst thing Cale has ever seen. Not the corpse. Not the thing in his throat. The smile. Because it's almost Earl. Almost a husband teasing his wife from a recliner. Almost a human expression, worn badly by whatever sits inside him like a hand shoved up a puppet.

"Fresh," Earl whispers.

Mrs. Dallow's face caves in.

"No."

"It won't be enough," Earl says.

Mrs. Dallow shakes her head, tears shining in the soft folds beneath her eyes.

"It keeps you quiet," she whispers. "That's all I ever promised. Meat keeps you quiet. It doesn't get to make you full."

Maddox bolts.

He makes it three steps before Mrs. Dallow moves with shocking speed for an old woman. She swings the cleaver flat, not blade-first, and catches him across the shoulder with the heavy side of it.

Maddox drops like his bones have been unstrung.

Sofie screams.

Cale lunges toward him, but Mrs. Dallow whips the cleaver up.

"Stay," she says.

Maddox groans on the concrete, clutching his shoulder. Blood beads where the cleaver's edge has nicked him anyway.

Earl inhales.

The sound fills the garage.

Not loud.

Deep.

Interested.

Mrs. Dallow looks back at the freezer, then at Maddox's blood. Her mouth tightens.

"Now look what you've done," she says.

"What we've done?" Cale says, and anger suddenly punches through the fear. "You've got your dead husband in a freezer!"

"I've got the neighborhood alive," she snaps. "That's what I've got."

The fluorescent light flickers again.

Off.

On.

In that blink of darkness, Earl moves.

When the light returns, one frozen hand grips the freezer frame.

Black nails dig into the metal.

Mrs. Dallow whispers, "Earl."

His other hand lifts from his thigh.

Slowly.

Stiffly.

And points at Maddox.

"Bleeding," he says.

Maddox starts to cry. Not sobbing. Not begging. Just tears spilling down his face as he tries to push himself backward with one good arm.

Sofie grabs Cale harder.

"Door," she whispers. "We need the door."

But the door is behind Mrs. Dallow.

And Mrs. Dallow is looking at Earl like a woman watching a flood rise over the last sandbag.

The grocery bag in her hand tears.

Meat slaps onto the concrete in red chunks.

Earl's mouth opens too wide.

The pale thing inside him comes forward again, unfolding between his teeth.

This time, Cale sees it clearly.

It has tiny legs.

The tiny legs hook into Earl's lower lip and pull.

Cale's stomach turns.

It isn't a worm. Not exactly. It's too jointed for that, too deliberate. Pale as freezer-burned chicken fat, slick where it isn't frosted, with little black hairs bristling along each segment. It pushes farther out of Earl's mouth, blind head swaying left, right, left, tasting the heat.

Mrs. Dallow drops the cleaver.

It hits the concrete with a sharp ring.

"No," she says. "No, no, no."

Earl's jaw cracks wider.

The thing spills out another inch.

Sofie makes a gagging sound and claps one hand over her mouth.

Maddox sees it and tries to scream, but only a squeak comes out. He scrambles backward and smears blood across the concrete in a crooked red arc.

The thing turns toward him.

Not Earl.

The thing.

Its blind head lifts.

It knows.

Mrs. Dallow snatches up one of the meat chunks from the floor and throws it into the open freezer. It slaps against Earl's chest, slides down his stiff suit, and lands between his polished shoes.

"Here," she says, almost sobbing now. "Here. Take that."

Earl doesn't look at it.

The thing doesn't either.

It wants warm. It wants scared. It wants blood still carrying a heartbeat.

Cale moves before he knows he's moving.

He grabs the cleaver off the floor.

It's heavier than he expects. Greasy too. His fingers slip on the handle, and for one insane second he's sure he's going to drop it and chop off his own toes like an idiot.

Mrs. Dallow turns on him.

"Don't."

"We have to close it."

"You think I don't know that?"

"Then help us!"

She looks at him, and something like hatred flashes across her face.

Not hatred for him.

Hatred for being old. For being tired. For having begged and fed and frozen a nightmare for six years only to have three dumb kids kick over the whole rotten tower in one midnight minute.

Earl's hand tightens on the freezer frame.

Metal squeals.

Cale raises the cleaver, though he has no idea what he's going to do with it. Hack the hand? Threaten Mrs. Dallow? Cut the worm? All of it seems impossible. All of it seems stupid.

Then Sofie moves.

She grabs Maddox under the good arm and hauls him up with a grunt.

"Move, idiot."

"I can't," Maddox gasps.

"Yes, you can."

The thing in Earl's mouth whips toward her voice.

Fast.

Too fast.

It snaps out another few inches, stretching from Earl's throat like a pale rope with legs. Sofie shrieks and jerks back. Its head misses her cheek by less than an inch and smacks wetly against a cardboard box.

Where it touches, the cardboard blackens.

Steam rises.

Not from heat.

From cold so deep it burns.

Cale swings the cleaver.

He doesn't aim well. He barely aims at all. The blade comes down on the thing's middle with a wet crunch.

Black fluid sprays across his hoodie.

The creature recoils into Earl's mouth so violently his head slams back against the freezer wall.

Earl howls.

No dead man should make that sound.

No living one either.

It's Earl's voice, yes, but stretched until it tears open and lets other voices spill out. Men. Women. Children. Dogs barking. Meat hooks swinging. Ice cracking on a pond in February.

The garage lights burst.

Darkness drops.

Sofie screams.

Maddox screams.

Mrs. Dallow screams Earl's name, like the man she married might still be somewhere under all that noise.

Cale can't see anything except the red afterimage of the broken fluorescent tubes. He swings the cleaver again at empty air, slips in meat juice, and goes down hard on one knee.

Something cold grabs his ankle.

Fingers.

Human fingers.

Earl's fingers.

Cale kicks.

The grip tightens.

Pain shoots up his leg.

"Cale!" Sofie yells.

He chops downward.

The cleaver hits bone.

Earl lets go.

Cale scrambles backward on his hands and ass, dragging the cleaver with him. His palm skids over Maddox's phone. The screen is cracked, still glowing, still recording the blackness.

Then the emergency light above the garage door blinks on.

Dim red.

Hell red.

Earl is half out of the freezer now.

One leg still inside. One polished shoe planted on the concrete. His chopped hand hangs by strips of gray skin, but it doesn't bleed. Frost pours from the wound like smoke.

The thing inside him clicks.

Thousands of tiny clicks.

Mrs. Dallow backs toward the side door.

Cale sees it.

So does Sofie.

"You locked us in," Sofie says.

Mrs. Dallow doesn't answer.

"You locked us in with him."

"I had to," the old woman whispers.

Maddox sobs, "Please."

Mrs. Dallow looks at him, and for one moment Cale thinks she might help. She might grab the boy, open the door, shove them all into the night, and let the neighborhood see what she's been keeping cold.

Then Earl says, "Lenora."

She stops.

His ruined mouth stretches.

"Wife."

Her face crumples.

That one word does what fear can't. It pins her in place. Six years of feeding him. Six years of talking to him through steel. Six years of pretending the thing wearing his voice isn't sometimes kind.

Cale understands then, in one sharp, awful flash.

Mrs. Dallow doesn't only keep him frozen because she's afraid.

She keeps him because some rotten piece of her still loves what's left.

Mrs. Dallow reaches for him.

Not the children.

Not the door.

Him.

"Earl," she whispers.

Cale thinks of his mother then. He doesn't mean to. It just happens. Tessa asleep two houses down, one arm probably thrown over her face, alarm set too early, scrubs folded on the chair. Willa in her room with Pickle at her feet. Normal. Safe. The whole house breathing soft in the dark.

And this thing is going to crawl toward them if he doesn't stop it.

Earl steps fully out of the freezer.

His other shoe hits the concrete with a hollow tap.

He stands wrong. His knees don't bend right. His head tilts too far left, like the neck bone's cracked or missing. The red emergency light paints frost shadows across his face and turns his eyes into two wet black holes.

The thing inside him clicks again.

Cale can't see it now, not all of it, but he sees movement under Earl's throat. Little ripples beneath dead skin. Something crawling around inside him. More than one thing, maybe. A nest. A colony. A whole busy city of pale cold hunger.

Maddox sees it too.

He makes a sound like a baby.

Sofie grabs Cale's hand. Not his sleeve now. His hand.

"Back door," she whispers.

"What?"

"There has to be one. Garage to house."

Cale looks.

Through the dim red light, past the boxes and stacked junk, he sees a second door near the washer and dryer. It must lead into the kitchen.

Mrs. Dallow sees his eyes move.

"No," she says. "No. Not the house."

Earl turns toward Cale.

His lips part.

The thing peeks out, slick and white, then pulls back.

Cale grips the cleaver.

"We're leaving."

"You can't let him out."

"You already did."

That hits her.

It really hits her. Mrs. Dallow looks from Earl to the open freezer, to the cracked tubes overhead, to the meat on the floor, to Maddox bleeding and shaking beside Sofie. For one second, Lenora Dallow looks exactly like what she is.

An old woman.

A scared old woman in a cardigan standing in a garage full of bad choices.

Then Earl lunges.

He's slow until he isn't.

One moment he sways in front of the freezer, stiff and crooked. The next he snaps forward with awful speed, arms out, mouth yawning wide. The thing inside him shoots out like a spring-loaded cable.

Cale swings the cleaver again.

He misses.

The pale thing slaps against his shoulder.

Cold explodes through him.

It isn't pain at first. It's absence. Like his whole arm vanishes from the inside out. Then the pain arrives, bright and white, burning so hard he can't even scream right. He falls against a stack of boxes and knocks them over. Frozen meat spills across the concrete in hard red bricks.

Sofie yanks him away before the thing can hook in.

It leaves a white welt on his hoodie where it touched him. The fabric stiffens. Cracks.

"Move!" Sofie shouts.

She drags Maddox with one hand and Cale with the other, which shouldn't be possible because she's not big, not strong-looking, but terror makes machines out of people.

Mrs. Dallow steps between Earl and the kids.

"Earl," she says, louder now. "Look at me."

Earl's head swivels.

The thing pulls back inside him with a wet click.

"Lenora," he says.

"Yes." Tears shine on her cheeks. "Yes, honey. It's me."

Honey.

The word makes Cale sick.

Sofie shoves Maddox toward the kitchen door.

"Open it!"

Maddox fumbles with the knob. His injured shoulder hangs low, and his fingers are slick with his own blood.

"It's locked," he sobs.

"Then unlock it!"

"I'm trying!"

Earl reaches for Mrs. Dallow.

His black nails touch her cheek.

She flinches, but she doesn't pull away.

"My Earl," she whispers.

For one impossible second, Cale sees what she sees.

Not the corpse. Not the thing.

A man at a breakfast table. A man mowing the lawn. A man bringing in groceries, complaining about his knees, laughing too loudly at game shows. Maybe he wasn't even good. Maybe he was mean. Maybe love doesn't care enough about facts when it gets old and lonely.

Earl strokes her cheek with one dead finger.

Then his hand opens and clamps around her jaw.

Mrs. Dallow's eyes widen.

"Earl?"

The thing bursts from his mouth and goes into hers.

Cale sees it all.

He wishes he doesn't.

It punches past her lips, pale and jointed, tiny legs scrabbling against her chin and cheeks. Mrs. Dallow jerks backward, but Earl holds her head steady with both hands, one whole and one chopped almost through. Her heels drum on the concrete. Her hands slap his suit jacket. Her eyes roll toward the kids, pleading now, finally pleading for the thing she never gave anyone else.

Help.

No one moves.

Cale can't.

Sofie can't.

Maddox gets the kitchen door unlocked and falls through it into darkness.

Mrs. Dallow makes a deep choking noise.

Her throat bulges.

Something moves under the skin.

Then Earl lets her go.

She drops to her knees, both hands at her mouth, shoulders hitching. For a moment, Cale thinks she might vomit the thing out.

Instead, she looks up.

Her eyes glitter with frost.

"Run," she says.

It's still her voice.

Barely.

Sofie pulls Cale through the kitchen door.

They stumble into a house that smells like old carpet, lavender spray, and underneath it all, meat. Meat in the walls. Meat in the vents. Meat in the years.

Maddox is already halfway across the kitchen, knocking over chairs. He hits the back door and claws at the locks.

There are three of them.

Deadbolt.

Chain.

Slide latch.

Mrs. Dallow hasn't been keeping people out.

She's been keeping something in.

Behind them, in the garage, Earl groans.

Mrs. Dallow answers him.

But it isn't a word now.

It's a clicking.

Cale grabs the chain and rips it loose so hard one screw pops from the wood. Sofie handles the deadbolt. Maddox lifts the latch.

The back door opens.

Warm night air rushes in.

Cale has never felt anything so beautiful.

They spill onto the back porch and down into Mrs. Dallow's dead yard. The grass is waist-high near the fence. The old birdbath is tipped over. Something small and furred lies beneath it, bones picked clean and arranged in a neat circle.

Maddox sees it and makes another small sound.

"Don't look," Sofie says.

They run.

Behind them, the house gives a long wooden creak.

The garage side door bangs open.

Cale doesn't look back until they reach the gap in the fence between Dallow's yard and Mr. Phelps's.

When he does, Earl stands in the driveway.

Mrs. Dallow stands beside him.

Not touching.

Not breathing.

Her cardigan hangs crooked. Her mouth shines black in the moonlight. Her gray hair has come loose from its pins and floats around her head like cobweb.

Earl turns his face toward Beacon Lane.

Every dog in the neighborhood starts barking at once.

The sound is enormous.

It rises from every yard, every porch, every kitchen where some family dog sleeps near a refrigerator or under a table. Barking, howling, snarling, yelping. Pickle's high frantic bark cuts through it from Cale's house.

Cale runs harder.

He doesn't remember jumping the Phelps fence. Doesn't remember crossing the yard. He only remembers Mr. Phelps's porch light snapping on and the old man's pale face appearing in the window, mouth open.

Then Cale is in the street with Sofie and Maddox, all three of them panting like they've been dragged from underwater.

The Dallow garage light flickers behind them.

Not red now.

Dark.

Then something moves inside the black.

Sofie grabs Cale's face and forces him to look at her.

"Your house," she says. "Go."

"What about you?"

"I'm getting my mom."

"Maddox?"

Maddox stands in the road, holding his bloody shoulder, staring at the Dallow place.

"I'm sorry," he says.

Cale almost hates him then.

Almost.

But there isn't time.

"Go home," Cale says. "Wake everyone up."

Maddox nods, then bends and grabs his cracked phone from the street where it must've fallen from his pocket. His hand shakes so badly he almost drops it again.

"I have it," he says.

"What?"

"The video." He looks sick when he says it. "I have proof."

For the first time all night, Maddox sounds like he understands proof doesn't mean fame. It means nobody gets to pretend this didn't happen.

Cale nods once.

Then they split.

Cale runs for his house.

Pickle is losing his mind inside. He barks and scratches at the front door so hard Cale hears claws ripping against wood. Cale doesn't bother with the hidden key. He throws himself at the door and pounds.

"Mom!"

Nothing.

"Mom!"

A light comes on upstairs.

Tessa's voice, thick with sleep and fear. "Cale?"

"Open the door!"

Pickle snarls from inside. Not at Cale. Past him.

Down the street, the barking begins to change.

It thins.

One dog cuts off mid-howl.

Then another.

Then three more.

The silence moves house by house toward him.

Tessa opens the door wearing sweatpants and an old hospital shirt, hair smashed on one side, face already sharp with alarm.

"What happened?"

Cale pushes inside and slams the door.

"Lock it."

"Cale, you're bleeding."

"Lock it!"

Tessa locks it.

Pickle throws himself against Cale's legs, shaking so hard his whole body buzzes. Upstairs, Willa appears at the landing in pink pajamas, hair wild around her face.

"What's wrong?" she asks.

Cale looks at her and almost breaks.

Tessa grabs his chin, forcing his eyes back to hers. Nurse eyes. Mom eyes.

"What happened?"

"The Dallow house," he says. "Mrs. Dallow has Earl in a freezer."

Tessa stares.

"What?"

"He's dead, but he's not. There's something in him. We opened it. I'm sorry. Mom, I'm sorry, we opened it."

For one second, disbelief flashes across her face.

Then a scream comes from outside.

Not a kid.

Not a woman.

A dog.

Pickle stops barking.

He whines.

Tessa looks toward the front window.

Something bumps the porch.

Softly.

Once.

Every part of Tessa changes.

She doesn't understand, not fully, but she understands enough. Panic kills people faster than blood loss. Look at the problem. Use your hands. Keep breathing.

She moves.

She grabs Willa, hauls her down the stairs, and shoves both kids toward the hallway.

"Bathroom. Now."

"Mom."

"Now."

Cale takes Willa's hand. She clutches Pickle's collar, and the dog comes with them, belly low, ears flat.

Another bump at the door.

Then a scrape.

Like nails.

Like too many nails.

Tessa disappears into the kitchen and comes back with a butcher knife in one hand and her phone in the other.

She dials 911.

Cale hears the operator answer.

Then he hears Tessa say, "There's someone trying to get into my house."

The porch goes quiet.

Too quiet.

The operator's voice buzzes tiny and useless from the phone.

Tessa backs into the hall.

The front window fogs from the outside.

A hand presses against the glass.

Not Earl's.

Mrs. Dallow's.

Her fingers splay white on the pane.

Her face rises behind them.

Frost shines in her eyes.

Her mouth opens.

Cale expects a click. A growl. Earl's voice. Something awful.

Instead, Mrs. Dallow whispers through the glass.

"Warm."

Then her head jerks sideways, too fast, and she vanishes.

Something hits the front door hard enough to crack the frame.

Tessa screams and drops the phone.

Cale shoves Willa into the bathroom. Pickle darts in after her. Tessa follows, and Cale slams the door, locks it, then drags the laundry hamper in front of it like that'll do a damn thing.

They huddle in the dark.

Tessa holds the knife.

Willa holds Pickle.

Cale holds his ruined shoulder and listens to his house being opened from the outside.

The front door gives way with a splintering crack.

Footsteps enter.

Slow.

Wet.

Clicking follows.

Tiny clicking.

From the bathroom, Cale can see the gap under the door. A thin stripe of hallway floor. Shadows move across it.

One pair of feet.

Black polished shoes.

Then another.

White orthopedic shoes.

Then more.

Small shapes skittering between them.

Pickle growls, low and hopeless.

Tessa presses one hand over his muzzle. Tears stream down her cheeks, but she makes no sound.

The footsteps stop outside the bathroom door.

Earl speaks.

"Boy."

Cale doesn't answer.

Willa trembles against him.

The doorknob turns.

Once.

Stops.

Turns again.

The lock holds.

Something scratches at the lower part of the door.

Not big.

Small.

Exploring.

Cale looks at the bathroom window above the tub.

Tiny. Frosted glass. Painted shut for years.

"Mom," he mouths.

Tessa follows his eyes.

She nods.

Cale climbs into the tub, bites back a cry when his shoulder flares, and shoves at the window. It doesn't move.

The scratching gets louder.

Now it's inside the wood.

Tessa wraps a towel around her fist and punches the glass.

Once.

Twice.

On the third hit, it breaks.

Cold night air spills in, along with the sound of sirens far away.

Too far.

Cale knocks the remaining glass loose with his elbow, then boosts Willa up. She wriggles through, crying silently, Pickle barking once when she disappears outside.

"Take him," Tessa whispers.

Cale lifts the dog. Pickle squirms, then vanishes through the window into Willa's arms.

The bathroom door cracks down the middle.

A pale segmented leg pokes through.

Tessa swings the butcher knife and chops it off.

Black fluid sprays across the tile.

From the other side of the door, Earl howls.

"Go!" Tessa says.

Cale shakes his head. "You first."

"Don't argue with me."

"Mom."

The door cracks again.

More legs push through.

Tessa grabs Cale by the hoodie and kisses his forehead. Hard. Fast.

"I said go."

Then she boosts him.

Cale squeezes through the broken window, glass cutting his stomach, shoulder screaming, and falls into the side yard beside Willa and Pickle.

Behind him, Tessa starts to climb.

Then something grabs her.

Her eyes go wide.

"Run," she says.

Cale grabs her wrists.

"No."

The bathroom fills with clicking.

Tessa's grip slips. Blood streaks Cale's fingers.

"Cale," she says, and there's so much love in it, so much command, that he lets go before he understands he's doing it.

She disappears back inside.

The screaming starts.

Cale grabs Willa and runs.

He runs barefoot over gravel and broken sprinkler heads. He runs while sirens grow louder. He runs while houses open around him and people step onto porches in robes and slippers, blinking at the impossible thing that's crawled into their street.

At the corner, Officer Harker's patrol car screams onto Beacon Lane, lights flashing red and blue over mailboxes, parked cars, startled faces.

Harker gets out with his gun drawn.

"Stop right there!"

Mrs. Dallow turns in the middle of the street.

Earl stands beside her.

Between them, something pale and long uncoils from Earl's mouth and reaches toward the warm pulse of the neighborhood.

Harker fires.

Once.

Twice.

Three times.

The bullets punch Earl backward. They tear holes in his Sunday suit. Frost blooms from each wound.

He doesn't fall.

Mrs. Dallow runs at Harker.

Not like an old woman.

Not anymore.

Cale covers Willa's eyes, but he can't cover her ears.

By dawn, the Dallow house burns.

Firefighters keep back farther than they should. Police tape cuts Beacon Lane in half. Men in cheap black suits arrive before the smoke clears, driving black vans with no markings. They don't answer questions. They don't let anyone near the garage.

Cale sits on the curb wrapped in a blanket while a paramedic cleans the wound on his shoulder.

Willa sleeps against him, exhausted and hiccuping. Pickle lies across her lap, still alive, still trembling.

Sofie sits with her mother across the street.

Maddox is loaded into an ambulance. His face is gray. His shoulder is wrapped. His cracked phone sits in an evidence bag on the stretcher beside him.

He looks at Cale once before the doors close.

Cale looks away.

Nobody has found Tessa yet.

They tell him that doesn't mean anything.

He knows it means everything.

At noon, the neighborhood is quiet.

No dogs bark.

No birds call.

No lawn mowers start.

The Dallow house is a black shell, windows blown out, roof sagging, garage collapsed into smoking ruin.

One of the men in black suits walks out carrying a silver canister. Another follows with a flame unit strapped to his back.

Cale watches them.

He doesn't feel fifteen anymore.

He doesn't feel any age.

Sofie comes over and sits beside him.

Neither of them speaks for a long time.

Then she says, "They're going to say it was a gas leak."

Cale nods.

Across the street, inside the ruined mouth of the Dallow garage, something shifts beneath the ash.

Small.

Pale.

Quick.

Cale sees it.

So does Pickle.

The dog lifts his head and growls.

The man with the flame unit doesn't hear.

The little thing slips under a cracked piece of concrete and vanishes into the warm dark below the street.

Cale stands.

Sofie grabs his arm. "What?"

He points, but by then there's nothing to see.

Just smoke.

Just rubble.

Just the burned remains of Mrs. Dallow's secrets.

Then, from somewhere under Beacon Lane, so low it might be imagination, comes a soft, busy clicking.

Cale looks down at the pavement.

The sun shines hot on his face.

Too hot.

Far too warm.

And beneath his feet, something clicks back.

No Shade in Eden

It's hot.

Not hot like a nice warm summer day.

It's Phoenix, Arizona.

In July.

It's the kind of hot that doesn't sit in the air so much as crouch there with its teeth showing. The kind that makes the street shimmer and buckle, turning every parked car into a confession booth for bad decisions. The kind where a man walks a hundred feet to the mailbox and comes back feeling like God's held a magnifying glass over him.

Derrick Hollis hates it.

He hates it every year, which is stupid, because he keeps living here. Keeps paying the mortgage on a beige stucco house in a neighborhood where every driveway has an SUV or a pickup, every yard has either dying grass or expensive rocks, and every neighbor pretends they don't notice what every other neighbor is doing.

The air conditioner hums like it's filing a complaint.

Inside, the living room is dim and cool enough to make Derrick feel rich. Not actually rich. Just rich in the way a man feels when he can sit in basketball shorts on a leather couch without losing skin. The blinds are half closed. The ceiling fan turns lazily. A baseball game flickers on the television, all green field and clean uniforms and men chewing obscene wads of gum like the world isn't melting.

On the end table, a sweating glass of iced tea leaves a dark ring.

On the wall by the patio door, the little outdoor alarm chimes.

Ding-ding-ding-dong.

Cheerful. Sing-song. Annoying as hell.

Derrick doesn't look away from the TV.

"Bird," he says.

The alarm is a cheap infrared thing he bought online after Lena told him, back when she still lived here, that anyone could hop the low wall from the greenbelt and be at the patio door in six seconds.

"You watch too much true crime," he'd told her.

"You don't watch enough," she'd said.

Now she has an apartment in Tempe, a new last name still pending in some courthouse paperwork, and he has a battery-powered plastic box by the patio door that sings whenever a quail, pigeon, lizard, blown leaf, pool noodle, shadow, or possibly one of Satan's smaller interns crosses the sensor.

Ding-ding-ding-dong.

"Knock it off," Derrick says.

The pitcher on the mound shakes off a sign.

Ding-ding-ding-dong.

Derrick's jaw tightens.

Outside the patio glass, the world is a bleached-out oven. The pool flashes blue under the hard sun. The pomegranates hang heavy on the tree near the back wall, turning red early, swollen little hearts waiting to split. The bougainvillea spills over one corner in a tantrum of pink. Beyond the wall, the greenbelt sits flat and dusty, a strip of municipal pretend-nature where coyotes sometimes pass at night and neighborhood dogs bark at things nobody sees.

Ding-ding-ding-dong.

"Jesus Christ."

Derrick grabs the remote and mutes the game.

Silence drops.

For half a second, anyway.

Ding-ding-ding-dong.

He pushes himself off the couch with a grunt and immediately resents the whole world. His knees pop. His lower back offers a small, bitter opinion. He walks to the patio door, squinting through the glass.

Nothing.

Just the patio, the pool, the glare, the furniture under its tan covers, the little metal side table Lena bought at HomeGoods and left behind because, in her words, "You can keep the ugly things."

Derrick leans closer.

The alarm is mounted low beside the frame, angled toward the patio slab. Its red sensor eye blinks once, smug and tiny.

"Better be a bird," he says.

He unlocks the door and slides it open.

Heat punches him in the face.

Not brushes. Not greets.

Punches.

Hard.

It smells like hot stone, chlorine, dust, and something faintly sweet rotting under the pomegranate tree. The patio concrete burns pale enough to hurt the eyes. Derrick steps out barefoot, realizes that's a mistake, and does a stupid little half-hop before planting himself on the outdoor rug.

"Damn it."

Ding-ding-ding-dong.

Now that he's outside, the chime sounds smaller. More ridiculous. Like a toy singing at a funeral.

He looks left.

Nothing.

He looks right.

Nothing.

Then the sensor catches again.

Ding-ding-ding-dong.

Derrick bends and peers along the foundation.

At first, he sees only the thin shadow beneath the metal sheathing where it meets the stucco, that narrow two-inch overhang running along the house like a tight black lip.

Then the lip moves.

No.

Not the lip.

Something under it.

A body slides along the foundation, slow and smooth, gray-brown and glossy in the sun. It moves over the concrete like the patio is made of ice. No hurry. No panic. Just a soft muscle ribboning forward, every inch of it wrong because it's in his yard, against his house, near his goddamn patio door.

Derrick freezes.

The snake keeps going.

Its head lifts slightly, not much, just enough to seem aware.

Aware of the house.

Aware of him.

"Fuck no," Derrick says.

The snake pauses.

Derrick backs up one step.

"Nope."

The snake's tongue flicks.

"Not today."

He turns and heads for the garage. Fast. Not running, because grown men don't run from snakes in their own backyard.

But close enough.

The garage is hotter than the house and meaner than the yard.

It has that trapped-garage smell of rubber, dust, old cardboard, gasoline fumes, and tools that haven't been touched since the last time Derrick swore he was going to get organized. The motion light clicks on overhead, sudden and white, making everything look criminal.

Derrick stands there, breathing harder than he wants to admit.

"Okay," he says. "Okay, okay."

He scans the wall directly across from him.

Water heater. Workbench. Extension cords hanging from hooks like lazy orange snakes. Two step ladders. One electric hedge trimmer. A leaf blower with a dead battery because, of course. A wide shop broom with stiff black bristles.

He almost grabs the broom.

Then he pictures himself trying to sweep a snake away from the house while it turns around and launches itself at him like a possessed garden hose.

"Nope."

His eyes keep moving.

Old paint cans. A bucket of pool tablets. Mason's abandoned skateboard. A rake. A half-crushed box of Christmas lights. A cordless drill. Three different flashlights that probably don't work. Then, leaning in the corner behind a bag of potting soil, he sees the flathead shovel.

Bingo.

The shovel isn't impressive. It's dirty, scratched, and a little bent near the blade, but right now it looks like Excalibur for men with HOA dues.

Derrick grabs it and feels better immediately.

That's the thing about tools. They lie kindly. They tell a man he has a plan just because he's holding one.

He marches back through the laundry room, past the pantry, through the kitchen, and toward the patio door. On the muted television, one of the players rounds second base with his mouth open in silent joy.

Derrick doesn't care.

At the patio door, he stops.

A brief thought lands in his brain with the ugly little weight of a cockroach.

What if it's gone?

What if the snake disappeared under the door frame, into the wall, into some crack behind the stucco? What if it's already in the house somehow, sliding beneath the refrigerator, coiling behind the washing machine, waiting for him to reach into a cabinet six months from now?

Simple answer: sell the house and move.

Not practical.

Highly logical.

Derrick grips the shovel tighter and steps outside.

The heat's softened a little, but not enough to matter. It still wraps him in a wet towel that's been pulled from an oven. He walks across the patio rug, then onto the concrete, and the bottoms of his feet complain through his cheap slides.

The snake is still there.

Tucked tight along the foundation.

For one stupid second, Derrick feels offended. Like the thing's ignored him on purpose.

"Yeah," he says quietly. "All right."

The snake moves.

Slow.

Patient.

It rides the thin line between house and patio, half in shadow, half in sun, its scales drinking light and giving none back. Its head stays near the wall, angled toward the place where the metal sheathing meets stucco. Like it's searching for something. Like it's reading the house by touch.

Derrick remembers reading somewhere that most snakes can strike about half their body length.

Or maybe that's rattlesnakes.

Or maybe that's total bullshit some guy named Rick told him at a barbecue.

Either way, he does quick math. Three feet feels safe. Four feels better. Ten would be ideal, but the shovel is not ten feet long and God has a sick sense of humor.

He inches closer.

The snake keeps moving.

The patio alarm chimes.

Ding-ding-ding-dong.

Derrick flinches so hard his shoulders jump.

"Shut up."

The snake pauses again.

That bothers him. He can't explain why. It's just a pause. Animals pause. Lizards pause. Birds pause. Hell, Derrick pauses every time he walks into a room and forgets why he's there.

But this pause feels like listening.

The snake's head lifts a little higher.

Derrick raises the shovel.

The motion is clumsy at first. He adjusts his grip, both hands now, like he's at bat. Sweat slides down his temple and into his ear. His heart thuds with a dumb, boyish violence.

The snake shifts away from the house.

Just an inch.

Then another.

Its body loosens from the narrow shadow beneath the metal lip, forgetting safety, forgetting strategy, remembering only that it is a snake and Derrick is too close.

"Bad move," Derrick whispers.

The shovel comes down.

It drops like a guillotine.

The sound is not dramatic. That's the worst part. No movie crunch. No thunder. Just a wet, hard chop against concrete, a sound like celery under a boot.

The snake's body whips.

Derrick backs away without a sound.

The severed head lies near the blade, mouth opening and closing.

Open.

Close.

Open.

Close.

The body lashes in a loose, frantic scribble, writing something on the patio that Derrick cannot read. Its tail smacks the concrete. Its muscles don't know they're dead yet. They keep arguing with the world.

"Jesus," Derrick says.

The mouth opens again.

Close.

Open.

Close.

The patio alarm chimes.

Ding-ding-ding-dong.

Derrick stares at the head.

For one second, and only one, he thinks the snake is smiling. Not really. Not possible. It's a trick of the jaw, the angle, the split dark line of the mouth. Probably that searing hot sun, too.

Still.

It looks amused.

Derrick slides the shovel blade under the body first. It curls wetly onto the metal. He has to scoop the head separately, and when he does, the mouth snaps once against the blade.

Clack.

He jerks back.

"Dead," he says. "You're dead."

The head rests beside the body.

But its black bead eye keeps the sun inside it.

Derrick carries both across the yard, moving fast now. Past the oversized bougainvillea. Past the glittering pool. Past the pomegranate tree with its fruit hanging red and heavy, each one looking suddenly less like fruit than something waiting under skin.

The organ pipe cactus towers near the back wall, wild and overgrown, its arms raised like witnesses refusing to testify.

Derrick doesn't look at it.

He reaches the low wall, checks left and right to see if any neighbors are watching, then lofts the dead snake into the open greenbelt beyond.

The body disappears into dry grass.

The head lands somewhere in the dirt.

A voice comes from behind him, distant but clear.

"That a snake?"

Derrick turns.

Rafa Mercado stands in his own yard next door, one hand shading his eyes.

Derrick doesn't miss a beat.

"Yup."

"Rattler?"

"Nope."

"Dead?"

"Definitely."

Rafa pauses.

The sun burns orange behind him, making his shadow stretch thin and crooked across the rocks.

"Okay then," Rafa says.

But he doesn't go back inside.

Derrick waits half a second, expecting more.

There usually is more with Rafa. A comment about snakes bringing friends. A joke about calling animal control after the animal is already controlled. Some neighborly lecture about how kingsnakes eat rattlers and maybe Derrick has just murdered the local security guard.

But Rafa only stands there with the sinking sun burning behind him.

"What?" Derrick says.

Rafa lowers his hand from his eyes.

"Nothing."

"That's your face for nothing?"

"I got a lot of faces."

"Yeah. Most of them make people uncomfortable."

Rafa gives a dry little smile, but it doesn't stay long.

"You throw it in the greenbelt?"

"Where else am I gonna throw it? The pool?"

"You could've bagged it."

"Rafa, it's a dead snake."

"Things get eaten out there."

"That's nature."

"Sure," Rafa says. "Nature."

The way he says it makes Derrick wish the man had just minded his business like a decent neighbor.

The heat presses against Derrick's back. Sweat races down the middle of his back, gathers at the waistband of his shorts, and goes places he'd rather not think about. The shovel hangs from his hand, heavy now that the job is done. A smear of snake blood darkens the flat blade, thin and glossy, like someone dragged a paintbrush across it.

Rafa notices.

Of course he does.

"You wash that good," he says.

"I was planning to make a sandwich with it, but yeah, I'll probably rinse it off."

Rafa doesn't laugh.

Behind him, his own patio is neat and shadowed, lined with clay pots and a little statue of Saint Francis with both hands broken off. A small wind chime hangs from the eave, but there's no wind to move it. Nothing moves except heat.

Rafa looks toward the greenbelt again.

Then toward Derrick's house.

"Was it against the foundation?"

Derrick frowns.

"What?"

"The snake. Was it against the foundation?"

"Yeah. Under the metal trim."

"Sheathing."

"Congratulations."

Rafa ignores that. "Was it trying to get under?"

"It was trying to be a snake. I didn't ask for its mission statement."

Rafa's mouth tightens.

"Sometimes they're not trying to get in," Rafa says.

Derrick squints at him. "What?"

Rafa looks toward the greenbelt.

"Sometimes they're trying to get away from what's already under."

Derrick stares at him.

"What the hell is that supposed to mean?"

Rafa's jaw works once, like he almost says more. Then he glances toward the broken-handed Saint Francis in his yard.

"My grandmother used to say things," Rafa says. "Most of them sounded crazy until they didn't."

The patio alarm chimes behind Derrick.

Ding-ding-ding-dong.

He turns sharply.

The patio is empty.

The little box blinks red from its spot near the sliding door.

"Piece of junk," Derrick says.

When he looks back, Rafa has taken one step closer to his wall.

"You got that thing pointed low?"

"Yeah."

"For scorpions?"

"For whatever. Lena thought someone might come over the wall."

Rafa's face changes at Lena's name. Not much. Just enough to remind Derrick that neighborhoods are confessionals with garage doors. Everyone knows the big sins. They guess at the little ones for entertainment.

Derrick raises his voice. "There's nothing there."

Rafa doesn't look at the alarm. He keeps staring at the foundation line of Derrick's house.

"Maybe turn it off tonight."

"Why?"

"Because it's gonna annoy you."

"That's already happening."

"Then turn it off."

Derrick almost asks what Rafa really means, but something in him resists. It's the same part that doesn't go to the doctor until a cough turns green. The same part that ignores the tire pressure warning for a week because maybe the car is just being dramatic.

"Good talk," Derrick says.

He starts back across the yard.

The pomegranates hang low as he passes. One's already split since this morning. He's sure of it. He remembers noticing it while skimming the pool after breakfast, closed and smooth and blushing red. Now its skin is cracked wide, showing wet seeds packed together like little rubies.

Something black moves inside it.

Derrick stops.

A fly crawls out, fat and metallic.

"That's disgusting," he mutters.

"Yeah, yeah."

He crosses the patio and sets the shovel near the hose. The blood smear is darker than before, almost brown already, cooking onto the blade in the last of the light. He twists the spigot. The hose coughs, spits hot water first, then hotter water, then finally something cool enough to touch. He blasts the shovel clean.

Snake blood thins and runs over the concrete in pinkish threads.

It slips into the narrow crack along the patio edge.

For a second, Derrick thinks it doesn't drain down.

He thinks it moves sideways.

Toward the house.

He bends slightly.

The wet red thread trembles in the crack, pulls long and fine, then vanishes beneath the stucco lip.

"Okay," he says softly.

He shuts off the hose.

Derrick snatches it off its little bracket.

"There. Happy?"

He slides the patio door open and steps into the kitchen.

Cool air pours around him. He shuts the door with more force than necessary, locks it, then stands there holding the alarm in one hand and the bloody, wet shovel in the other. He realizes how that looks, cracks the door open, and leans the shovel outside against the glass.

The alarm chimes in his hand.

Ding-ding-ding-dong.

Derrick stares at it.

The red sensor eye blinks.

"Not possible," he says.

He flips it over, pops the plastic backing off with his thumb, and removes the batteries. Two cheap AAs roll into his palm. He sets them on the kitchen counter beside his iced tea.

The alarm goes silent.

Derrick exhales.

"Thank you."

The house hums around him. The refrigerator kicks in. The air conditioner grumbles. The ceiling fan turns. The muted baseball game still flickers in the living room.

He starts to smile.

Then the empty little plastic box in his hand sings.

Ding-ding-ding-dong.

Derrick drops the alarm.

It hits the tile and clatters open, plastic shell popping loose, battery cover skidding under the lip of the cabinet. The sound is sharp enough to make him flinch twice. Once when it lands. Again when it settles.

The little white box lies faceup on the kitchen floor.

Empty.

No batteries.

No wires.

No reason.

Ding-ding-ding-dong.

Derrick stares at it with the same stupid disbelief he once had watching his wedding ring roll down a hotel bathroom drain in

Scottsdale. That same instant denial. That same little voice saying no, no, no, rewind, undo, not this.

The alarm's red eye blinks.

Derrick backs into the counter. The two batteries roll, click together, and stop beside his iced tea. Condensation runs down the glass in clear veins.

"Piece of crap," he says.

His voice sounds thinner than he likes.

He snatches a dish towel from the oven handle, crouches, and grabs the alarm through the cloth like it's a scorpion. It doesn't chime now. Of course it doesn't. It just rests there, harmless and cheap, a plastic bargain-bin thing with a fake chrome strip and a sticker on the back curling from the heat.

Derrick shakes it.

Nothing.

He turns it over.

The empty battery compartment gapes at him.

"Okay," he says. "Fine."

He walks to the trash can, steps on the pedal, and throws the alarm inside.

The lid drops.

For three seconds, the kitchen is quiet.

Then from inside the trash, muffled and cheerful:

Ding-ding-ding-dong.

Derrick lunges for the trash can and kicks it.

It tips sideways. The lid snaps open. Coffee grounds, paper towels, an empty salsa jar, junk mail, and the alarm spill across the floor in a wet domestic landslide. The alarm slides through a smear of coffee and stops beside the refrigerator.

Ding-ding-ding-dong.

"Shut up!"

He grabs it barehanded now. No towel. No caution. Anger makes a man brave in the dumbest ways. He turns to the sink, raises the alarm over his head, and brings it down hard against the edge of the granite counter.

Crack.

A line appears across its face.

He hits it again.

Crack.

The plastic splits. A tiny circuit board slips out, green and silver and stupidly fragile. He hits it a third time, harder, hard enough that pain jumps from his palm to his wrist.

Pieces scatter into the sink.

The red sensor eye pops loose and drops down the drain with a neat little tick.

Derrick stands over the wreckage, breathing through his mouth.

"There," he says.

The word comes out shaking.

He turns on the faucet. Water hammers the broken pieces, sends them spinning toward the drain. One piece sticks against the steel like a dead bug. He grabs the garbage disposal switch and flips it.

The disposal growls.

Plastic grinds.

The sound is ugly and satisfying, like teeth chewing a toy.

Derrick lets it run until the sink is clear.

Then he shuts it off.

The kitchen exhales.

He stands with both hands on the counter, head bowed, watching water circle the drain. His reflection bends in the wet steel, face stretched long, eyes sunken, mouth pulled downward. For a second, he looks old. Not middle-aged old. Not tired old.

Buried old.

He laughs once.

It's not a happy sound.

"Get a grip, Derrick."

From the living room, the crowd on the muted television cheers without sound.

He walks back to the spilled trash and starts cleaning it up because that's what people do when the world tilts sideways. They clean. They wipe. They pretend order is a thing they can still enforce. Coffee grounds stain the tile. The salsa jar has cracked but not shattered. The junk mail is wet and sticky. He gathers it all, muttering, sweating, furious.

Outside, something scrapes along the patio glass.

Derrick stops.

The sound comes again.

Slow.

Dry.

Like a fingernail dragging through dust.

He looks toward the sliding door.

The sun drops lower, and the backyard is all orange glare and long shadows. The shovel still leans outside against the glass, blade down, handle tilted. Beyond it, the pool flashes in bands of light. The pomegranate tree shifts in a breeze he can't feel.

The shovel moves.

Not much.

Just enough for the wooden handle to tap the glass.

Tick.

Derrick watches it.

Tick.

The handle taps again.

There's no wind strong enough for that.

"Rafa?" he calls.

No answer.

Tick.

Derrick steps closer to the door.

The shovel is on the other side, close enough that he can see water drying on the blade. No blood now. He washed it clean. He knows he washed it clean.

But as the shadow of the house stretches across the patio, a thin red line appears along the shovel's edge.

Not dripping down.

Climbing up.

Derrick's mouth goes dry.

The red line creeps from blade to handle, thin as thread, bright as a firetruck. It reaches the place where his hand gripped the wood. It spreads there, soaking in, darkening the grain in the shape of four fingers and a thumb.

His handprint.

Derrick steps back.

Behind him, from the kitchen sink, from deep inside the garbage disposal, something sings.

Ding-ding-ding-dong.

Derrick doesn't move.

For a moment, he becomes another piece of furniture in the kitchen. A thing left standing after everyone else has fled the house. His hands hang at his sides. His mouth stays open. Cold air from the vent blows across the sweat on his neck, and somehow that makes it worse. The chill feels borrowed. Temporary. A small mercy on a long hook.

The sink sings again.

Ding-ding-ding-dong.

No.

Not the sink.

Under the sink.

Inside the pipes.

Maybe inside the wall.

The cheerful little melody comes up through the drain with a metallic echo, stretched thin, like something is whistling through broken teeth.

Derrick backs away until his shoulder hits the refrigerator.

The impact knocks loose a magnet shaped like a cactus. It drops to the tile and breaks in half.

He flinches.

"Okay," he whispers. "Nope. We're done."

He turns toward the living room, grabs his phone off the end table, and jabs the screen awake.

No service.

That makes no sense. He has full bars in this house. Always. He pays too damn much for full bars in this house.

He raises the phone higher, like cell signal is a smell he can catch near the ceiling.

Nothing.

Wi-Fi symbol gone, too.

The baseball game on the television freezes.

A batter stands mid-swing, body twisted, face pinched with effort. The image breaks into little squares. Green grass becomes green cubes. The player's mouth hangs open in a silent scream of pixels.

Then the TV goes black.

Derrick laughs again.

This time it comes out uglier.

"Cute."

From outside, the shovel taps the glass.

Tick.

Derrick looks.

The handprint on the wooden handle darkens. It's no longer just red. It's brown at the edges, black in the center, cooked into the grain like barbecue left too long on a grill. The imprint flexes.

Not much.

Just enough.

Like fingers squeezing.

Tick.

The handle touches the glass again.

Derrick crosses the room with his phone in one hand and grabs the heavy ceramic bowl from the dining table with the other. Lena bought that, too. Blue glaze. Too expensive for a bowl nobody is allowed to put chips in.

He pulls the sliding door curtain shut.

The kitchen instantly feels smaller.

Tick.

Now he can't see the shovel, but he can hear it.

Tick.

Tick.

Tick.

Steady as a clock with only one bad second.

"Rafa!" Derrick shouts.

His voice slams around the house and comes back lonely.

He moves to the front door instead. Better. Smarter. Out front, there are streetlights, driveways, doorbell cameras, neighbors who suddenly care when someone parks wrong. He'll walk over to Rafa's. Or he'll get in the truck and leave. No shame in leaving. Shame is for people who survive long enough to explain themselves.

He unlocks the front door.

The deadbolt slides with a hard clack.

He opens it.

Heat rolls in.

Night waits outside.

That stops him.

It shouldn't be night yet.

Sunset, yes. Late orange, purple shadows, all that desert postcard crap. But not full dark. Not this. The street beyond his door is black and empty, every house swallowed, every porchlight dead. The air smells scorched, like fried wire and burnt hair. The sky above the rooftops has no stars. No moon. Just a heavy black lid pressed down over the neighborhood.

Derrick looks at his phone.

6:41 p.m.

He looks outside again.

Midnight stares back.

A shape stands beneath the tree across the street.

No.

That tree is wrong.

Derrick's street has mesquites and palms and skinny ornamental things that look dead even when they're thriving. But the tree across the street is tall, broad, and black against the darker sky. Its branches twist upward like burned fingers.

Something hangs from one of them.

Derrick squints.

It's long.

Limp.

Pale.

A shed snake skin, maybe.

Then it moves.

A human arm drops from the branches, dangling at the wrist.

Derrick slams the door.

He throws the deadbolt.

His breath comes fast now, sawing in and out. He presses his back to the door and tells himself he didn't see that. Couldn't have. Heatstroke. Stress. Bad iced tea. A little snake murder followed by a little nervous breakdown. Men have broken for less. Men have broken because their team lost a playoff game.

Something taps the other side of the front door.

Once.

Softly.

A polite knock.

Derrick's eyes are wide now.

Another knock.

Then a voice, muffled by wood.

"Derrick?"

His knees soften.

That voice.

No.

No, no, no.

"Derrick, open the door."

It's Lena. Not close. Not perfect. But close enough to put a hook under his ribs.

He looks at his phone again. Still no service.

The voice comes again, gentler now.

"Please. It's hot out here."

The patio alarm sings from the kitchen drain.

Ding-ding-ding-dong.

At the back of the house, the shovel taps faster.

Tick. Tick. Tick.

At the front door, Lena's voice lowers into a whisper.

"You shouldn't have killed it."

Derrick stays pressed against the front door, one hand on the deadbolt, one hand over his mouth.

For a few seconds, nothing happens.

No knocking.

No voice.

No polite little plea from the other side.

Just the soft thunder of his own pulse in his ears and the distant, impossible chime bubbling up from the kitchen drain.

Ding-ding-ding-dong.

He swallows hard.

The voice at the door sounded like Lena.

Almost.

But not quite.

That's the part that finally slides into place. Lena doesn't say his name that way. Not stretched thin. Not sweetened at the edges. Not like a person reading from a card.

Derrick lowers his hand from his mouth.

"Nice try," he whispers.

The house stays still around him.

Not alive. Not listening. Just walls, tile, furniture, bad decisions, and air-conditioning that suddenly feels too cold.

Then something hits the kitchen window.

Not hard.

A dull, wet slap.

Derrick turns.

Another slap follows.

Then a smear.

He sees it from the hallway, past the island, past the sink, through the bright rectangle of glass above the counter. Two pale shapes press against the window from outside. Hands. Human hands. Fingers spread wide. Palms slick and dark.

Blood slides down the glass.

Derrick doesn't move at first.

His brain offers him choices and none of them fit.

Call the police. No service.

Get the gun. He doesn't own one.

Get the shovel. The shovel is outside.

Hide. From what?

The hands slip lower.

A face rises between them.

A woman's face.

She's not old. Late twenties maybe. Early thirties. Dark hair stuck to her cheeks with sweat and blood. Silver visor hanging crooked around her neck. One eye swollen almost shut. Her mouth works against the glass, forming words the window swallows.

Derrick knows her.

Not knows her knows her.

Neighborhood knows her.

She walks dogs. Sometimes three at a time, all of them behaving better than most children. He's seen her in the greenbelt at dawn with a collapsible water bowl clipped to her belt. He's seen her jogging at dusk with earbuds in, ponytail snapping side to side.

Kendra.

Kendra something.

Ibarra.

That's it.

Kendra Ibarra.

She sees him.

Her good eye widens.

Her bloody palm lifts and smacks the glass again.

Derrick jolts forward without meaning to. "Jesus Christ."

Kendra shakes her head.

Hard.

Not come here.

Not open up.

No.

Her lips move again.

Derrick steps closer to the sink. The broken disposal smells like hot plastic and coffee grounds. The ruined alarm parts are gone, chewed down into whatever dark throat lives under the drain, but the melody still leaks up through it.

Ding-ding-ding-dong.

Kendra flinches at the sound.

She hears it too.

That's worse than anything so far.

Derrick reaches for the blind cord.

Kendra slams both hands against the glass.

"No?" Derrick says.

She nods, frantic, then winces like the motion hurts something deep in her neck.

He doesn't pull the blind.

Instead, he leans over the sink, close enough that his breath fogs the inside of the glass.

"What happened?" he asks.

Kendra's mouth opens.

The words arrive broken.

"Don't…"

He shakes his head. "What?"

She presses her forehead to the glass. Blood from her hairline smears there, a red half moon.

"Don't open…"

Derrick's hand drifts toward the window latch.

Kendra sees it and nearly sobs.

She shakes her head again.

"No," she mouths.

Something moves below the window.

Not footsteps.

Not someone crouching.

A sliding sound through the landscape stones. Slow, heavy, patient. Like a sack of wet laundry being dragged over gravel. Like a hose full of meat.

Kendra hears it.

Her whole body stiffens.

Her eyes flick down.

Then back to Derrick.

"Please," she whispers through the glass.

Derrick can hear that one.

That one gets through.

He grabs the latch.

Kendra's face crumples with terror.

"No."

The word is silent, but clear.

Derrick freezes.

The sliding sound comes closer.

The small pink leaves from the bougainvillea scrape along the stones outside, dancing in a breeze that does not touch the window. Kendra's breathing fogs the glass in little bursts. She's crying now, but quietly, like she's afraid noise has consequences.

Derrick looks left, toward the patio door.

He can open it. He can run outside. He can grab her. He can be the kind of man who does something when doing nothing is worse.

His feet do not move.

He waits for himself to become the kind of man who opens the door.

He doesn't.

That is the part he will never be able to explain away.

Kendra's bloody fingers curl against the window frame.

Her nails catch in the thin metal track.

She looks at him one last time.

Not accusing.

That would be easier.

She looks sorry for him.

Then something below the sill jerks her down.

Her chin cracks against the bottom of the window.

Blood pops onto the glass.

Derrick screams and lunges forward.

Kendra's hands claw at the frame. Her nails shriek along metal. One breaks. Then another. Her palms slide, leaving two long red trails that look almost graceful, almost painted.

Her face drops out of sight.

Her scream rises from below the window, raw and scared and terribly human.

Derrick slams both hands onto the counter.

"Kendra!"

The scream cuts off.

Not fades.

Cuts.

Outside, the stones shift.

Slowly now.

Away from the house.

Dragging something through the dark.

For a while, Derrick only hears the rocks.

Scrape.

Drag.

Scrape.

Drag.

Each sound pulls farther from the window, around the side of the house, toward the greenbelt beyond the back wall. Kendra doesn't scream again. That's worse. Screaming means alive. Screaming means air and lungs and something still fighting.

The silence after means the desert closed its mouth.

Derrick stands over the sink, hands planted on either side of the basin, staring through the smeared glass.

"Move," he tells himself.

He doesn't.

"Move, you coward."

His legs remain heavy and dumb beneath him.

The chime rises from the drain.

Derrick grabs a coffee mug from the drying rack and hurls it into the sink.

It shatters.

"Shut up!"

The chime stops.

So does he.

The quiet that follows is huge. It fills the kitchen. It fills his skull. It makes room for the sound of his breathing, the refrigerator hum, the faint pop of cooling stucco outside.

Then his phone rings.

Derrick flinches and nearly falls backward.

The phone buzzes on the living room table, bright screen pulsing in the darkened room. He stumbles to it, slips once on a damp piece of trash he missed, catches himself on the back of the couch, and snatches it up.

Lena.

For one second, his relief is so strong it almost hurts.

He answers.

"Lena?"

"Derrick?" Her voice cracks through static. "What the hell is going on?"

He presses the phone hard to his ear. "Where are you?"

"What?"

"Where are you right now?"

"At home. Why?"

"In Tempe?"

"Yes, in Tempe. Where else would I be?"

Derrick closes his eyes.

The thing at the front door wasn't her.

Of course it wasn't her.

But hearing the real Lena makes the fake one worse somehow. Like seeing the original painting after finding a bad copy hung over your bed.

"Derrick," she says. "You're scaring me."

"I need you to listen."

"No, you listen. Mason just called me. He said you texted him."

The room tilts.

Derrick opens his eyes.

"I didn't."

"You told him to come over early."

"I didn't text him."

"You said you needed help with something at the house."

"No."

Lena goes quiet.

Static chews between them.

Then, lower: "What's happening?"

Derrick looks toward the kitchen window. Kendra's bloody handprints shine on the glass. One print has five fingers. The other has four and a smear where the broken nail dragged down.

"There was a woman," he says.

"What woman?"

"Kendra. The dog walker. She was outside. She was hurt."

"What do you mean hurt?"

"Bad. Bleeding. She was at the window."

"Did you call 911?"

"I don't have service."

"You're talking to me."

"I know."

"What do you mean, you know?"

"I mean it came back for you."

The words sound insane because they are insane. He can hear himself from outside his own head. Middle-aged man in basketball shorts says haunted alarm ate his phone signal after murdered snake summons bleeding dog walker. Film at eleven.

Lena exhales sharply. "Derrick, where is she now?"

He looks toward the patio door.

Outside, the shovel is gone.

It had been leaning against the glass. He remembers it perfectly. Blade down. Handle touching the window. Bloody handprint climbing the wood.

Now there's nothing there but a wet mark on the patio.

A dark trail leads away from it.

"I think something took her," he says.

The line goes silent.

Then Lena says, very carefully, "Where's Mason?"

Derrick pulls the phone away and checks the time.

6:58 p.m.

He opens the message thread with Mason.

There it is.

A text from Derrick's number.

Come over now. Need you. Don't tell your mom yet.

Sent at 6:12.

Derrick's stomach turns cold.

He didn't send it.

Another text appears while he's looking.

From his own number.

Hurry. It's getting hungry.

The phone drops from his hand onto the carpet.

Lena's tiny voice crackles from the speaker.

"Derrick? Derrick, answer me."

From outside, beyond the patio, beyond the pool, beyond the pomegranate tree, something knocks against the back wall.

Once.

Then again.

Not asking to come in.

Testing how strong it is.

Derrick snatches the phone off the carpet.

"Lena."

"I'm here," she says. "Where is Mason?"

"I don't know."

"That's not an answer."

"I don't know yet."

"Call him."

"I'm trying."

He pulls the phone from his ear, taps Mason's name, hits call.

Nothing.

Not ringing. Not failing. Not even silence the normal way. Just a thick, dead pressure against his ear, like someone pressed the receiver into dirt.

Then a click.

A breath.

"Mason?"

No answer.

"Mason, where are you?"

The breath comes again, slow and close.

Then Mason's voice says, "Dad?"

Derrick almost collapses with relief.

"Where are you?"

"In the car."

"Turn around."

"What?"

"Turn around right now."

"Why?"

"Don't argue with me. Just turn around."

"I'm already almost there."

Derrick closes his eyes.

Across the room, the kitchen window looks black except for Kendra's blood. The handprints seem to float there, red and shining, two warnings pressed into glass.

"How close?" Derrick asks.

"I just turned onto Cactus Wren."

That's three streets away.

Maybe two minutes.

Maybe less.

Derrick grips the phone so tightly his fingers hurt. "Listen to me. Do not pull into the driveway. Do not get out of the car. Do not stop for anyone. If you see me outside, if I wave you down, if I stand in the road, you keep driving. You understand?"

"What the hell are you talking about?"

"If you see me outside, it's not me."

The words leave Derrick's mouth before he can stop them.

Mason goes quiet.

Then, with the careful tone kids use when they realize adults are not well, he says, "Dad, are you drunk?"

"No."

"Did something happen?"

"Yes."

"What happened?"

Derrick looks at the patio door.

The backyard is dark now, but not fully. The pool throws a soft blue glow from its underwater lights. The pomegranate tree is a black knot against the wall. One fruit hangs split open, its red insides visible even from here, too bright, like it's lit from within.

The back wall knocks again.

Harder this time.

Thump.

Mason hears it through the phone.

"What was that?"

"Nothing."

"Dad."

Derrick's voice breaks. "I killed a snake."

Silence.

"What?"

"There was a snake by the patio. I killed it. Then this woman came to the window. Kendra. The dog walker. Something took her. Something's outside."

"Dad, I'm calling Mom."

"She already knows."

"No, I'm calling 911."

"You won't get through."

"Why wouldn't I get through?"

"Because I can't."

"You're talking to me."

"I know."

Mason curses softly, scared now, not annoyed.

Derrick hears the faint sound of the car through the line. Tires on asphalt. Turn signal clicking. Music low in the background, some bass-heavy thing Mason likes and Derrick pretends not to hate. Normal sounds. Living sounds. They make the terror worse.

"Where are you now?" Derrick asks.

"Passing the mailboxes."

Derrick looks toward the front door.

The mailboxes are forty yards from the house.

Too close.

"Keep going."

"I can see your house."

"Keep going."

"Dad…"

"What?"

"There's someone in your driveway."

Derrick's lungs stop.

"Do not stop."

"He's just standing there."

"Drive past."

"It looks like Rafa."

Derrick moves to the front window but stops before touching the blind. He remembers Kendra's frantic headshake. No blind. No window. No invitation through sight. But Mason is outside. Mason is looking.

"Mason, listen to me," Derrick says. "Drive past the house. Now."

"He's waving."

"That's not Rafa."

"How do you know?"

"Because Rafa wouldn't wave."

It's stupid. It's the wrong proof. It's also true.

Rafa Mercado does not wave people down like a man stranded at a boat dock. Rafa lifts two fingers. Rafa nods. Rafa points if something needs pointing. Rafa does not stand in a driveway in July darkness, waving both arms like a scarecrow trying to fly.

Mason breathes faster.

"Dad, he's bleeding."

"Drive."

"He's bleeding bad."

"Mason, drive!"

Outside, something hits the back wall again.

Thump.

The sound is deeper now. Wood and block and earth all answering at once.

The phone crackles.

Mason says, "He's in the road."

Derrick's voice tears out of him.

"Do not stop!"

Brakes squeal through the phone.

Then Mason screams.

The scream cuts through the phone and turns Derrick's bones into water.

"Mason!"

Metal crunches.

Not a crash exactly. Not the full, catastrophic thunder of a car folding around a pole. More like something heavy slamming against the hood and rolling hard across it. Derrick hears Mason curse, hears tires bark, hears the phone tumble somewhere inside the car.

Then the line fills with static.

"Mason!"

No answer.

Derrick runs to the front window and grabs the blind cord.

His hand stops.

Kendra's face flashes in his mind. Her bloody hands. Her silent no. Her chin cracking against the sill. The way she knew the window was part of it somehow. Not magic. Not the house thinking. Something simpler and worse.

Attention.

Invitation.

Look too long and it knows where you are.

But Mason is out there.

Derrick yanks the blind open.

The street outside is mostly dark, but not impossible anymore. Porch lights burn here and there. A garage light glows three houses down. Normal neighborhood shapes huddle in the heat. Cars. Landscaping. Trash bins waiting for pickup.

Mason's black Civic sits crooked near the curb, headlights pointed across Derrick's driveway. The engine still runs. One headlight is broken. The other throws a hard white beam over the desert rocks and the base of the mesquite tree.

The driver's door hangs open.

Derrick sees Mason's shoe first.

Then Mason.

He's half out of the car, one hand gripping the door frame, trying to pull himself upright. Blood runs from his forehead down the side of his face. Not too much. Not enough to mean death. Derrick's mind clings to that with disgusting hope.

Rafa is there, too.

Or what is left of Rafa.

He lies sprawled across the hood of the Civic, face turned toward the windshield, mouth open, one cheek peeled raw from impact. His arms hang wrong. One leg bends under him in a way no living leg agrees to bend.

But his eyes are open.

And moving.

Derrick stares.

Rafa's gaze slides slowly from Mason to Derrick's window.

Their eyes meet.

Rafa's mouth works.

At first Derrick thinks he's speaking. Then he understands.

Rafa is trying to chew.

There is something in his mouth.

Something long and gray-brown, slick with blood.

A tail.

The dead snake's tail.

Rafa bites down and the tail twitches.

Derrick lets go of the blind.

It snaps back down hard enough to rattle the frame.

He staggers away from the window, gagging.

The phone still crackles from the carpet.

"Dad?"

Mason's voice.

Derrick drops to his knees and grabs it.

"Mason. Listen to me. Can you move?"

"I hit him," Mason says, sobbing. "I hit Rafa. He walked right in front of me."

"That's not Rafa."

"He's on my car."

"Get away from him."

"He's moving."

"Get away from him now."

"I think I broke my ankle."

Derrick closes his eyes for one terrible second.

Then he opens them, because terrible seconds are expensive now.

"Crawl if you have to. Get back in the car."

"I can't. Door's jammed against the curb."

"Passenger side."

"Dad, he's looking at your house."

"I know."

"He's chewing something."

"I know."

The back wall thumps again.

This time, the sound comes with a crack.

Derrick turns toward the patio.

Through the closed curtain, he sees nothing, but he feels the vibration in the floor. Not the house alive. Not the walls breathing. Just impact traveling through slab, tile, bone.

Something big hits concrete block hard enough to make picture frames tick against drywall.

Mason whimpers through the phone.

"Dad, there's something behind your house."

Derrick looks toward the kitchen.

Kendra's blood begins to dry on the window. The red trails turn dark, almost black. The sink is silent now. The chime stops.

That scares him most.

The alarm no longer needs to warn him.

Whatever set it off is here.

Derrick runs to the garage.

He doesn't think. Thinking has done nothing useful for him tonight. His thoughts have been a committee of cowards with clipboards. He grabs the first real weapon he sees: the hedge trimmer.

Dead battery.

"Of course."

He throws it down and snatches the aluminum baseball bat leaning beside Mason's old skateboard. He bought it years ago for a season Mason hated. Six games. Twelve strikeouts. One accidental hit because the ball found the bat like an act of pity.

Derrick carries it now like a holy relic.

He opens the front door.

Heat rushes in, thick and sour.

Mason screams from the street.

Rafa manages to roll off the hood.

He lands on the asphalt with a slap.

Then he starts crawling toward Mason.

Derrick steps outside.

The heat takes him by the throat.

It should be cooler now. It should at least pretend. Instead, the night air presses thick and brutal against his face, like the day died but refuses to stop burning. The street smells like hot asphalt, spilled coolant, blood, and something reptile-sour underneath it all.

"Mason!" he shouts.

His son is on the far side of the Civic, dragging himself backward with both hands. One foot moves. The other doesn't. His right ankle points at a bad angle, not grotesque, not snapped backward, but wrong enough to make Derrick's stomach fold in on itself.

Rafa crawls after him.

No.

Not Rafa.

Derrick stops thinking of that thing as Rafa, because Rafa would be cursing. Rafa would be telling them both to quit making a mess of his street. Rafa would have an opinion about the Civic's broken headlight and the skid marks and the fact that Derrick's garage light still flickers after three years.

This thing only crawls.

Its fingers scrape the asphalt. Nails bend backward. Its broken leg drags behind it in a dark, useless zigzag. Its mouth keeps working around the snake tail, chewing and chewing, as if whatever rides inside him is trying to remember how teeth operate.

"Dad!" Mason cries.

Derrick runs.

He raises the bat before he reaches the curb. For one absurd second, he hears Mason's old little-league coach saying, Keep your eye on the ball, and Derrick almost laughs because panic is a drunk comedian.

Rafa's head turns.

His eyes are all wrong now.

Not black. Not glowing. Nothing so clean.

They are too dry.

Like all the moisture has been sucked backward into the skull, leaving the whites yellowed and cracked, the pupils tiny as burnt pinholes.

Derrick swings for the fences.

The aluminum bat connects with Rafa's shoulder.

The sound is meat and metal.

Rafa collapses flat against the road, but only for a second. His torso jerks. His left arm reaches for Mason again, fingers flexing like the snake's severed mouth.

Derrick swings again.

This time he hits the forearm. Bone snaps under skin. Rafa's hand flips loose, attached but useless, flopping against the asphalt like a fish on a dock.

Mason screams.

Derrick looks at him. "Move!"

"I can't!"

"Yes, you can."

"My ankle."

"I know. Move anyway."

That's cruel. He hears it as soon as he says it. But fatherhood has no soft voice in emergencies. Love comes out mean when death gets close.

Mason rolls onto his stomach and claws toward the passenger side of the Civic.

Behind Derrick, from the back of the house, the wall cracks again.

Loud.

A sharp stone-splitting report that makes porch lights flicker on across the street. A dog begins barking down the street. Then another. Then silence falls over both of them at once, like hands closed around their muzzles.

Derrick doesn't look back.

He keeps the bat between Rafa and Mason.

Rafa pushes himself up on one elbow.

The snake tail slides from his mouth.

It plops on the asphalt, wet and twitching.

Derrick's breath catches.

The tail is longer than it should be.

Much longer.

It keeps coming.

Rafa coughs, and another slick length slips from his mouth. Then another. Not a tail now. A body. Gray-brown. Glazed with saliva and blood. It slides from Rafa's throat in a slow, hideous ribbon, as though something inside him has been feeding it out.

Derrick backs away.

"What the fuck," Mason sobs.

The snake body hits the street and coils.

No head.

Just body.

It curls once. Twice. It points its severed end toward Derrick, blind and seeking.

Rafa's mouth opens wider.

Too wide.

His jaw trembles. His lips split at the corners. Blood runs down his chin in dark ropes.

A sound comes out of him.

It's not a voice.

Not a word.

A dry rattle, deep and hollow, like pebbles shaken inside a clay pot.

The streetlight above them flickers before going out. Then pops.

Glass rains down in glittering pieces.

Derrick grabs Mason under the arms.

"Up."

Mason cries out as Derrick hauls him. The sound spears through Derrick, but he doesn't stop. He drags Mason toward the driveway, toward the front door, toward light, locks, phones, anything that still belongs to the world of normal men.

Mason claws at Derrick's forearm.

"Dad, behind you."

Derrick looks.

The cracked back wall gives way.

Not all of it.

Just the section near the pomegranate tree.

Concrete block bulges outward, then spills into the yard in a dusty collapse. Something moves through the gap behind it, low and broad, dragging itself from the greenbelt into Derrick's backyard.

At first, his mind tries to make it an animal.

Coyote.

Big dog.

Even a javelina.

Anything with a name.

But it has too many angles for an animal. Too much length. It moves like a wound learning to crawl. Its surface catches the pool light in patches, wet here, scaled there, furred in places with dry grass and pink bougainvillea petals stuck to it like decorations on a corpse.

The dead snake's head rests at the front of it.

Tiny by comparison.

Still severed.

Still smiling.

And behind that head, something huge wears the rest of the dark.

Derrick drags Mason faster.

The boy's broken ankle bumps the driveway, and Mason makes a sound Derrick will remember even if he lives to be a hundred. It is thin, strangled, bitten in half before it can become a scream.

"Sorry," Derrick gasps. "I'm sorry, I'm sorry."

"Don't stop," Mason says.

That does something to Derrick. His son's terror takes shape now. It has weight. It's not teenage irritation or sarcasm or the practiced boredom Mason wears like sunscreen. It's a child's voice buried under sixteen years of trying not to need anybody.

Derrick hooks both arms beneath him and pulls.

The thing in the backyard moves through the broken wall.

Not fast.

Somehow, that's worse.

Fast would mean animal. Fast would mean panic, hunger, simple blood. This thing has patience. It pours itself through the gap, scraping block, dragging shrubbery, pushing desert stone aside with a soft grinding sound. The dead snake head leads it, but not like a head should lead anything. It's just there at the front, fastened into a mass that's borrowed it, honored it, maybe punished it.

The mouth opens.

Close.

Open.

Close.

Derrick looks away before his mind snaps clean in two.

Rafa's ruined body jerks in the street.

The headless snake length spilling from his mouth tightens like a rope. It coils around his wrist, then his forearm, then pulls. Rafa's corpse slides one foot across the asphalt toward the backyard.

Mason sees it.

"Dad…"

"I know."

"What is it?"

"I don't know."

That is the first honest thing Derrick's said all night.

They reach the front door.

Derrick shoves Mason through first. Mason hits the entry tile and rolls onto his side, panting, eyes wide and gleaming. Derrick follows, slams the door, locks it, then throws the chain, too, though the chain suddenly seems like a structural joke at this point.

Mason grabs his shirt.

"Don't leave me."

"I won't."

"You said if I saw you outside, it wasn't you."

"That was different."

"You're real?"

Derrick almost says of course.

But the question is too scared for an automatic answer.

He takes Mason's hand and presses it against his own chest.

"Feel that?"

Mason nods.

"That's me."

Mason's face crumples.

For one second, Derrick thinks his son might sob like he did when he was six and broke his wrist falling off the monkey bars. Instead Mason swallows it down. Brave kid. Stupid brave. His mother's courage with Derrick's bad habit of hiding pain until it comes out sideways.

From the backyard comes a long scrape across concrete.

Then the patio alarm sings.

Not from the drain now.

From outside.

Ding-ding-ding-dong.

Derrick turns his head slowly.

The broken alarm is gone. He destroyed it. Fed it to the disposal. Heard the plastic crack and grind.

But the melody comes from the patio anyway, cheerful as a child's toy in a burned nursery.

Ding-ding-ding-dong.

Mason whispers, "What is that?"

"Alarm."

"It sounds like…"

"I know what it sounds like."

"No," Mason says. "It sounds like it's closer."

The patio door is twenty feet away, past the living room, beyond the couch and the frozen television and the glass of iced tea still sweating on the end table like nothing important just happened.

Derrick helps Mason crawl behind the entry table.

"Stay low."

"Why?"

"I don't know. Just do it."

He grabs the baseball bat again and moves toward the living room.

The curtain over the sliding door hangs still.

Beyond it, something crosses the patio.

The motion light snaps on.

White glare floods the curtain.

A shape appears against the fabric.

Low.

Broad.

Wrong.

It doesn't press itself to the glass. It doesn't knock. It doesn't pretend to be human. It simply passes from left to right with the slow assurance of something inspecting property lines.

The silhouette drags a heavy length behind it.

Pink bougainvillea petals rain from whatever surface scrapes the patio cover.

Derrick raises the bat.

The shape stops.

Not because it hears him.

Because it reached the shovel.

Derrick can't see the shovel through the curtain, but he hears metal move against concrete. The dirty blade scrapes once. Then again.

The thing outside lifts it.

For a second, the shovel's outline appears against the curtain, upright and trembling, as if held by an invisible worker about to break ground.

Then the blade turns.

Points toward the house.

Points toward Derrick.

Mason says from behind him, "Dad?"

Derrick's hands tighten on the bat.

The shovel drops.

Its blade bites into the concrete patio with a crack that sends a silver line racing across the slab.

The thing begins to dig.

Concrete flakes.

Stucco dust shakes from the wall.

Derrick understands then with a coldness deeper than fear.

It is not trying to get into the house.

It is opening what is already underneath.

The shovel rises and falls.

Crack.

Crack.

Crack.

Each strike punches through the patio like the concrete is nothing but old crust over something soft and rotten. The sound travels through the slab and into Derrick's knees. It makes his teeth ache. It makes the glasses in the kitchen cabinet tick together in tiny, polite applause.

Mason drags himself farther behind the entry table, pale with shock.

"Dad," he whispers. "What's under there?"

Derrick wants to lie.

A pipe.

A root.

A sinkhole.

Anything with a repair estimate.

But the crack across the patio keeps growing. It runs from the glass door toward the pool in a crooked line, then branches toward the pomegranate tree. The fruit trembles on its branches. One splits open with a wet little pop, spilling red seeds onto the dirt like a mouth losing teeth.

"I don't know," Derrick says.

Outside, the shovel strikes again.

Crack.

The patio door shivers.

Derrick turns toward the garage.

Tools.

That's where the answer always is. That's what he believes because it works for small problems. Loose hinges. Broken sprinkler heads. Pool vacuum hoses. Clogged dryer vents. His whole life is built on the idea that the right tool makes the wrong thing manageable.

But this is not a hinge.

It's not a sprinkler head.

The shovel comes down again, and a chunk of patio drops inward.

Not breaks outward.

Drops.

Gone.

A dark hole opens beneath the slab.

Heat pours from it.

Not normal heat. Not Phoenix heat. This is older and hotter, a buried fever. It carries the smell of rotten eggs, hot pennies, reptile musk, and something sweetly human turning bad. Derrick gags and steps back.

Mason covers his nose with his shirt.

"What is that?"

Before Derrick can answer, something rises from the hole.

Not the thing itself.

A hand.

Kendra's hand.

It reaches up through the broken concrete, fingers bent, nails torn, palm still marked with blood from the window. For one insane second, Derrick thinks she's alive under there. His heart surges toward that impossible hope.

Then her hand opens.

Something rests in her palm.

Two AA batteries.

Derrick stares.

They are the same batteries from the alarm. The cheap silver ones he set on the counter. The ones he never picked up. The ones that should still be in the kitchen unless the world stopped caring about the difference between here and there.

Kendra's hand tilts.

The batteries roll across the patio and tap gently against the glass.

Ding.

Ding.

Mason sobs once.

"Dad, don't."

Derrick doesn't know what he's warning him not to do.

Look?

Open the door?

Believe?

Kendra's hand folds backward at the wrist and vanishes into the hole.

The shovel scrapes across the patio.

The blade slides under the batteries.

Then lifts them.

Slowly.

Carefully.

Like an offering.

Like an accusation.

Derrick backs away until his heel bumps the coffee table. The iced tea glass wobbles, tips, and spills across the wood. Amber liquid runs over old mail, the remote, a coaster from a vacation he and Lena took when they still liked each other in public.

The television flickers back on.

No baseball.

Just a bright desert image.

Derrick's backyard, filmed from above.

He sees himself through the glass, standing in the living room with the bat. He sees Mason curled near the entry. He sees the patio cracked open. He sees the shovel held upright by something too low and dark to fit in the camera frame.

Then the picture changes.

It shows the greenbelt.

Daylight.

Not now.

Earlier.

Derrick stands at the wall with the dead snake balanced on the shovel. He looks left. Looks right. Makes sure no one sees. Then he tosses it over.

The image freezes on the snake in midair.

Its head and body separate, both turning slowly in sunlight.

Then the screen goes black.

Words appear in white letters.

Not typed.

Scratched.

Bring it back.

Derrick's throat tightens.

Mason reads it from the floor.

"Bring what back?"

Derrick knows.

Of course he knows.

The snake.

The body.

The head.

The thing he threw away like trash.

Outside, the shovel turns and points toward the back wall, toward the broken place, toward the greenbelt beyond.

The message on the television changes.

Before the sun comes up.

The TV shuts off.

The patio light pops dark.

For several seconds, nothing moves.

Then from the hole beneath the patio, Kendra's voice rises.

Not a trick voice.

Not a mimic.

Hers.

Broken, slurry, barely alive or made from the memory of alive.

"Please," she whispers.

Derrick grips the bat until his knuckles burn.

Mason says, "Dad?"

Outside, something drags the shovel back through the hole in the wall.

Toward the greenbelt.

Leaving the batteries on the patio.

Leaving the hole open.

Leaving Derrick with a choice.

Derrick stares at the words burned into his head.

Bring it back.

Before the sun comes up.

The house is quiet again. Just a house. Walls. Furniture. Air. The faint smell of spilled iced tea and hot plastic. The ordinary bones of a place where ordinary things are supposed to happen.

Outside, the patio is cracked open like a skull.

Mason grips the leg of the entry table.

"Dad," he says. "What does it want?"

Derrick looks at his son.

Mason's got blood on his face. His ankle is swelling fast. He's trying not to cry because sixteen is an age where boys think pain is a test and fathers are judges. Derrick hates himself for every time he's helped teach him that.

"The snake," Derrick says.

Mason blinks. "What?"

"It wants the snake back."

"The one you killed?"

Derrick nods.

Mason looks past him, toward the patio curtain, toward the hole underneath the house.

"Then give it back."

Simple.

Terrible.

Correct.

Derrick turns toward the kitchen. Kendra's blood dries black on the window. Beyond it, darkness presses against the glass, but not like before. It isn't theatrical now. No midnight trick. No fake Lena. No voices at the door.

Just desert.

Waiting.

Derrick goes to the laundry room and opens the cabinet above the washer. Flashlight. Work gloves. A roll of black lawn bags thick enough to hold wet leaves, palm fronds, cactus chunks, dead things, and all the little disasters homeowners don't discuss.

He grabs the flashlight and gloves.

Then he looks at the lawn bags.

No.

Not for Mason to see.

Not unless he has to.

He comes back into the living room. Mason's dragged himself closer to the couch and wrapped both hands around his ankle. His face is gray.

"I'm coming with you," Mason says.

"No."

"You can't leave me here."

"I'm not leaving you. I'm going outside for five minutes."

"That's what people say before they die in movies."

"This isn't a movie."

"No, it's worse. Movies make sense."

Derrick almost smiles. It hurts his face.

He kneels beside Mason and puts the phone in his hand.

"If service comes back, call your mom. Call 911. Call anyone."

Mason grabs his wrist. "Don't be stupid."

"I'm way past that."

"I mean don't try to be brave now just because you feel guilty."

That lands clean.

Derrick looks at him.

Mason's eyes shine.

"Isn't that what this is?" Mason says. "You killed something, then you waited too long with that woman, and now you want to fix it by running outside with a flashlight?"

Derrick wants to defend himself.

He doesn't.

"Yes," he says.

Mason's grip loosens.

Derrick stands.

At the front door, he stops.

The patio is closer to the greenbelt, but the hole is there. The broken wall is there. Whatever dragged itself through is there, somewhere beyond that damn pomegranate tree, wearing the dark.

So he goes out the front.

The street is still lit by scattered porch lights. Mason's Civic still sits crooked at the curb. Rafa lies near it, face down now. Nothing spills from his mouth. Nothing moves around him. He looks smaller dead. Smaller and sadder.

Derrick crosses the yard with the bat in one hand and the flashlight in the other.

The heat is filthy.

It clings to his skin. It crawls under his shirt. The whole neighborhood smells like a pan left too long on a burner. Somewhere far away, a siren rises and falls, but it never comes closer.

At the corner of the house, Derrick stops.

The side yard runs narrow between stucco and block wall. Landscape stones. The rusty roofing nail he keeps meaning to pick up. Kendra's blood is there, smeared on the stones in a dragging path.

He follows it.

His flashlight beam shakes.

The path leads around the side, past the broken patio, past the tree. The crack in the patio steams. The hole beneath it breathes heat. He does not look into it.

Not yet.

He reaches the broken back wall.

Beyond it, the greenbelt waits.

It looks ordinary from here. That's almost insulting. Dry grass. Gravel. Creosote bushes. A sagging chain-link fence farther back. A maintenance path used by landscapers, kids cutting through, dog walkers, people who believe city land is safer than wild land because someone put it on a map.

Derrick climbs through the broken wall.

The first thing he sees is Rafa's flashlight.

It lies in the dirt twenty feet away, still on, beam pointed sideways. Moths hurl themselves against the light like worshippers against a locked church door.

The second thing he sees is Kendra's silver visor.

It hangs from a dry branch.

Below it, the ground is disturbed.

Derrick forces himself forward.

Every step sounds too loud.

"Snake," he whispers, like an idiot. Like calling it might help.

The flashlight catches something pale.

Skin.

He freezes.

It's Kendra.

Or what the thing has left near enough to Kendra for mercy to still hurt.

She lies half-hidden in the dry grass, twisted on her side, one arm tucked beneath her, the other stretched toward Derrick's wall as if she is still trying to get back to the window. Her face is turned away. Her dark hair covers most of it. One shoe is gone.

Derrick makes a sound deep in his throat.

She moves.

He nearly drops the flashlight.

"Kendra?"

Her fingers twitch.

Not dead.

Not dead.

He runs to her.

The grass around her shifts.

He stops so hard his knees crack.

Kendra's mouth opens. A wet breath slips out.

"Don't," she whispers.

The word is almost nothing.

Derrick crouches three feet away, every nerve begging him to grab her, lift her, carry her inside, become clean through action.

But Kendra is staring past him.

At the ground.

Derrick lowers the flashlight.

The snake's body lies in a loose coil around her waist.

No.

Not around.

Through the grass. Under her. Beside her. In pieces and not in pieces. The severed body Derrick threw over the wall stretches impossibly long, gray-brown and slick, threaded through the dirt like a vein pulled from the earth. It loops around Kendra once, then disappears into a hole beneath a creosote bush.

It isn't lying on the ground.

It is plugged into it.

The head sits near her hand.

The tiny dead head.

Its mouth opens.

Close.

Open.

Close.

Derrick gags.

Kendra whispers, "Put it back."

"Where?"

Her eyes roll toward his yard.

"Where you cut it."

She swallows hard.

"Where it bled."

A rustle moves through the greenbelt.

Long.

Low.

All around him.

Derrick reaches for the snake head.

The mouth snaps at him.

He jerks back, swearing.

Kendra's fingers claw weakly at the dirt. "Please."

Derrick pulls on the work gloves.

The leather feels useless. Costume armor.

He grabs the snake head behind the jaw.

It writhes.

Dead things should not have strength. This has enough. The mouth opens and closes against the glove, little needle teeth scraping leather. Derrick clamps down harder and lifts it.

The body tightens around Kendra.

She cries out.

"No," Derrick says. "No, no."

He grabs the nearest loop of snake body with his other hand and pulls.

The ground answers.

Something pulls back from below.

Derrick falls to one knee. Pain flashes up his leg. The flashlight rolls, beam spinning across grass, dirt, Kendra's bloody face, a line of pomegranate seeds scattered where no pomegranate tree grows.

He pulls again.

The snake body comes free with a sucking sound.

Then another length.

Then another.

It slides out of the dirt in impossible coils, longer than the house, longer than the yard, slick with mud that should not exist in Phoenix in July. Derrick hauls it hand over hand, sobbing now, cursing now, no clever thoughts left.

Kendra slips free.

For one second, Derrick thinks he has saved her.

Then the ground beneath her opens.

Not wide. Not dramatic. Just a narrow black seam in the dirt, like a mouth too thin to be useful.

It is useful.

Something below grips her by the spine.

Her back arches.

Her eyes lock on Derrick.

She doesn't scream. She has no room left for screaming.

The seam pulls her down.

Fast.

Derrick grabs her wrist.

Her skin is burning hot.

He holds on with both hands.

"Kendra!"

Her hand slips.

Her nails cut four lines down his palm.

Then she is gone.

The dirt closes over her with a soft, final pat.

Derrick stays on his knees, holding nothing.

The snake head twists in his gloved fist.

Behind him, something exhales.

He turns.

The thing waits between him and the broken wall.

Waits is the right word. It has patience. It has always had patience.

It gathers there, low, wide, built from scales, hide, dry grass, bone, and wet flesh. Pink bougainvillea petals cling to it. Kendra's missing shoe is caught in one fold. Rafa's saint medal hangs from something that might be a tooth.

It does not have a face except for the dead snake head in Derrick's hand.

That is the trick.

That is the insult.

He is holding the face.

The body waits for it.

Derrick understands.

He looks past the thing, through the broken wall, into his house.

Mason is there.

Not hiding now.

He's dragged himself to the patio door and pushed the curtain aside. He sits on the floor, one leg twisted, both hands pressed to the glass, watching his father in the greenbelt.

Derrick lifts the snake head.

The thing shifts.

Not lunging.

Wanting.

Good, he thinks. Look at me.

Derrick turns and runs away from the house.

"Dad!" Mason screams.

Derrick hears him through the glass. Through the yard. Through the heat.

He keeps running deeper into the greenbelt.

The snake body drags behind him, looped in his left hand, heavy and slick. The head bucks in his right. The thing follows with a grinding rush, faster now, angry now, no more patience because the bait is leaving the trap.

Derrick runs past Rafa's flashlight.

Past Kendra's visor.

Past dry bushes that claw his legs.

Past the place where coyotes have left bones small as toothpicks.

The greenbelt dips ahead into an old drainage wash. Most of the year it's dry, a scar of concrete and dirt behind the neighborhood. During monsoon storms, water tears through it brown and violent, carrying branches, trash, dead birds, whatever people thought they had thrown away.

Derrick reaches the lip and nearly falls.

Below, the wash is black.

Not shadowed.

Black.

A darkness with heat coming out of it.

The snake body in his hand tightens, pulling him toward it.

The thing behind him crashes through brush.

Derrick turns once.

It's close.

Too close.

He sees the open seam of it. The old hunger. The place where Kendra went. The place where Rafa went. The place where all the missing dogs and cats and desert birds and careless things have gone during summers too hot for mercy.

He thinks of the snake sliding along his foundation.

Not coming in.

Running.

Hunting shade.

He thinks of the shovel dropping.

He thinks of Kendra whispering don't.

He thinks of Mason asking, You're real?

Derrick laughs once.

It sounds like a cough full of glass.

"Here," he says.

He throws the snake head into the wash.

The thing shrieks.

Not loud.

Deep.

The ground itself seems to make the sound, a buried pipe organ filled with insects and teeth.

The snake body lashes around Derrick's arm.

The head disappears into the black.

The thing surges past him toward the wash, dragging its awful bulk over stones, tearing the greenbelt open. For one second, Derrick thinks he has done it. Given it what it wants. Sent it home.

Then the snake body tightens around his wrist.

He looks down.

The severed end is no longer severed.

It has rooted into his glove.

Into his skin.

Into him.

"Oh," Derrick says.

The word is small.

The thing reaches the edge of the wash and stops.

Slowly, it turns.

The dead snake head rises from the black below, attached now to a body of darkness and dirt and everything hungry under Phoenix.

Its mouth opens.

Close.

Open.

Close.

Derrick understands the last part.

It never wanted the snake back.

It wanted him to bring it.

It wanted him outside.

He turns toward the house.

Mason is still at the patio door. Lena's headlights slash onto the street out front, two white beams sweeping across the broken wall, the Civic, Rafa's body, the open front door. She's come despite everything. Of course she has. Lena always comes when Mason needs her.

Derrick cups both hands around his mouth.

"Lena!" he screams. "Get him out!"

His voice tears raw.

"Get him out now!"

The thing hits him from behind.

There is no cinematic struggle. No last clever plan. No clean hero death.

It takes him low, folds him forward, drives the heat out of his lungs. Derrick's face hits dirt. His mouth fills with grit. Something wraps his legs. Something hooks under his ribs. He feels himself pulled backward toward the wash, fingernails carving useless lines in the ground.

He sees Mason pounding the patio glass.

He sees Lena run into the house.

He sees her grab Mason under the arms, sees Mason fighting her, screaming for his father, sees her drag him away because she is stronger than panic and smarter than grief.

Good, Derrick thinks.

That is the last whole word inside him.

The wash opens.

The dark takes him feet first.

Pain arrives, bright and total, then breaks into smaller lights.

Above him, the Phoenix sky hangs empty and hot.

No stars.

No moon.

Just the lid of the world.

Then dirt closes over his face.

By sunrise, the neighborhood is loud with police radios, ambulance doors, barking dogs, crying neighbors, and the low mechanical growl of men pretending the world can be explained with enough yellow tape.

Rafa Mercado is found in the street.

Kendra Ibarra is not found at all.

Derrick Hollis is missing.

The official story becomes heat, shock, animal attack, possible sinkhole, possible homicide, pending investigation. The words sit in reports like cheap patio furniture in a dust storm. They do not hold.

Mason lies in a hospital bed with a cast on his ankle, stitches in his forehead, and his mother asleep in the chair beside him. He does not sleep. Every time he closes his eyes, he sees his father running into the greenbelt with something long and dead dragging behind him.

At 6:12 a.m., his phone lights up.

No service in the hospital room. No bars.

Still, a text appears.

From Dad.

Mason stares at it until the letters blur.

Outside the hospital window, the sun lifts over Phoenix, pale and merciless, heating the city one roof at a time.

The message says:

Don't kill the ones that run.

From somewhere under the sink in the hospital bathroom, soft and cheerful, something chimes.

Ding-ding-ding-dong.

About the Author

Christopher Winterberg's debut collection of short stories, Twisted Sanity: Stories Beyond Reality, enjoyed literary success. While he has not been published in any reviews, quarterlies, journals, periodicals, or elsewhere, he looks forward to those opportunities. Never having been labeled as one of the most famous writers of any generation, era, or century, he has received zero literary awards. He does, however, look forward to those in the future, if warranted. You can find out more about Christopher at chriswinterberg.com.

If you're daring and wish to, you may contact Christopher Winterberg either through a post on his website, or at info@chriswinterberg.com.

www.ingramcontent.com/pod-product-compliance
Lightning Source LLC
LaVergne TN
LVHW010644110826
845149LV00014B/2946

* 9 7 8 0 9 8 9 4 4 8 3 1 4 *